AVALON SUMMER

David Matson Hooper

AVALON SUMMER

iUniverse books may be ordered through booksellers or by contacting:

iUniverse LLC
1663 Liberty Drive
Bloomington, IN 47403
www.iuniverse.com
1-800-Authors (1-800-288-4677)

ISBN: 978-1-4917-4146-7 (sc)
ISBN: 978-1-4917-4147-4 (e)

Library of Congress Control Number: 2014912639

Printed in the United States of America.

iUniverse rev. date: 07/28/2014

"I found my love in Avalon, beside the bay.
I left my love in Avalon, and sailed away.
I dream of her and Avalon, from dusk till dawn
And so I think I'll travel on to Avalon."

AVALON
V. Rose/A. Jolson/B. Desylva

"Twenty-six miles across the sea
Santa Catalina is waitin' for me
Santa Catalina, the Island of Romance."

26 MILES (Santa Catalina)
G .Larson/ B. Belland

CHAPTER 1

▼

WAXIE AND BLACKIE

"This is Emperor Hudson, baby, on KRLA, where the hits just keep comin' at ya! It's twelve minutes before high noon in the City of the Angels, a beautiful seventy-two degrees, and the surf is up at the beaches. Stay tuned for the Casey Kasem show coming up next, but first, here's the latest from the Rolling Stones."

"I can't get no satisfaction...."

The song seemed to jump out of the radio on Waxie Shein's dresser and through the open doorway, to where he stood in front of the medicine cabinet mirror searching his face for zits, and gratefully finding none on this cheerful Saturday morning. He slicked some Brylcreem into his black hair and parted it on the right, dragging a lock across his forehead.

Although he'd just turned eighteen, Waxie still didn't need to shave more than twice a week, if that often. He skipped that ritual today, but nonetheless splashed on after-shave lotion. "Chicks dig English Leather," he mused, as the Stones finished singing and Bob "Emperor" Hudson went to commercial break on the 50,000-watt station.

Waxie finished grooming himself before the mirror, satisfied that he was as presentable as could be to meet the day. Although he only stood five feet nine inches in bare feet, he figured since his father was over six feet, he still had room to grow. He adjusted the belt on his white Levis, into which was tucked a sharply pressed red and white striped shirt. He checked the shine on his brown loafers for scuff marks, and found none.

Waxie switched off the light and stepped through the doorway, reached for the radio, shutting it off in the middle of a Coke commercial, and palmed the key ring lying on top of the dresser. The ring held the key to his brand new Vespa motor scooter, which waited outside, along with the promise of an Avalon summer. The scooter had been a combination birthday and graduation gift (Avalon High, Class of 1965), and now he was eligible for membership in the Islanders Motorcycle Club. No matter that the Vespa was a poor cousin to a motorcycle, in a town the size of Avalon, some formalities were overlooked. Yes, in Avalon, where cars were discouraged and the preferred mode of travel was by golf cart, the Vespa would actually be an attention getter. Avalon, as any local knew, was only about a square mile in size, just about walking distance to anywhere. And this was a good thing, as the price of gasoline was steep, due to its having to be shipped from "over town" (as the mainland was called) by barge.

The Vespa had been shipped over from a dealership in Long Beach and stashed at Ben and Mollie's house, hidden until graduation night. The extended Shein family, which included sister Sarah, and an aunt and uncle from over town, had been on hand for the ceremonies, and the party later in the ballroom of the Casino. The event had been one of shared family pride, and no one seemed happier than Waxie. Knowing, however, that his carefree summers of youth were about to end, he intended to savor this one to the fullest measure.

Waxie walked down the hallway past his folks' room, and through the doorway into the office of the hotel that doubled as home and family business. Blackie glanced up from the counter where he was busily entering figures into a ledger. He removed his reading glasses and said, "Morning, son. Where're you off to in such a rush?"

"Just down to the steamer pier, Pop. I want to watch the boat come in."

"Is it that late already?" he said, glancing at the wall clock. "Got all your chores finished?"

"Yes, sir. Well, most of them. I won't be long. Besides, I want to give the scooter another test spin."

Blackie's face lit up in a smile as he said, "Okay, son. I guess you deserve that. But don't stay long. I may need you now that the season's really underway."

"Sure, Pop," Waxie said as he headed out the front door.

Blackie was an optimist. He still believed, as he did each summer, that business would finally pick up, and the Travel On Inn (named for a line in the song "Avalon") would once again prosper as it had in the "good old days". In truth, those good old days were long gone, and something he had only heard about from his wife, Ruth. She had described how it was back then, before World War Two. The Big Bands, like Kay Kaiser and Benny Goodman, had played for the weekend dances at the Casino. Tourists filled the massive ballroom, and every hotel in town filled to capacity. Movie stars like Clark Gable, she had told him, and the rich and powerful, used Avalon as their playground for secret getaways far from the confines of Hollywood. Yes, thought Blackie, those had been the golden days of prosperity.

But Blackie would have to live in the shadow of those times. For now the paint was peeling, the carpet worn, and the Travel On Inn was run down at the heels and relegated in the more generous guidebooks, to one star status. Truly, it was now the end of the line, a place fit only for those on a tight budget, or for overflow from over-booked hotels. It was a small, two-story affair, with a dozen rooms to each floor, and it was an exceptionally good day if most rooms were occupied. The rooms were basic, even sparse. Each contained a bed, nightstand, dresser, chair, tiny closet, and a bathroom shared by two adjoining rooms. No television, heater, or air conditioner, and no carpet on the floor. But the rooms were kept clean. That was something Blackie and Ruth took pride in.

But there was little pride associated with their other business concern, the Annex, which hid itself away up the street as if ashamed, with only a small number on the building and no name to identify it. Nor was the place listed in any guidebooks or Chamber of Commerce pamphlets. A poor excuse for a hotel, it served the purpose of providing summer housing for many of Avalon's minimum wage workers, who could afford little else. The rooms were even more Spartan than those of the Inn. There were a dozen tiny rooms lined up in a row along a boardwalk. At the end of the building were communal toilets and showers. Each of the rooms held a single bed, a small table and chair, a dresser, a small sink, and a couple of hooks on the door to hang clothing on. Although the Annex was nothing to brag about, it's income helped keep the Travel On Inn afloat. Blackie reasoned that what the family business needed was fresh blood and new ideas, so he was grooming his son to follow in his footsteps. But the boy just couldn't seem to get with the program. He was more interested in chasing girls, summer tourist girls at that.

Outside the Travel On Inn, gleaming in the sunlight, sat the blue Vespa of Italian design. Waxie noted again that the seat had a cushion behind it for riding double, and included footrests for a passenger. This would improve his dating chances. There weren't many local girls of his own age (his graduating class had only numbered about a dozen), but with the tens of thousands of visitors expected on the island between now and Labor Day, his chances of picking up girls improved considerably. Waxie straddled the scooter, slipped the key in the ignition and turned it, then kicked the starter over with his foot. The 50 cc engine purred sweetly. He kicked up the stand, slipped in the clutch, and put it in gear. A puff of blue smoke blew out the pipe and dissolved into the air in a swirl.

Waxie jumped the curb and headed slowly downhill on Sumner Avenue toward the bay. He passed the Hotel Atwater, and its adjacent coffee shop, then souvenir and clothing shops, the Bamboo Lounge, and Hotel Glenmore. When he reached the burger stand on the corner of Crescent, he made a slow left, keeping an eye out for pedestrians. A short block later he was at Metropole, where the steamer pier jutted out like a finger pointing toward the mainland.

Waxie parked the Vespa at the foot of the pier, and began walking its length, taking in his surroundings as he went. The morning fog had burned off, and now everything was bathed in the golden sunshine that made the water sparkle like myriad jewels.

The waterfront of Avalon spread out in a crescent shape. To his left, half the crescent led to a steep bluff that dropped down to a rocky spit of land, man-made and shaped like a crab's pincher, known as Casino Point. On top of this sat Avalon's picture postcard landmark, the Casino. It was a massive circular monolith, Mediterranean-looking and gleaming white with a red–tiled roof. It derived its name from the Italian word for "a place of gathering", and had no association with gambling.

Between the Casino and the steamer pier, along the recently reinforced breakwater, both the Tuna Club and the Yacht Club hung out over the water with attached docks. Out in the bay, gently bobbing at anchor, gathered a plethora of water craft moored in every available space.

Waxie walked over to the other side of the pier, where the other half of the crescent spread out. In addition to the yachts, cabin cruisers, sailboats and dinghies in the harbor, another structure, the Green Pleasure Pier, sat on pilings atop the water. At its end was a small floating dock where the Grumman Goose seaplanes tied up and dropped off their passengers. At the end of the bay, closing off the crescent, was a spit of land known as the Cabrillo Mole and gave the impression of another crab's pincher. Along most of the waterfront ran Crescent Beach, narrow with gleaming white sand, which gave way to pebbles as one entered the water. Waxie gazed along the length of the beach, looking for the tan and supple bodies of girls and young ladies sunning themselves.

"Not many chicks out yet," he thought as his eyes searched the beach. "But I'll be back later to scope things out. There'll be more action after the boat comes in."

Waxie strode to the end of the pier and looked toward the horizon, where a brown smoggy haze hung over the Los Angeles area. Dead ahead, getting ready to enter the harbor, the Great White Steamship, *S.S. Catalina,* was cutting through the glassy water, making twelve knots, black diesel smoke spewing from her stack, her wake fanning out behind. The ship had left San Pedro two hours earlier and would be docking momentarily. As she tied up, children of Avalon would be in the water alongside, diving for the coins and trinkets tossed overboard by passengers. Waxie recalled a time when he had donned swim fins and mask to join in the treasure hunt as well. But that had all ended by the summer of his Bar Mitzvah. "You're a man now," Blackie had stated solemnly, "and you'll take up your place in the family business, and handle more responsibilities." But the earnest speech had just been an acknowledgement that Waxie would be spending more time at home during the summer months, helping out.

The *S. S. Catalina* was slowing now as it entered the harbor, something it had been doing since 1924, with the exception of the war years. A long blast on the ship's steam whistle signaled its arrival. Its engines reversed, churning up water at the stern, and it sidled into the dock, it's landing cushioned by a row of tires that hung off the side of the pier. There was a flurry of activity as ropes were tossed over the side to uniformed men who grappled with them and wound them tightly around posts fore and aft. Soon, the gangways went down, and tourists poured forth like a flood.

Waxie watched intently as the mob rushed past him, until he caught sight of a beautiful young redhead who made his heart jump. But when she flew into the waiting arms of one of the boat handlers, disappointment sucker punched him. This blow was quickly replaced by expectation as he noticed a cute young brunette. His heart caught in his throat as she brushed past him in the company of her parents. He started to follow her, but remembered his promise to Blackie that he would quickly return home. "Maybe I'll see her this afternoon on the beach," he thought excitedly. "Or maybe she'll be at the dance at El Encanto."

Waxie turned into the flow of the crowd and walked briskly back to his scooter in anticipation of the day, the summer, and hopefully, a summer romance. His senses sharpened as he looked around at the crowds, and at the little snapshot views of his town. In the immediacy of the moment, everything seemed sharper, brighter, and more brilliant to the boy. He watched the light play on the water, heard the screech of gulls, and the sound the water made as it lapped against the pilings and the sand. He felt the warmth of sun on his face, and the fresh crispness of the ocean air. He smelled noonday smells as they wafted in the air and mixed together. It was a heady blend of salt water and fresh fish, sizzling bacon and burgers, onions and fries, diesel fuel mixing with baby oil and suntan lotion, and the smoke from a cigarette.

Looking up, he saw the little cottages and houses of all sizes and colors, but mostly white, dotting the hills above Avalon. Little roads wound and climbed and meandered, tying the houses together in a kind of mosaic. And where the roads did not wander, and the houses did not stand, were the green and brown earth tones of the dry grasses and chaparral, oaks and cacti that had been there long before Avalon had a name.

Waxie reached the Vespa, straddled it, and kicked the engine over. It purred into life.

CHAPTER 2

▼

SALT AND PEPPER

"You're listening to the Casey Kasem show on KRLA. On a hot August day in 1957, Bruce Belland cut his summer school class at Hollywood High to go surfing with his buddies. While at the beach, a friend pointed out Catalina Island in the distance and speculated it was about twenty-six miles away. Bruce pulled out his ukulele and began composing this next song, which took his group The Four Preps to the top of the charts in 1958."

"Twenty-six miles across the sea, Santa Catalina is waitin' for me, Santa Catalina the island of romance."

The song drifted out of a radio and into the ears of one Robert Wayne Silenski, who had more on his mind at the moment than romance, as the *S. S. Catalina* pulled into Avalon Harbor. Bob Silenski had a motto, and if you will, a creed. If he had a coat of arms it would read: "Never in Love, Only in Heat." He was, at this very moment, in heat.

He had been eying the current object of his lust for a good five minutes, planning his move. She was a well-built redhead leaning against the railing of the steamship, gazing at the approaching town of Avalon. Bob was mesmerized by her profile, the breeze blowing her long hair away from her face, accentuating her full red lips, her girlish upturned nose, soft chin, and rosy, slightly freckled complexion. Then his eyes took a walk all over her.

"Cute little thing!" he said to himself. "Nice face. Nice bod. Tight ass. I shall have this saucy wench before the day is done. Yes! She shall be mine!"

His attention was momentarily diverted as a teenage kid crossed his line of sight. The kid had a transistor radio tuned to KFWB (AM 98), and Bob caught a lyric from a familiar song by the Four Tops. This gave him the sudden inspiration for his opening line. He made a wavering beeline (because of the rolling of the deck) toward the girl, and sliding up next to her, casually leaned in and smiled broadly.

"Hey, sugar pie honeybunch," he began. "You're looking nice today. Beautiful and intriguing, in fact, like this ocean full of dolphins and flying fish and other mysteries of the deep. Speaking of mysteries, you mystify me. What's your name? Mine's Bob, but everyone calls me Sil."

"Rhonda," she said, with an air of irritation.

"Well, help me Rhonda! I'm a stranger to Avalon. What about you--first time here?"

"No," she replied.

"Good. What are you doing later? Maybe you could show me around."

"Sorry," she said. "I'll be having lunch with my boyfriend."

"Ouch! You really know how to hurt a guy."

"You asked for it."

"Yeah, I guess I did. But where is this alleged boyfriend?" he said, looking around.

"He's waiting on the dock. He's a boat handler. After the boat makes its turnaround, he'll be off work and we can go out on the town."

As her face broke into a smile, Sil's smile faded.

"Well, if he stands you up," he said, "just look for me. I'll be around."

"Goodbye," she said frostily, turning her gaze back toward Catalina Island. Sil waited a moment, getting one last glimpse of her profile, and then walked away. Suddenly, a familiar voice called out.

"Guppy!"

Sil looked over to see his buddy J.T. approaching.

"Puma head!" he shouted back.

They continued the greeting as they walked toward each other.

"Gremmie!"

"Hodad!"

"Flatus breath!"

"Flatus breath?"

"Flatus--a gaseous odor excreted from the anal cavity. In other words, I called you fart breath."

"How long is it?"

"Long as my arm, hard as my fist, and up to here." Sil made a chopping motion with his right hand against his left elbow. He had lifted the quote from Errol Flynn's autobiography, *My Wicked, Wicked Ways,* which he had read twice. You see, Sil was not only a fan of Errol Flynn, but he also fancied himself a protégé of the ultimate man's man and babe magnet. The two men faced each other now, near the stairway that led to the main deck.

"I saw you in action just now. What happened?"

"Major wipe out."

"What, the mighty Sil shot down? Well, don't worry, buddy, there's plenty more where that came from. I mean, just take a look around," said J.T. with a broad sweep of his arm. "What do you see?"

Sil's head, which had been lowered in mock shame, now snapped erect as he glanced madly about.

"Chicks!" he shouted.

"Babes!" added J.T.

"And we'll have fun, fun, fun till daddy takes the woody away." The woody was a reference to Sil's surf wagon, which he'd left behind on the mainland.

By now, some of the passengers on deck were staring at the pair, either overtly, or discretely. This was something Sil had noticed before. People would sometimes refer to them as "Salt and Pepper", because on first glance, they appeared to be mirror opposites. Both were tall and athletically built, but Sil was fair skinned, while J.T. was a black man. Sil had clear blue eyes and long blond hair that he was growing out into a Beatle cut. He had a straight nose, sharp facial features, and an angular jaw line. J.T. had coffee-colored eyes, short kinky hair, a flat nose, and soft, rounded features. Someone once remarked that they resembled a black and white photograph and its negative. And out in public, such as they were today, they would often get double takes.

Sil and J.T. had not grown up together, but had become friends as high school seniors, at a Varsity football game. Sil had been a tight end and wide receiver for Mira Costa. J.T., a tackle for Lynwood High, met Sil on the ten-yard line when he took him down with a little too much force. Above the noise of the crowd and the players, J.T. heard a crunch and a sharp scream, and saw Sil's face screwed up in pain. He had broken his collarbone. Feeling remorse, he'd taken himself out of the game to ride along in the ambulance with Sil and keep him company.

"Man, you didn't need bail on the game," said Sil, as the morphine began to kick in, while the doctor prepared to re-set the bone. "But I'm glad you did. No hard feelings, huh?"

"Look," said J.T., jotting down his phone number on a scrap of paper, "call me later and let me know how you are."

Sil did call, and the two became friends. This summer, they were just renewing their friendship, as J.T. had been in the Army for the past two years, and was looking forward to a couple of carefree months. It was good to be just Jay Tee again, instead of Pfc. Joshua Thomas Taylor.

They boat was reversing engines now, and J.T. said, "Hey, Sil, let's dig the view before we dig the action."

They walked to the bow and looked out on a town that seemed to be a cross between the South Pacific and the Mediterranean. The massive round, red tiled building to their right created an Italian look, while the palm trees lining the shore lent a tropical touch. And anywhere they looked convinced them they were no longer in L.A.

"No waves," said Sil.

"Say what?"

"No surf, hodad."

"Man, is that all you ever think about? Besides women, I mean."

"It's just that I'm going to miss surfing over here. It's such a rush. Better than football. You ought to try it sometime."

"Not me, partner. Maybe when you show me some other Negroes, some of the brothers out there, maybe, just maybe, I'll get my feet wet. But ol' Jay Tee ain't gonna be the Rosa Parks of surfing."

"No, really man. You ought to check it out. You'll be stoked. Dig it… just you and your board and the elements---the sun, the cool water, shooting the curl, and then cutting back, in the tunnel, then the soup. Maybe get some real boss tubes. Oh yeah, and don't forget the chicks, the honeys."

"Shit, I knew this part was comin'," groaned J.T.

"Yeah, those surfer chicks are so much hipper than the pom-pom rah-rah girls in high school. They're friendly, uninhibited, and down to earth. And they all got that golden California tan."

"So you say. I like my women with a natural tan all over."

Bob Silenski had spent the previous summer surfing around his hometown of Manhattan Beach, and up and down the South Coast, from Trestles to Paradise Cove. Then a fraternity brother had hipped him to Catalina.

"Huntington Beach may be 'Surf City,'" he'd been told, "but Catalina is the 'Island of Romance'." Naturally, Sil decided he should check it out, and when J.T. had looked him up after his discharge, they decided to head over together and see what developed.

"Looks like we're tying up," said J.T.

"Let's go get our gear," said Sil.

They picked up their backpacks at the baggage storage room. Sil's had a transistor radio tucked inside. He may have to live without a surfboard, but he wasn't going to be without tunes. The Top 40 was the soundtrack to his life.

The steam whistle blew loudly from its mount in front of the great funnel as the boat sidled into the dock. Soon, the two were walking down the gangway and onto the pier. Sil caught sight of his redhead locked in the embrace of a uniformed man. "Oh, well," he thought, "can't win 'em all."

They jostled their way through the surging crowd to the foot of the pier, where across the narrow street a large sign read: U DRIVE RENTALS, and behind it was a lot filled with golf carts and bicycles.

"Let's go find us some digs," said J.T.

"Yeah," said Sil. "But first I need to pick up some new shades."

They popped into Molly's Gifts and Souvenirs where a rack of sunglasses stood just inside the doorway. Sil picked out a pair of Ray Bans, while J.T. settled for a cheaper brand. They paid the sales clerk, and joined the flood of humanity on the street.

The pair stopped by the Hotel MacRae to check on rooms, but Sil decided it was out of their price range. Next they tried the Hotel Catalina, but decided to pass on it, too. The desk clerk suggested they try the Hotel Atwater, but it was booked up. However, the Atwater desk clerk was helpful. "You might try the Travel On Inn, just up the street," he said. "They usually have some vacancies."

In the same building as the Atwater was a bustling coffee shop, the Skipper's Galley.

"Let's get us some chow, Sil. I am one hungry muthafucka."

"I could go for a bite, but let's get some rooms first. Anyway, it's just too crowded right now." Then Sil noticed the HELP WANTED sign in the window. "Hmmm. Yes, let's definitely stop back here and check it out," he said.

Presently, they were standing in front of an older wooden structure with a VACANCY sign in the window, and faded, peeling paint on the siding.

"Say, J.T., how would you describe the color of this place?"

"Baby shit green."

"Yes, exactly what I was thinking, too---baby shit green. Let's see what they got."

Two steps up to the porch, through the rickety screen door, and into the lobby they went, vaguely aware of the rack of postcards next to the counter, and the signs on the wall behind it.

WELCOME TO THE TRAVEL ON INN.
CHECK OUT TIME 11 AM
NO PETS. NO VISITORS AFTER 8:00 PM

No one was about, so Sil tapped the bell on the counter. Moments later, a door in the wall behind the counter opened, and out stepped a tall thin man with a neatly trimmed mustache.

"Afternoon, boys," he said pleasantly. "How can we help you?"

"Two rooms, my good man; one for myself, and one for my (ahem) man-servant here. Fetch me my bags, boy."

"Shut up, Sil," said J.T.

"So, a comedian we have here," said Blackie, a little embarrassed, and a little annoyed.

"But you DO allow colored folk here, don't you?" said Sil, pressing the issue.

Blackie forced a thin smile. "Look, boys, I don't care what color you are---black, white, or purple, just so long as your money is green, and you behave yourselves. Understood? Now, rooms are three dollars a night or twenty a week. What'll it be?"

"What do you say, my man?" said Sil.

"Let's try a couple nights." J.T. replied.

"Fine," said Blackie. "That will be twelve dollars, payable in advance. Now if you'll just sign the register, I'll get your keys."

While they were signing their names, Blackie plucked two keys from the pegboard on the wall, and notated their numbers in the book.

"Rooms seven and eight," he said. "You'll share a bathroom. Which one of you is Joshua?"

"I prefer Jay Tee. Joshua's too Biblical."

"I know what you mean," said Blackie. "My given name is Jacob, but everyone calls me Blackie."

"Hey," said Sil to J.T., "that ought to be your name."

"Shut up, Sil," he said, glaring. Then, "Why Blackie?"

"Well, son, you see, it's like this: when I was in the Navy, one of my shipmates found out I was from Boston, and he stared calling me 'Boston Blackie', after the movie detective. Then it got shortened to Blackie, and just stuck. To this day, I sometimes forget I was ever Jake. So there you have it. You'll be in room seven, J.T. And you, mister wise guy," he said, eyeing Sil, "you're in eight---and no funny business, understand? I'll be watching you. The rooms are just down this hall," he gestured. "I'll see if my son remembered to stock fresh sheets and towels."

He opened the door behind him, and hollered down the hallway. "David- -we have guests checking into seven and eight. See they have everything they need."

"Okay, Pop," came the reply.

"If you need anything else, just ring the bell," said Blackie before disappearing back through the door in the wall.

A few minutes later, as Sil was finishing his unpacking, there came a light knock at the door.

"Enter if you dare," said Sil.

"Here's some fresh towels. Sorry I forgot them earlier," said the kid with the bundle in his hand. "I got sidetracked."

"No problem. Is your name David?"

"Yeah, but everyone calls me Waxie."

"Everyone calls me Sil", he said, offering his hand to shake. "Say, Waxie, this business about no visitors—how well is that enforced? I mean, suppose I wanted to bring a girl by?"

"Well," said Waxie, after a pause, and a quick look over his shoulder, "my mom's on the desk at night, but she usually turns in by ten. And my dad's not out front till seven or eight in the morning. Does that answer your question?"

"Yeah, thanks. Oh, and where's the best place to pick up chicks around here?"

"Are you kidding?" said Waxie, beginning to blush. "Just about anywhere. The beach, the Pleasure Pier, the streets---"

"What about tonight?"

"There's a dance at El Encanto."

"El Encanto?"

"Yeah. It's kind of a plaza at the end of Crescent, up a little hill. You can't miss it--you'll hear the music. It starts around eight."

"Well, thanks for the tip, Waxie. Maybe we'll see you there."

"Oh, I'll be there," he grinned.

Before chasing women, though, Bob Silenski had two important items on his agenda, the first involving food. He collared J.T., and the two headed over to the coffee shop, which by now wasn't quite as crowded. Even so, they could only find seats at the counter. They ordered up two lunches and two job applications from the waitress, and handed them in when they paid their bill. While Sil was lingering over a cup of coffee, a middle-aged woman, small and wiry, approached and told them if they stopped by tomorrow, they could interview with her husband. "Just ask for the Skipper," she said curtly.

Now it was time to scope out the town, to which they set about with relish. They hung out on the beach awhile, admiring the tanned and sunburned girls in various states of undress, striking up a few casual conversations. Then they joined in on a pickup volleyball game, and finished up at a fish and chips stand before heading back to the hotel to shower and change into what J.T. called "evening attire".

Just before eight o'clock, they headed out again. Sil had changed into a light yellow sport shirt and powder blue Levis, but kept his sneakers. He also splashed a little Canoe cologne on his face. J.T. wore a pin striped shirt, black slacks, and Italian shoes. He wore the odor of Brut aftershave.

The sun had dipped below the hills of Avalon and a twilight glow bathed the palm-lined streets they strolled along. They wandered along the waterfront, listening to the evening birds and the lapping of wavelets. Then they began hearing a new sound, that of music coming from El Encanto. As they entered the plaza, Sil began singing along with Sam the Sham and the Pharaohs.

"Wooly bully, wooly bully, wooly bully!"

They passed through the entryway and into the Spanish tiled plaza, enclosed by various tourist shops, now closed up for the day. At one end of the plaza, a teenager spun records on a phonograph hooked up to a sound system. Couples and singles stood around the outside, chatting and watching the dancers in the center, one of whom was Waxie Shein. Sil spotted him with a cute brunette and nodded. Sil and J.T. scanned the whole of the plaza before turning to each other.

"What's it remind you of?" asked Sil.

"High school, only with white chicks."

"Uh huh."

"Wanna split?"

"No rush. Let's hang out awhile and see what happens," said Sil.

Before long, a mousey teenage girl approached and shyly asked Sil to dance. Her girlfriends watched from a corner of the plaza, whispering and giggling, while she and Sil slow danced to the Rolling Stones. It was a song about a spider and a fly, and Sil pondered whether he, in this case, was the spider or the fly. When the song ended, he bowed to the girl, who blushed, and ran off to her girlfriends. Sil returned to his friend.

"Where I come from, that's jailbait," said J.T.

"Funny, where I come from, it is too."

"Split?"

"Yeah."

As they walked back through the archway, J.T. said, "Where to now?"

"How 'bout we check out that building over there?" he said, pointing down the Via Casino toward the huge, round building at the end of the bay.

When they reached the Casino, they discovered a movie theater in the front of the building. Curious, they walked around back, where the land ended and water washed up against the rocks.

"Well, that's where we were this morning," said Sil, pointing to the horizon.

"I'm beginning to wish we were still there," said J.T. softly.

"What do you mean?"

"C'mon, man, just look around. You see any other Negroes around here? I see nothin' but white chicks at that dance. I mean, my daddy used to tell me to lighten up, but this is too much."

"Lighten up?" said Sil, with a puzzled look.

"Yeah, man. You know, he used to say, 'Josh, let me clue you in on sumpin'. This here is Whitey's world, and if you wanna get by you got ta lighten up. Walk white, talk white, dress white, to be right. Otherwise, you just goin' ta end up like one of them geechee niggers'".

"You don't have to worry about that, Jay. I never think of you that way."

"Bullshit, Sil. What was all that jive about me being your boy earlier, huh?"

"Oh, that. Hey, I was just joking. I didn't mean anything by it."

"Yeah, Sil, I know. You just ignorant to the ways of the world, that's all. Let me ask you this---how many Negroes did you have at Mira Costa, huh? I'm bettin' zero".

"It's true," said Sil, looking down at his feet.

"Yeah, I knew it. You wanna know why? I'll tell you. Because they won't let us into those beach towns. That's for whites only. Oh, it ain't like there's signs up, like down in the South; it's more subtle than that. The Man just lets you know you ain't wanted, especially once the sun goes down. It's the same everywhere, even in the Army. No official policy of segregation, but each group hangs with it's own kind. And that, my friend, is a fact of life."

Sil looked up hopefully. "Maybe it'll be different now," he said. "What with the Civil Rights Act and all that."

"Maybe. I hope so. But you can't just legislate prejudice away. You don't just pass a law and expect everyone to change their thinking overnight. I don't see any 'No Colored' signs around this tourist trap, but I don't exactly feel welcome here, either."

"Well, hey," said Sil, "we just got here. Give it a few days. See what develops. Maybe you'll find yourself an Ebony Goddess before the week is out."

"Okay, Sil, I'll give it a week. One week. Things don't pick up by then, I'm gone like a cool breeze."

"Fair enough," Sil agreed. "Now, what say we find a bar, and I buy you a cold beer?"

"Now you talkin', brother."

The first bar they found, the Waikiki, didn't entice them, mainly because it was filled with an older crowd, mostly married couples by the look of it. So they ambled on, and as they turned the corner at Sumner, they heard music coming out of the Bamboo Lounge. It was Burl Ives, singing on the jukebox.

"Pearly shells, from the ocean..."

They walked through the open door and into what was known as a Tiki Bar. Everything was decorated in a Polynesian theme---wooden Tiki gods and Tiki torches, bamboo and rattan furniture. On the walls were paintings of Hawaiian Islands and hula girls. The middle-age bartender, wearing a loud Hawaiian shirt over his beer belly, was putting miniature parasols into a pair of tropical drinks in wide-rimmed glasses.

They eased up to the bar stools, and Sil ordered a gin and tonic and a Coors beer. He gazed about the dimly lit room, and then nudged J.T. with his elbow. He nodded over to a darkened booth, where a couple of young ladies were engaged in conversation.

"Don't look now," he said, "but your prayers have been answered."

J.T. peered over to the booth and found the two brunettes. Both were very attractive. One was white, and one was black.

"Chocolate and vanilla," said Sil.

"Shut up, Sil," said J.T. before cruising over to the jukebox, dropping in a coin, and punching up a song by Marvin Gaye. When the upbeat sounds of "I'll Be Doggone" came spilling out of the speaker, J.T. sauntered over to the girls' booth, Sil in tow with the drinks, and said, "Evening, ladies. Mind if we join you for a while?"

"No, not at all," said the black girl, moving over to make more room. "We were sort of hoping you would".

Sil ordered drinks for them, and after introductions all around, he found that they were both stewardesses for United Airlines.

"And now, we're all united," he quipped.

They all hung out in the corner for a while drinking, chatting, dancing to the jukebox. Then Sil looked at his watch and suggested they all continue the party at the Travel On Inn. However, the stewardesses both demurred.

"I'm sorry, we'll have to take a rain check," one said. "We're getting up pretty early."

"That's right," the other concurred. "We're going snorkeling in Lovers Cove, and then we're catching the Inland Tour. After that, we have to get back to LAX."

"You're welcome to join us tomorrow," offered the first girl.

"Thanks," said a disappointed Sil, "but we've got to see a man about a job."

They offered to walk the girls back to their hotel, and stalled the time a little by taking a stroll along the beach on the way, holding hands in the moonlight.

"Now I know why it's called the Island of Romance," said the girl walking alongside Sil, as they approached the Hotel Catalina. In the lobby, the night clerk eyed them suspiciously as they said their goodnights.

"Thank you for rescuing us from a dull evening," said the girl with Sil, squeezing his hand. "It's been an evening to remember."

"That it has," he answered. "Now here's something to remember me by." He pulled her close, and gave her a long, passionate kiss.

Pretending not to see the kiss, J.T.'s date said, "Thanks for a lovely time, Jay. I hope we'll meet again some time." Then she gave him a peck on the cheek, and the girls headed to their room, while the guys watched from the lobby.

Later, Sil lay in bed listening to the radio, volume down low, remembering the feel of the kiss, and wondering why he hadn't pushed harder to score. J.T. lay in the next room, past the shared bathroom, staring at the ceiling. Then he closed his eyes and tried to picture a German girl he had dated when he was stationed in Mannheim.

Around Avalon, things were slowing down. The action had either moved to a few boats out in the harbor, or to the few bars still open. When they also closed, a few night owls would make their way over to the Skipper's Galley for either a late dinner or an early breakfast, or just coffee and conversation. Eventually, the lights all over town dimmed and died, and the running lights on boats winked off, until all that was left out on the ocean was darkness, and above, a canopy of bright reassuring stars. The last day of spring was beginning on the mainland, but in Avalon, summer had already begun.

CHAPTER 3

▼

THE SKIPPER AND
THE BEATNIK

Bob Silenski was gazing out of a rectangular opening in the wall before him, into the dining room of the Skipper's Galley. He was dressed in a white cook's coat, with a row of large buttons down the side, and a white cook's hat. Behind him were a grill and a broiler. Directly in front of him was a stainless steel counter forming the bottom part of the rectangular opening, and hanging from the top of the opening was a wheel, onto which were clipped a half dozen order tickets. Standing next to Sil was another man similarly attired, a few inches shorter, and stocky. His name was Phil Munday, and he was the regular swing shift cook. He was a few years older than Sil, and sported a goatee on his chin. Sil had been working under his tutelage and supervision for the past couple of hours. Just prior to that, he and J.T. had been sitting at a table in the dining room with the Skipper, who was studying their job applications.

The Skipper, whose legal name was Jack O'Hara, looked the part of a sea captain, with his black-brimmed blue nautical cap, and the unlit cigar stub clamped in the side of his mouth. He squinted behind the dark rimmed glasses he wore. He had a ruddy complexion and slightly puffy face. He was middle-aged and pudgy around the waist. "They call me the Skipper," he'd said when they were introduced, "because I run a tight ship." Then he'd laughed and winked, as if it was an inside joke.

"I see you have short order experience--Burke's Coffee Shop in Hermosa Beach and the Pioneer Pancake House at Lake Tahoe. I also see that second job only lasted a few weeks. Why?" The Skipper looked over his glasses at Sil.

"I was on semester break. I was trying to get in a little skiing, and paying for it by working nights there. That's their busy season, so they hire on extra temporary help."

"Well, this is our busy season," said the Skipper. "If I hire you, I need to know that you'll stay the summer, through Labor Day."

"No sweat. The next semester doesn't start till then anyway."

"Good," said the Skipper. "What I need is a breakfast and lunch cook. The hours are seven-thirty to three-thirty. Think you can handle that?"

"Sure," said Sil, "no problem."

"Good. You can start tomorrow. I'd like to get you trained now, though. Can you stick around a few hours?"

"Sure, why not?"

"Good. I'll hook you up with Phil. He can show you the ropes and get you shipshape."

Now the Skipper turned his attention to J.T. "Joshua," he said, looking at the name on the application.

"I prefer Jay Tee."

The Skipper continued, without acknowledging the nickname. "I see your only restaurant experience was in the Army. What exactly were your duties?"

"Well, sir, I did a lot of K.P. duty. Peeling potatoes, scrubbing pots and pans, that sort of thing."

"I know all about that," said the Skipper, smiling. "I learned how to cook in the Army during World War Two. I can't hire you as a cook, Joshua, but I do need a dishwasher right now. It would be the same hours as your friend here. It only pays minimum wage, but if you work out, I might train you to become relief cook. What do you think? You want the job?"

"Yeah. Okay. Sure."

"Good," said the Skipper. "And since you've already had some experience, you don't need to hang around any today. I'll show you the ropes in the morning. Seven-thirty sharp."

"Yes, sir."

"You can call me Skipper. We'll have another new kid coming in tomorrow to work with you. Name's Jimmy. He was out here Memorial Day weekend, and I liked the cut of his jib, so I tried him out. He had to go home to take his finals, but he's supposed to be flying back out today. Well, lads, welcome aboard. I've got some paperwork to finish up, but Phil will show you around. That's him behind the order window. Just go introduce yourself and tell him I said to train you." Then the Skipper stood up and headed for his office.

Now it was a couple of hours later, and Bob Silenski was gazing out the order window, past the horseshoe shaped counter to the dining room on his right. Each side of the counter had a separate dining room, serviced by a different waitress. Sil's eyes were glued on the younger, more attractive one.

"Cute little thing!" he said.

"Who?" said Phil.

Sil pointed, and Phil smiled and said, "Oh, yeah, Shelly. I'm hip to that grove, daddy-o. She's one cool kitty. I'm getting' down with her order right now, and it's comin' up. Why don't you call her over?"

Sil picked up the microphone, pushed the switch, and said in his deepest, sexiest voice, "Shelly." Now he practically purred in his most suggestive bedroom voice, "Order up."

Phil chuckled as he placed the order in the window, pulled the ticket, and placed it beside the plate. "Like, Coolsville, man."

Shelly finished pouring a cup of coffee, returned the pot to its station warmer, and hurried up to the window, smiling self-consciously.

"Don't embarrass me, you," she said good-naturedly, as she picked up the club sandwich with fries.

"Hanky panky, no, no, no!" said Sil, as she walked off.

"You are one gone cat," said Phil, and then added, "Glom a menu before you split, and try to memorize it, so you won't be bugged about it tomorrow. By the way, where you crashin'?"

"At the Travel On Inn."

"Like, that's cool. But tell Blackie to hip you to the Annex, dads. You'll save some bread. Tell him you're sailin' with the Skipper. He'll dig."

Phil Munday had been at the Skipper's Galley for three years now, and it was the closest he had ever been to having a steady gig. Now he was beginning to think it was a real nowhere scene, and was getting restless for change. He'd been thinking about The City lately. Frisco, you dig? It had been nearly four years since he'd split out on that groovy scene. And it wasn't like he'd been real cool about splittin'. But it had been either Splitsville or the steel bar hotel. A Bohemian friend of his had dropped by his North Beach pad one evening to give him the word. And the word was his scene was blown.

"Friday's been asking about you, Munday." Friday was a reference Joe Friday, the cop on television's Dragnet series.

"The fuzz? I don't dig."

"Joe the Glom got busted and he's ratting out everyone he ever so much as sold a joint to. Now the Man's got eyes for you, daddy-o."

Joe the Glom happened to be Phil's pot connection, and Phil scored more than joints from the cat. Like lids and kilos, so he could have a little pocket bread from doing some dealing on the side. I mean, like, hip artists either starved, did the square thing, or got imaginative and did a little pot dealing. No harm in that, he'd thought at the time. But now he wasn't so sure.

"Thanks for the tip, man. And now I must become a real gone cat. Like Splitsville."

He gathered up what possessions he could in the middle of the night, leaving behind canvases and paintings, taking only a pallet, brushes, and paints, a few clothes, and some books by Jack Kerouac; and caught the Greyhound bus for L.A. Phil had a hipster friend, Dave Baum, who was living down in Venice, so he crashed a while with him, sleeping on the couch at night, and painting on or around the beach during the day. By and by, he migrated to Torrance, where he learned the trade of short order cook. It was to have been only a temporary gig. Then one day he went over to Avalon for an art show and dug the scene so much he stayed on and went to work for the Skipper.

Phil knew that the Skipper's Galley was just another greasy spoon, but working there had its advantages. With a steady paycheck, he didn't need to prostitute his art by painting portraits and landscapes for the tourists. How lame was that, he thought. But with the bread of a steady paycheck, he could afford a little cottage on Catalina Avenue. It was large enough to include a little room he used for a studio. Occasionally, he would sell a painting, and he currently had one on display at the art gallery in the Casino, and another in the lobby of the Hotel Saint Catherine.

Each winter, the Skipper's Galley closed down for a few weeks for repairs and maintenance, and for the O'Haras to have a little vacation. This gave Phil an opportunity to split to the mainland to do an art showing with a couple other hip artists. Then he would take a trip down to Tijuana and score some Benzedrine pills from a pharmacy where he was known, and smuggle the pills across the border. He would divide the "bennies" into three plastic bags. One would get stuffed down his pants, the others into his motorcycle boots. He would then hit the Kentucky Bar, have too many drinks, and stagger a few blocks to the border, where the guards would peg him as just another drunken tourist on a whoring excursion, and wave him across. He would then catch the Greyhound to San Diego, change buses for Long Beach, and trade the pills for pot through a dealer he knew. No money would change hands, but he would end up with enough dope to smoke for the rest of the year. Phil found it very relaxing to get a little high and listen to a good jazz recording. Lately, though, he'd been digging an LP by this folk singer cat he'd been turned on to by the name of Bob Dylan. Phil dug Dylan's lyrics. They reminded him of Beat poetry.

It was only recently that Phil had received a letter from an old bohemian friend in The City. The cat had given him the word, and the word was good. There was a brand new scene in the Haight-Ashbury section, by Golden Gate Park. North Beach was now Deadsville, man, like nowhere. Topless bars and square tourists had taken over. But the Haight was like, cool, in a new kind of way. This friend had been hanging out with some cats that called themselves the Merry Pranksters--a group of writers, artists, and hipsters. Among them was one Neal Cassady, an old beatnik who'd been the real-life model for Dean Moriarty in Jack Kerouac's *On The Road*. To Phil, this was a cosmic message to him to return to San Francisco, and pronto. Only one thing kept him from packing his bags immediately, and that was his loyalty to the Skipper. He had pledged to hang on at the Galley through Labor Day.

Now Phil turned his attention back to Sil, the new cook he was training. Since this was Sunday afternoon, and most of the tourists had already split the scene, the pace was slower in the kitchen, and he and Sil were finished filling orders. Phil used this opportunity to show Sil around the place, and how things were set up in the reach-in cooler under the work counter. Then he showed him the walk-in and the dry goods storage area. As they passed the dishwasher's station, they heard music spilling out of the transistor radio, which was tuned to KRLA.

"What's new, pussycat, oh, woh woh oh oh..." sang Tom Jones.

"Are you married, or are you happy?" asked Sil.

"Happy, daddy-o," said Phil. "I was hooked up with this cool kitty for a while, but she split for over town. I'm gonna go out on a limb here and guess that you're single."

"Bingo," said Sil. "Never in love, only in heat."

"Snatch hound, huh?"

"Long as my arm, hard as my fist, and up to here."

"Crazy, man, crazy."

Phil pointed out the laundry basket where they were to toss their dirty uniforms, and the room where they changed clothes. Then he showed Sil the time clock.

"You'll get a time card in the morning, after you fill out your W-2. For now, I'll just tell Skip you worked half a shift."

"Thanks."

"Hungry?"

"I could eat something."

"Have a seat out front, and I'll lay some eats on you. Cheeseburger and fries okay?"

"Sure."

"Just don't hip the Skip. You're supposed to work a full shift. Dig you later, daddy-o."

Sil grabbed a seat in Shelly's section, and then motioned her over.

"What's new, pussycat?" he said.

"You the new breakfast cook?"

"Bingo. Name's Bob, but everyone calls me Sil."

"Hi," she said, shaking his hand. "I'm Shelly, but you already knew that. Can I get you some water or coffee?"

"Both, thanks. Also your phone number."

"You're a fast mover," she laughed. "Sorry, but it's unlisted."

"Hey, I'm serious. Let's go out sometime. I need someone to show me the town. When's your night off?"

"Tuesday and Wednesday, usually."

"Well, sugar-pie, honeybunch, I'll catch you tomorrow and ask again."

After polishing off his meal, Sil left Shelly a generous tip, waved to her and winked, and headed out the door. Back at the Travel On Inn, he questioned Blackie about the Annex.

"I'll have my son show you what we've got there," Blackie said cheerfully.

After a quick look around the Annex, Sil decided to stay put where he was. After all, his cook's income would allow him a little more comfort than the Annex had to offer.

J.T., however, decided his minimum wage would go further at the Annex, so he reluctantly moved his belongings over there that evening. He was not happy with his new digs. It reminded him of an Army barracks. A nagging voice crept into his head. It sounded like his father's voice.

"Look at you, Josh," the voice chided. "Living in Whitey's ghetto, washing his dishes, cleaning up his messes. You just an Uncle Tom--a geechee nigger."

He shut the voice up. "I'm a man," he declared. "Furthermore, I'm going to City College in the fall. I got me a damn future."

Then J.T. recalled that not only was he a veteran, but that he'd taken and passed the Civil Service exam recently. This might get him a job at the post office, if there was an opening. He'd check on it tomorrow, after his shift at the Skipper's Galley.

Meanwhile, at the Travel On Inn, Sil had showered and changed and was ready for the nightlife. He collected J.T., and together they went rambling along the waterfront. After a gin and tonic for Sil and beer for J.T., they went poking around in tourist shops, before ambling toward the Casino. They heard chimes ringing from a tower high on a hill above them, and decided to investigate. After a long steep hike, they reached the Chimes Tower. From where they stood, they had a bird's eye view of Avalon, spread out and glittering below them. The Casino was all lit up, as was the town and harbor, causing Sil to exclaim, "Man, check it out! This beats the hell out of L.A. for atmosphere. Looks like we could be at the French Riviera or Monte Carlo, or some other exotic place. I say, Jay, I almost feel like the Prince of Avalon, of the Kingdom of Catalina."

"Shit, Sil," groaned J.T. "Where do you come up with jive like that, man? It's just a white bread tourist trap, that's all."

"Yeah, man, but just think of the possibilities the place holds. Think of all the women. And we've got the whole summer ahead of us."

"So you say."

When he was in high school, Sil had perfected a Tarzan yell, Tarzan having been one of his childhood heroes. He had more or less retired the yell, except for a drunken encore at a frat party just before semester break. Now, feeling on top of the world, he suddenly felt inspired to let out a long primal call.

"AHEEAEEAHEAEOO! AHEEEAHEEAHEHAEOO!"

The call carried much as the chimes had, echoing off the hills and ricocheting through the narrow streets below. Down below, startled passers-by turned their heads in all directions, looking for Tarzan.

"You flippin' out, Sil?" said J.T., a little concerned.

"No, man, just feeling good. Look at that sparkling little scene down there, Jay. It's like a gift package, all tied up in ribbons and bows, waiting to be opened."

"So you say," said J.T. But he wasn't at all convinced.

CHAPTER 4

▼

JIMMY FONTANA

"Trains and boats and planes…."

The lyrics to a recent song by Billy J. Kramer rolled round and round in Jimmy Fontana's head as he nervously chewed gum and hummed along. He was strapped into the co-pilot's seat of a Grumman Goose on the tarmac at Long Beach Airport. It was only the second time he'd been in an airplane, and he was as nervous today about flying as he'd been the first time.

On Memorial Day weekend, he'd flown in another Catalina Airlines seaplane, except that then he'd been in the passenger cabin and hadn't had to look out the window, thereby risking vertigo or airsickness or just plain panic. On the return trip from that long weekend, he'd opted to sail on the *S.S. Catalina*, a slower but safer means of transportation. Now he was back, hoping to overcome his fear of flying, and this time there was no getting around it by shutting his eyes. Due to his last minute arrival at the terminal, he'd been assigned the last available seat, which turned out to be next to the pilot, since there was no need of a co-pilot on such a short flight. Jimmy uneasily checked the tightness on his seat belt, while chewing gum and humming nervously. *"Trains and boats and planes…."*

He looked ahead through the windscreen and saw the runway. He looked out the side window and saw the control tower. Pilot Warren Stoner, wearing sunglasses, communicated with the tower through the microphone attached to his set of headphones, as he taxied into position for takeoff. Then he reached up and pulled the handle of the throttle, revving up the twin Pratt and Whitney engines. The plane lurched forward, picking up speed. Once the Goose was airborne, Captain Stoner hand cranked the retractable wheels up into the body of the plane.

There was a queasy feeling in Jimmy's stomach as the amphibian lifted off and took to the sky over Long Beach, with buildings and cars becoming smaller as it gained altitude. Jimmy had the sensation of being on a fast elevator. In quick succession, they were passing over Long Beach Harbor and out into the San Pedro Channel. Jimmy looked down on fishing boats, sailboats, and cabin cruisers scattered widely across his line of sight. He noticed a freighter headed out for deeper water, its wake fanning lazily out behind. Jimmy realized he was no longer nervous, and he let out his breath and started to enjoy the flight and the unique view of Catalina Island to the northwest.

The sky was a light blue with scattered, puffy white clouds, and below was the deep blue Pacific Ocean. Dead ahead, the island rose out of the water, dotted with green patches on the dry, brown and green summer vegetation that was common to Southern California. As they approached, and the plane began its descent, Jimmy could make out the town of Avalon and its little harbor quickly becoming larger in his view. Boats bobbed at anchor, and assorted little buildings dotted the crescent-shaped village. The small sleek plane flew low, circled Avalon, and headed back out over the harbor, splashing down just outside to miss the anchored boats. It bounced twice, and then became like another boat in the bay, churning up a wake behind, the pontoons providing balance. Captain Stoner began changing the pitch on both motors, using the propellers now to steer the Goose. He gradually throttled back on the power until the engines sputtered and quit near the end of the Pleasure Pier. The plane glided up to the floating landing and dock at the end, and bumped the row of rubber tires. Young men in blue shirts and white shorts, known as dock boys, scurried about, helping tie down the plane, then assisting with the unloading of passengers, baggage, and supplies for the town.

Jimmy thanked the pilot and shook his hand, then made his way through the passenger cabin and out the door. A dock boy helped him up along the landing onto the floating dock where he pulled his gear from a pile. He hefted the backpack onto his shoulders, then picked up a guitar in one hand, and a portable record player in the other, and walked up the ramp to the Pleasure Pier. He leaned against a railing, set down the guitar case and record player, and pulled out the pack of Marlboros from his shirt pocket. He shook one loose, lit it, and took a deep drag while he watched passengers and baggage being loaded for the return trip.

While he smoked, he looked the Pleasure Pier over. Beside him stood the fish market building, with the Harbor Master's office above it. Farther along, he noticed the office and ticket stand for Catalina Airlines, as well as a couple of fast food stands, a bait and tackle shop, boat rental stand, public rest rooms, showers, lockers, and the Chamber of Commerce office. Also lined along the wooden walkway were the ticket booths for the glass bottom boats and other boat cruises, which departed from the side of the pier. Then Jimmy took a long look at Avalon and its surroundings, turning his head in a 360 degree arc until his gaze returned to the blue and white Grumman Goose which had brought him to his new home. He realized with gravity that he wouldn't be boarding a plane again for nearly three months.

Jimmy ground out his cigarette with a brown wing tip shoe, hefted up his belongings, and began walking purposefully down the pier along Crescent and up Sumner Avenue. At the Skipper's Galley he stopped and looked through one of the windows. Inside were customers, a hostess, two waitresses, a busboy, and a pair of cooks behind the order window. The one with the goatee he recognized, although he couldn't remember his name. He'd never seen the other cook before. More importantly, he did not see the Skipper or his wife, Samantha, so he continued on his way until he reached the Travel On Inn.

He stepped through the front door and dropped his belongings by the front desk. He rang the bell, and Blackie soon appeared,

"Well, hello," said Blackie. "You're the kid who plays the guitar. Jimmy, isn't it?"

"You remembered," said Jimmy, smiling.

"Here for the summer now?"

"Yeah. I'll be back at the Skipper's Galley. Can I get a room?"

"Of course, young fella. We're glad to have you back. David will be happy to see you. I'll let him know you're here. Let's give you a nice quiet room in the back." He searched the pegboard, found a key, and handed it to Jimmy. "Number twelve," he said. "How far in advance do you want to pay?"

"How 'bout a week? I'm not sure when payday will be."

"That'll be fine," said Blackie. "That's twenty dollars. If it gets to be too steep for you, we can put you up in the Annex."

"I think I'll be fine here, thanks. One more thing—mind if I use your phone?"

"Local call?"

"Yeah. I want to let the Skipper know I'm here."

"You bet," said Blackie, passing the telephone across the counter. "Use it anytime you need to."

Jimmy fished a scrap of paper from his shirt pocket, and dialed the number on it.

"Hello," he said when the woman answered. "Is this Sam? Is the Skipper in? Jimmy Fontana from Fullerton. He's not? Well, would you tell him I'm at the Travel On Inn, and I'll be ready to start work in the morning, seven-thirty? Thanks. Yeah, I'm glad too. Bye now."

"Everything okay?" asked Blackie.

"Yeah, thanks. Well, guess I'll get unpacked."

"You need anything, just ring the bell. I'll send David over when I find him."

Then Blackie disappeared through the doorway behind the desk.

A few minutes later, Jimmy had unpacked and removed his Martin guitar from its case. It had a beautiful blond finish and wore new strings. When he'd quit the rock band after high school, Jimmy had sold his electric Fender guitar and bought the acoustic Martin. At the time, he'd thought it a bit expensive, but soon realized it was worth the money, as it had such a rich, warm tone. Anyway, he was more of a folk singer than a rocker, and other than the Top 40 on KRLA, he listened mostly to folk music these days. He seated himself with the guitar balanced on his leg, and began to sing a melancholy Donovan song. It gave him a perverse pleasure to sing sad songs.

"Ah, but I may as well try and catch the wind..."

There came a tap-tap-tap at the door.

"Come in," said Jimmy.

Waxie threw the door back and said, "Hey Jimmy, welcome back."

"Thanks."

"So, you're here for the summer?"

"That's the plan."

"Then what, back to Fullerton College?"

"No, I'm afraid not. I'm going in the Navy."

"The Navy?"

"Yeah. I flunked out of school and lost my student deferment. May as well join up than wait around to be drafted."

"Wow," said Waxie, sitting on the edge of the bed, "that's a drag."

"Tell me about it."

"Well," said Waxie philosophically, "maybe it won't be so bad. Pop was in the Navy."

"Did he like it?"

"I don't know. It was World War Two. He was just doing his duty. He met my mom when he was in the Navy."

"Really?"

"Yeah, at a USO dance. During the war, they closed down Avalon to tourists and put some military installations on the island. So my mom went over town to live with my aunt. She got a job at the North American Aviation plant in Inglewood. She said when she'd go to the beach sometimes on her day off, she could see Catalina off the coast. Anyway, my pop's ship was home ported in Long Beach, and he met my mom before he shipped out. They kept in touch, and got married after the war. But instead of him taking her to Boston, she brought him to Avalon."

"Well, at least that story has a happy ending."

"Do you have to go in the Navy? Maybe you could get your deferment back."

"Too late. I already enlisted. It's a four-month delay program. Sort of like sign now, pay later."

"Well, at least you can have a fun summer. I got a Vespa for my graduation present. Let's take it for a spin after I have dinner with my family."

"Sure. You know where I'll be."

Jimmy had only recently met Waxie, during the Memorial Day weekend, but they had hit it off immediately. He was a year older and an inch taller than Waxie, but in other ways bore a resemblance to him. His hair was a shade lighter, wavy, and unlike Waxie, he combed it straight back. His eyes were blue, not brown, but he had a similar build to Waxie, slender and evenly proportioned. They had a similar gait when they walked--long strides, not quite a swagger, but sort of a carefree bounce. And both were currently single, without girlfriends.

It hadn't always been that way for Jimmy. He had gone steady for two years with Diane Fisher. But that had ended suddenly a few months ago, when she'd told him she'd been seeing his best friend Vince. She gave him back his ring, but still wanted to be friends. Friends? How unfriendly the word now seemed.

Jimmy had gone into a deep depression and seemed to lose interest in everything. Unable to focus on his classes, he just stopped attending school. He would instead head down to the beach where he would watch the waves roll in for hours at a time. Or he'd hang out at the park, trying to study but soon giving up. He began to take notice of couples everywhere, and felt sad. Often at night he cruised around aimlessly in his '57 Chevy and sooner or later would wind up on Diane's street. He would drive slowly by her house. If her bedroom light was turned off, he knew she was out with Vince. If the Mustang was parked out front, he knew they were inside, and he'd imagine them close together, making out. If the Mustang was gone, and her light was on, he'd crush an impulse to park and knock on her door just to see her again. But he knew it was useless, so he'd drive away. And then his song would come on the radio.

"Well, here it comes, here comes the night...."

When he finally realized he was flunking out of school, Jimmy joined the Navy. After he'd enlisted, he'd remembered the Laurel and Hardy short "Beau Hunks", in which the pair join the Foreign Legion so Hardy can forget his unfaithful lover, only to find out that every man on the post they're assigned to carries a photo of the same woman, and all pining away for her. Jimmy knew he had to get far away, and a long ocean voyage seemed just the ticket out.

Jimmy had had a part time job as a cook's helper at a restaurant near his home. One day toward the end of the semester, a young cook on the line asked him what was wrong.

"You look as if you've lost your best friend," he said.

"I have," said Jimmy glumly. "He ran off with my girlfriend."

"That's tough," said the cook. "No wonder the long face. But hey, I have just the cure for that."

"What, suicide?"

"Nothing so drastic. You just get your ass over to Catalina Island for the summer. The place is packed with women. You need to get back on the horse."

"Yeah, right. Good idea, but I don't have that kind of dough lying around."

"You don't need bread, my friend. Just get a plane ticket—five bucks one way—and get on over to Avalon. Then go over to the Skipper's Galley and tell the Skipper you want a cook's job for the summer. Tell him Larry Kilgore recommended you."

"But I'm not a cook."

"I know that, but he doesn't. I'll show you a few tricks of the trade, enough to get you in the door. Then just keep your eyes open and fake it till you make it."

Jimmy took Larry's advice and landed the job for the summer. He'd worked a couple of days alongside the Skipper and had pulled it off. Now it would just be a matter of learning enough to keep his foot in the door. And he would take care of that problem when it arose. For now, he was in Avalon, and it seemed as if an ocean separated him from his old flame, and every familiar thing he knew.

While Waxie enjoyed dinner with his family, Jimmy got a bite to eat at the Skipper's Galley. When he returned, Waxie was ready to show off the Vespa and soon the two were puttering around Avalon's side streets. Jimmy had changed into more casual clothing: brown corduroys, desert boots, a black tee shirt, and a windbreaker. Waxie wound the scooter up and down hills, then along Crescent, past Lovers Cove, and out to Pebbly Beach. Up Wrigley Road he shot, past the Holly Hill House (another picture postcard landmark), finally ending up behind the Casino. Waxie parked the scooter and the two stood overlooking the clear water of the bay. Jimmy lit a cigarette as they walked along the breakwater and found a large rock to sit on that faced the bay.

"So you're out of high school now," said Jimmy. "Congratulations. Now what?"

"I don't know. Just keep working at the Travel On Inn, I guess. It's the family business. Pop wants to do some renovations in the winter."

"Yeah, I noticed it needed a paint job. Don't you want to do anything else with your life?"

"I don't know. Sometimes I think I'd like to go over town for a while and see what that's like. It gets kind of old sometimes, living in a small town where everyone knows you and you've done pretty much all there is to do. It can get boring in the winter."

"Living on the mainland isn't that great either," said Jimmy. "Traffic, smog, crime. Everybody seems to be going in the fast lane. That kind of life can wear you out. I think that's why my dad has ulcers."

"Yeah, I guess every place has its ups and downs," agreed Waxie.

Then the talk turned to girls. Waxie already knew Jimmy's sad story, so they talked about Waxie's love life instead.

"I just met this really neat girl at El Encanto," he said. "Really cute and fun to be with."

"How'd it go?"

"Great! We danced, we talked, went for a ride. Then I walked her to her hotel and kissed her goodnight."

"Nice. You going to see her again?"

"I wish. She went back on the boat today. Story of my life. Meet someone I really dig, and then she's gone. But there's always tomorrow."

"Speaking of tomorrow," said Jimmy, "I start bright and early at the Galley. I guess we ought to head on back."

"Okay,' said Waxie, stretching his legs. They reached the Vespa and were about to climb on, when suddenly they heard a long primal call followed by another, echoing all around.

"What the hell was that?" said Jimmy.

"It sounded like Tarzan."

"Where'd it come from?"

"I think up there," said Waxie, pointing toward the Chimes Tower.

"Should we check it out?"

"Nah," said Waxie. "We might find out it's not Tarzan after all. Probably just some weirdo."

"Maybe you're right," said Jimmy, climbing on back of the scooter. "Home, Jeeves, and don't spare the horses."

Later that night, Jimmy lay in bed thinking about Diane and wondering if he should send her a postcard. Would she appreciate it? Would she even care if she heard from him at all? Doubtful. He pushed these thoughts out of his head, and tried to imagine what the summer in Avalon would be like. He tried, but the screen of his imagination was blank. Well, tomorrow is a fresh day, he thought, closing his eyes and rolling over on his side. He waited for sleep to come and numb out all his pain and confusion.

CHAPTER 5

▼

LUNCH RUSH

"You're tuned to the Reb Foster show on KRLA at fifteen past the hour. It's a beautiful seventy-five degrees on this groovin' Monday morning. Coming up next--Herman's Hermits with 'I'm Henry The Eighth'. Peter Noone forgot the second verse in the recording studio, so he just sang the first verse twice, which didn't stop it from becoming a hit, and it's still climbing the charts."

The song made its way into the air from the little radio by the dishwasher's section, where Joshua Taylor (Jay Tee to his friends) was up to his elbows in dirty dishes, and was struggling to keep up. To him, the radio was just a distraction. But over at the cooks' station, whenever Sil and Jimmy would get caught up with orders, they would strain their ears to listen. This was one such moment. Jimmy, who was sweating from the heat, needed a cigarette break, and this looked like his chance. He ducked out of sight of the order window, removed his cook's hat, wiped his forehead with the apron tied to his waist, and said, "Now that we're caught up, mind if I take five?"

"Sure, man, go ahead," said Sil. "I've got it covered."

And indeed he had. Jimmy was grateful to be starting off the day working with Sil, so he could learn a few things without having the Skipper around. He was also grateful that when the rushes came, Sil would take charge and give him simple things to do, like make toast or pancakes or fry bacon. When things slowed down he'd pick Sil's brain about such things as how to fold an omelet or flip an egg, or how to tell the difference between over-easy and over-medium. He was already seeing Sil not only as his mentor but also his boss. Hence, he'd asked permission to take a smoke break.

Jimmy excused himself as he scooted past J.T. and made his way through the back of the kitchen, past pots and pans and dry goods, to the screen door that led to the parking lot out back. It was an open area that connected Sumner Avenue with Metropole Avenue. Stepping outside, he squinted in the bright sunlight of late morning, and took in a deep breath of fresh air, which was scented with the aroma of eucalyptus trees from Island Plaza across the street, and ocean breeze. Then he took in a lung full of cigarette smoke as he lit one up, and the first drag made his throat sting and his eyes water. He watched as a carefree couple in shorts and sunglasses strolled through the parking lot, oblivious to him.

Jimmy's head was swimming with names and numbers of orders, names of waitresses and busboys, and the clatter of cups and plates, and spatulas scraping against grills, and all the other coffee shop sounds that had made up his morning. But now, watching the couple walk away, another thought and another face came into his mind. Diane Fisher. Thoughts of her didn't stay buried very long, he knew. He could almost conjure up her sparkling eyes and coy smile, and he wondered where she was and what she was doing at this moment. And then he felt the pain of separation, of abandonment again, almost like a bitter taste in his mouth. He flicked the Marlboro butt across the lot and slammed the screen door behind him as he stepped back inside the Skipper's Galley, to bury himself in work. He arrived at his station only moments before the Skipper showed up.

The Skipper had traded in his yachtsman's cap for a white sailor cap, something Jimmy would be wearing in a few months. The Skipper had the brim turned down, like Gilligan on television.

"Okay, mates," said the Skipper in an authoritarian voice, "time to get serious. That little breakfast rush was like a little foreplay for a mermaid. Time to put away the breakfast stuff and get ready for the lunch rush. You can keep the bacon out for BLTs, but don't fry any more. Jimmy—there's a pot of clam chowder in the walk-in. Bring it and the six pack of beer on the shelf next to it. Put the pot on the stove, and the beer in the reach-in."

"Right!"

"Bob—bring a case of hamburger patties and a couple bags of fries. I'll get the rest."

"Aye, aye, cap!" said Sil.

"That's what I like to hear," said the Skipper, clamping down on his half smoked, but cold cigar. A couple of minutes later, he gave them fresh instructions.

"Turn on the steam table and start tossing patties on the broiler. When they're done, toss 'em in the steam tray, Jimbo. Then start dropping baskets of fries and toss 'em in the other one. We'll sandbag it all. In a few minutes the boat will dock, and all hell will break loose. We'll have a big line at the door and the idea is to get 'em in and out as quick as we can, so we can turn the tables over. Understand?"

"Got it Skip," said Sil. "How do you want to run the show?"

"Like this—Jimmy will take care of the broiler and the fryer. You got the grill and the toaster. I'll cover the wheel, call out orders, and put the plates together. Make sure you got plenty buns and patties up here at all times."

"Aye, aye," said Sil. "Anything else?"

"Yeah, make sure you drink plenty of water. I got some salt tablets if you need 'em. I don't want anyone passing out from heat exhaustion, that clear?"

"Yes, sir," said Jimmy.

"You don't have to call me sir. Just Skip or Cap or boss."

High noon came shortly, and with it pandemonium as hordes of tourists first filled the streets, then shops and restaurants, and into the Skipper's Galley they came.

The hostess at the door was the first to be overwhelmed by the mob. Then the waitresses got hit. They frantically scribbled orders in their ticket books. Then the parade of girls began, lining up at the order window, tickets in hand, and it was the cooks' turn to join in the mad scramble. The Skipper began barking orders.

"Burgers a pair--make that four, hold the onion on one, fries on all of 'em. Keep those fries comin', Jimbo! Okay--one BLT on wheat, one fish basket, one shrimp basket. Chowders, a pair. Rail 'em!"

"Aye, aye," said Sil.

"One chili size, medium rare. Better fire that one fresh."

"Okay," said Jimmy.

"One grinder, medium!"

"I'm on it."

"Taylor," he called out to J.T., "we need more dinner plates up here on the double!"

"Okay, boss."

"Marilyn, order up! Here you go, dear. Francie--order up! Cheeseburgers, a pair! Bob--one grilled cheese and a tuna salad sand."

"On the way."

"Linda, order up."

"Hey," said Linda, "that's not my order, it's supposed to be a number five."

"Our mistake. We'll put it on the rail. Jimmy, chicken basket—rail it!"

"Okay, boss."

"And keep those fries comin'! Marilyn, order up."

And so the frenzy continued like this for the next two hours without a let-up. Every so often, the Skipper would pull out a beer from the reach-in, duck out of sight, and chug it. Then he would expertly toss the empty can across the room into the trashcan by the dishwasher's station. His face was flushed and he sweated profusely. Whenever they could catch their breaths, Jimmy and Sil grabbed a glass of water from the big sink. Eventually, the flood of orders slowed to a stream and then a trickle. The Skipper had timed the lunch rush down to the last beer, and when it had been polished off, he removed his sailor hat, mopped his balding head with a hand towel and removed his apron.

"Okay, mates," he said, "you got the helm. Dump the extra fries, but save the burgers still in the steamer. We can still sell those, or at least chop 'em up and throw 'em in the chili. I don't like anything to be wasted. Clean up before Phil and Dan come on. Be sure to stone the grill and brush the broiler. Well," he added, before heading off to his office, "ya done good for the first day. See ya back here tomorrow morning."

Jimmy and Sil cleaned up as the Skipper asked, and at three-thirty the swing shift showed up. A young guy named Hector took over for J.T., who said wearily, "Shore am happy to see you, brother."

Phil Munday and Dan Burton, a twenty-one year old Pierce College student, relieved the cooks.

"You cats can get real gone now, and make the beach scene," said Phil behind the sunglasses he had yet to remove. "But before you split this crazy scene, dads, cop a seat and I'll lay some eats on you."

Sil, Jimmy, and J.T. clocked out, washed up, and then commandeered the unofficial employees table in the dining room. An older waitress named Betty, who worked at Avalon School during the rest of the year, took their orders. When the food arrived, Sil said to J.T.,

"Hey, hodad, how 'bout doing me the favor of scrounging me up a clean fork. This one's a little grody, and I believe you were (ahem) the guy who washed it."

"Sure, Sil, no problem."

As soon as he stood and turned his back to the table, Sil lifted J.T.'s hamburger bun and dashed a liberal amount of Tabasco sauce on the patty. J.T. returned momentarily with a clean fork for Sil, then sat to enjoy his meal. He took a big bite out of the burger, made a face, swallowed, and took a long drink of water, while Sil cracked up.

"Sil you muthafucka! I'll get you for this, just wait."

"Puma head!" said Sil.

"Flatus breath," countered J.T.

"Flatus—a gaseous odor excreted from the anal cavity," said Sil.

"In other words, Sil, I called you fart breath. And you'd better not turn your back on me, cause now I owe you one."

"Okay," said Sil with a shit-eating grin, "I'm sorry, my man, even though it was pretty funny. I'll make it up to you, though. I'll buy you dinner later."

"Better be steak and lobster, flatus breath," said J.T., picking up a French fry and eyeing it suspiciously.

"We can go someplace romantic," said Sil, raising an eyebrow.

"No way, unh, uh. Not less you bring a date for me. Of the female persuasion only."

"Is there any other kind?" asked Sil, taking a sip of Coke.

As he ate, Sil turned his attention in the direction of the other dining room, on the other side of the horseshoe counter. His gaze locked on Shelly Green, the waitress he had met the day before. He studied her as he grazed through his shrimp basket. He liked what he saw. Oh, she wasn't what he would call a classic beauty, but he thought she looked pretty cute in her waitress uniform, with the full-length blue apron over it and the white tennis shoes. Casual, but classy, he thought. She had a natural and wholesome attractiveness that began with the sincere smile that lit up her dimpled oval face. Her hair was straight and fine and of a color that Sil liked to think of as dishwater blond, and she had it tied back in a ponytail. Her eyes were also a light color, a shade of brown, close to amber. He guessed her to be about five-foot six, on the slender side, but with curves in all the right places. Then he noticed her legs, or what he could see of them beneath the length of her dress. If the calves were any indication, he must check out her thighs as well. On the beach, and the sooner, the better.

"Cute little thing!" he said, turning back to his meal.

"Hey, Sil," said J.T., wiping his mouth with a napkin, and pushing away his plate, "I think I'll find the post office and pick up an application. Want to meet up later?"

"Yeah. I'll probably be down on the beach. What do you say, Jimmy, wanna go scope out the chick action?"

"Okay."

"I'll knock on your door once I get changed. But first, I've got to go visit that cute little thing over there." He nodded in Shelly's direction, then stood and wandered over to her section and sat at an empty table. She flashed him a smile, then finished taking a customer's order and walked the ticket up to the order window. She picked up a menu from her wait station and brought it over to Sil.

"I've already eaten," he said with a smile.

"Can I get you anything else?" she asked.

"Of course, beautiful. Your phone number."

"It's unlisted, remember?"

"Okay. Then how about going out with me tomorrow night?"

"Sorry, I'm busy tomorrow."

"Then how about Wednesday? I'll keep asking until you say yes."

"You're awfully persistent, aren't you?"

"Only when I want something badly. Believe me, I won't be able to sleep at night until you say yes."

"I've got a cure for that," she said. "Take a cold shower."

"You really know how to hurt a guy, don't you?" he said.

"Oh, all right," she laughed. "You win. Wednesday night it is."

"Thank you," he said, taking her hand and kissing it. "What time shall I pick you up?"

"There's a movie at the Casino Theater at seven. How about we meet a quarter till?"

"Where do you live?" he asked.

"We can just meet here," she said. "It'll be a nice walk."

"Of course," he agreed. "Thank you. You won't regret it."

"We'll see about that," she said. "Well, I'd better get back to work. I'll see you later. Now go home and take that cold shower," she said, wagging a finger.

At six forty-five Wednesday evening, June 23rd, Bob Silenski appeared in the doorway of the Skipper's Galley, freshly showered, shaved, and groomed. He looked around, and not seeing Shelly, took a seat at the counter. Before he could be waited on, she walked in from the street wearing a green summer blouse and tan knee length skirt. Her ponytail was gone and her hair now fell loosely about her shoulders. Bob lifted his hand in greeting, and she flashed him a smile in return as she walked toward him. He stood to meet her, giving her a quick hug and remarking, "You look clean out of sight."

She shyly looked down and nearly blushed as she said, "Thank you. Well, all set to go?"

"Lead on, princess," he said, gesturing broadly toward the door.

They strolled along in the pleasantly cool Avalon evening, enjoying a gentle breeze, and each other's company. The talk was casual as they walked, Shelly pointed out sights and stopped to look into a couple of shop windows.

Sil asked her about herself and her family, finding out that she was a sophomore at Orange Coast College, majoring in Education. She also mentioned that she and her brother John had worked at the Skipper's Galley the previous summer.

"Where is he now?" Sil asked.

"He's in the Army. He was drafted. He's taking Advanced Infantry Training at Fort Benning. I miss him a lot."

"Sorry to hear that," said Sil.

"I'm hoping he'll get sent to Germany, not Vietnam," she said.

"Maybe he'll luck out," said Sil. "J.T. spent his tour of duty in Germany."

"Who's J.T.?" she asked.

"My buddy who got the morning dishwasher job. You know, the black guy."

"Oh, yeah," said Shelly. "I haven't met him yet, or the other new cook for that matter."

"You will. They're both cool guys."

"What about you, Sil. What do you do on the mainland?"

"I'm a junior at Long Beach State. Pre-Med. My turn ons are surfing, partying, traveling, and beautiful women, like you. My turn offs are gremmies, hodads, suits and ties, and wipe outs."

"Very cute," said Shelly.

They had now walked down the Via Casino past the Tuna Club and the Yacht Club, and were rounding the point to the Casino. They walked up to the box office, and Sil bought the tickets for a second run Rock Hudson and Doris Day movie. A poster announced the coming attraction of the new James Bond movie, *Thunderball*.

"At this theater," said Shelly, "you have two choices. One--take it, or two--leave it."

After the movie, and a short walk along the breakwater, Shelly offered to show Sil the Hotel Saint Catherine just around the bend from Casino Point.

"How'd you like the movie?" she asked as they walked.

"It was okay. Tony Randall was funny. But I got the impression that the battle of the sexes never ends, not even with marriage."

"Are you against marriage, Sil?"

"No, not in theory. But I'm too young and (ahem) innocent to strap on the ball and chain."

Shelly laughed before changing the subject. "Did you know that Doris Day is filming a movie here this summer?"

"Here in Avalon? Where'd you hear that?"

"I got it from a reliable source."

"The gossip mill?"

"Yes, but also from The Islander. There was an article in last week's paper."

"No kiddin'?" said Sil. Then he added, "Would it make you jealous if I went out with Doris Day?"

Shelly laughed. "I don't think so. Besides, she's old enough to be your mother."

"That's an image I don't want to contemplate," said Sil in mock seriousness.

Shelly linked her arm in Sil's and said, "Well, there it is, the Hotel Saint Catherine."

It was a large, stately building, decades old and still bearing a hint of grandeur. The couple walked through the entrance and into the lobby where they looked around at the décor and furnishings and paintings hanging on the walls. Sil made a face at the abstract painting.

"Don't you like modern art, Sil?"

"No, can't say I do."

"Too bad. Our swing shift cook, Phil Munday, did that one. They say he's quite an accomplished artist."

"Couldn't prove it by me. But I'll make sure to ask for his autograph when I see him again."

Back outside in the star studded night, Sil asked if he could walk Shelly back to her house.

"Of course you can," she said, taking his arm again.

"So, where do you live?"

"Not far from the Galley. I'll give you directions when we reach it."

They made a slow, circuitous return trip, trying to cheat the time, but it eventually brought them back to the Skipper's Galley. As they passed the Bamboo Lounge, they could hear the strains of "Pearly Shells" coming from the jukebox. "Must be the bartender's favorite song," thought Sil.

At the Skipper's Galley, Shelly said, "Okay, we go another block and then turn right at Beacon."

Soon, they were standing in front of a white frame house with a little picket fence out front.

"Well," said Shelly, "here we are. My little summer home."

"Nice," said Sil. "Got this place all to yourself?"

"No, I rent a room in the back from the Schusters. I have my own key, but I don't like to stay out tool late. Afraid I might wake them." She pressed her finger to her lips for emphasis.

"I'll remember that the next time we go out," he said.

"Thanks for a great time," she said. "It was really fun. I enjoyed your company."

"And I, yours," he said, pulling her into him and kissing her lightly on the lips. She pulled back a little, and then gave him a quick hug.

"I should go in now," she said. "Goodnight, and thanks again."

"How about a repeat engagement?" he asked.

"Ask me again at work. I'll see you there." With that she turned and walked to the door. As she closed it, she turned to see him still standing there. He waved then walked away.

Up at the Annex, Joshua Taylor tossed and turned, thinking about piles of dirty dishes and feeling alone in the world. In his room at the Travel On Inn, Bob "Never in love, only in heat" Silenski had a hand wrapped around his erection, thinking of Shelly Green and about how he'd like to nail her.

Jimmy Fontana sat on the stoop on the Travel On Inn, smoking a cigarette and trying to recall Diane Fisher's face to mind with some kind of clarity. Her memory was beginning to get fuzzy around the edges.

Inside the Travel On Inn, in the room where he grew up, David "Waxie" Shein slept the sleep of the innocent, dreaming about rosy-cheeked girls, Vespas, and Avalon summer dances.

CHAPTER 6

▼

THE SAN DIEGO GIRLS

"Help me if you can, I'm feelin' down...."

Jimmy Rabbit, disc jockey on KGB, San Diego's Boss Radio, was spinning the latest Beatles song. Donna Forte heard it coming out of her bedroom radio speaker, and reached over to the night stand to shut if off. She didn't need the Beatles to remind her she was feeling down. Her feelings, in fact, were a little more complicated than that. They wove a quilt of anger, fear, anxiety, heartbreak, confusion, and helplessness. And how about this--she was late. The only person she felt safe to confide in was her best friend, Lynn Robinson. She had tried to confide in Father Paul during confession at Sunday mass earlier.

"Bless me Father, for I have sinned," she said to the priest behind the thin partition of the confessional.

"When was your last confession?" he asked.

"Two weeks ago," she said.

"How have you sinned?"

And she had told him. She hadn't wanted to, but she couldn't keep it to herself, either. She was no longer a virgin. She'd had intercourse with her boyfriend. She held a thin hope that Father Paul, in absolving her of her sin, would make everything all right again, would even bring Chuck back to her. What an empty word intercourse was. It didn't seem like it meant sex, any more than the act itself had felt like sex should. She wanted the priest to give her old self back to her. Instead, he gave her the Prayer of Contrition, and the Our Fathers and Hail Marys, and she felt just as empty and confused as before. And she was still late.

It seemed no one could help her. She played back that night in her mind, trying to see what she could have done differently, if only she could live it over again for real, instead of just in her fearful, guilt-ridden thoughts.

It had started out as such a special evening, that night after graduation. She and Chuck would both be going off to college in the fall, Chuck on a football scholarship to San Diego State, she to San Diego City College. They had gone out to dinner at a nice restaurant in Mission Bay, then out dancing at the Cinnamon Cinder. Later they parked, as they often did on their dates. Chuck found a nice secluded spot in Torrey Pines, overlooking the Pacific Ocean, with moonlight dancing on the waves. They made out, the kisses became more passionate, and Donna had to roll the backseat window down in order to get some fresh air. She reclined on her back and let Chuck feel her up under her bra. When his hand wandered down to her bell-bottoms and gave a tug at the zipper, she gripped his wrist and pushed his hand away. She'd never let him get to third base before and wasn't going to now, either.

"Please, darling, let's wait," she said anxiously. "Let's make it special."

Chuck's face was flush, his skin warm, and his breathing heavy. He took Donna's hand and placed it in his lap, so she could feel the stiffness.

"Oh, please, honey," he said. "What could be more special than this? We love each other. We've been going steady nearly two years and now we're adults. Besides, with us going to different schools in the fall, I wouldn't want us to drift apart."

"That could never happen, sweetheart. I love you too much."

"Do you, Donna? Sometimes I wonder. If you really loved me, you'd prove it by giving yourself to me completely. Then I'd know you belonged to me and no one else."

That old argument again, thought Donna. Well, that's just how boys were. Oversexed. And it was the girl's responsibility to say no, to keep them from going all the way. And up until now, she'd managed to do just that.

"But what if I get pregnant," she countered, "what then? We're too young to get married, you said so yourself. You want to finish college first."

"You won't get pregnant," he said. "I've taken care of that. Look," he said, reaching in his back pocket for his wallet, and fumbling out something small, square, and wrapped in foil. "I brought a condom. It'll protect you. I just can't wait any longer to seal our love."

"No, Chuck, it's not right."

"Well, okay, if that's what you want. I guess if you can't satisfy my needs I need to find someone who can."

Now Chuck was playing dirty. He was hitting her hot button, the one that tapped into her insecurities. She'd never felt good enough for Chuck. And whenever she saw other girls staring at him in his Letterman's jacket, she felt jealous and threatened.

Chuck Belton. He was more than a big man on campus at Point Loma High. He was like king of the place. Captain of the football team, president of the senior class, and voted "most likely to succeed." She, on the other hand, had lesser credentials in the popularity pyramid: Vice-President of the Pep Club, Song Leader (one rung down from Yell Leader), and Homecoming Princess (one of several in the queen's court). She was also voted "Most School Spirit." This last accolade, she knew, was just a consolation prize mostly because she was Chuck's girl. She knew he could do better, and most of the girls at school thought so too. Excepting Lynn. Dear, sweet Lynn. Now here was Chuck playing his trump card on her. Go all the way or I'll leave you. It was the wrong night to argue---post graduation, moonlight dancing on the water, Chuck's strong arms holding her and at the same time threatening to let go. She said yes.

Later, they drove home in silence. Sex in the back seat of Chuck's car had been a let down. She wasn't sure either one of them had done it right. It had been rushed, forced, and painful for her. Chuck had groaned, pulled out, pulled up his pants, and tossed the rubber out the window. And then instead of holding her and cuddling her, he'd gotten behind the wheel and started the engine. The silence as they drove home was what hurt the most.

In short time, he had dropped her off in front of her house, not even offering to walk her to the door, which she found very strange. She had leaned over to kiss him goodnight and whispered, "Goodnight, darling. Call me in the morning before we go to mass, okay?"

Sunday morning came and went, but no phone call from Chuck. Sunday night, still no phone call. She began to fret. Maybe something bad had happened to him. By Monday evening, Donna could stand it no longer. She picked up the telephone and called. His mother answered.

"Hello, Mrs. Belton."

"Hello, Donna. Did you want Chuck?"

"Please."

"Just a minute, dear. I'll call him."

A few moments later, he answered.

"Oh, hi Donna."

"Chuck, are you alright? I hadn't heard from you, so I began to worry."

"I'm okay," he said flatly.

"You don't sound okay," she said after a pause. "What's wrong? Tell me. Please. Maybe I can help."

"Nothing's wrong, Donna," he said, sounding a little irritated.

"Are you sure?"

"Yeah. It's just that, well, I've been doing some thinking."

"About what?"

"Well, uh, I really didn't want to discuss this over the phone, but since you asked, it's like this—maybe we shouldn't see each other for awhile."

"What?"

"Yeah. I was thinking we ought to see other people for the summer."

"See other people—what are you trying to say?"

I'm saying this, Donna," he said after a long pause. "There are two kinds of women in this world-- virgins and whores. And we both know which you are."

"I can't believe you just said that!" she said, trying not to get hysterical.

"Yeah, well, that's the way it is," he said tersely.

"But you said you loved me. I thought we were going to be married," she sobbed.

"If I marry anyone, Donna, she'll be a virgin."

"But you said if I went all the way, it would seal our love."

"Maybe you should have said no," he said coldly. "Listen, I have to go now. I'm sorry, Donna. Maybe I'll see you around."

"Wait," she cried into the receiver, "don't go. I love you, Chuck. You can't leave me this way."

But there was no response, just the whine of a disconnected call ringing in her ears.

Later, when she didn't come down for dinner, Donna's mother checked in on her and found her sobbing into her pillow.

"What's the matter, sweetheart?" asked her mother, Angie. "Why are you crying?"

"Oh, Mom," she said, choking back tears, "Chuck and I broke up."

"Oh, honey, I'm so sorry. When did this happen?" she asked, sitting on the edge of the bed and placing her hand on Donna's.

"Just now," she sobbed.

"Oh, dear. Do you want to talk about it? No? Can I do anything for you?"

"Not right now. I just have to think."

"I guess you don't feel like coming down to dinner," Angie said. "I'll bring you up a plate later."

"Thanks, Mom."

"If you want to talk about it later, I'll be here for you. And remember, you can always give your troubles to God. Maybe saying the Rosary will help."

But Donna knew it wouldn't help. Nothing would.

Now here it was another Sunday, and she was late. Besides Father Paul, she'd confided in Lynn, whom she knew wouldn't judge her. If she really were pregnant, though, everyone would know. Then what? And what would Chuck do about it?

As these thoughts swirled around in Donna's troubled mind, the telephone rang. Maybe it was Chuck, she thought. Maybe he's finally come to his senses and wants to make up. She picked up on the third ring.

"Hello?" she said tentatively.

"Hi, Don! How are ya, girlfriend? Feelin' any better?"

"No."

"Whatcha doin'?"

"Painting my nails."

"What color?"

"Black."

"Ha! Well, at least I see you haven't lost your sense of humor. So, uh, did you get your period yet?"

"No, and I don't know what to do. I'm going crazy."

"Don't worry, Don. Lots of girls are late at times. I wouldn't worry unless you start having morning sickness. You haven't had that, have you?"

"No, but I haven't been sleeping much all week, and I've lost my appetite."

"Well, hey girl, that's your problem right there. Stress. That can really mess up a girl's cycle. Ain't no big thang, Don. Anyway, I have the cure for that."

"What is it?" asked Donna.

"Road trip! Girls' day out! I'll pick you up in half-an-hour in the Beast."

"I don't know, Lynn. I don't feel like going anywhere."

"Hey, Don, ain't no big thang. It's either road trip or slit your wrists. Come on, we'll have fun. We'll go out to Coronado and meet millionaires or movie stars. And if that doesn't pan out, there's always O.B. And you know there's cute guys there."

"Oh, okay," said Donna, managing a small laugh. "You've sold me. But make it forty-five minutes."

"That's more like it. Wear something sexy and lots of makeup. We need all the help we can get if we're going to trap rich men."

"Thanks, Lynn, for always being such a good friend."

"Ain't no big thang," said Lynn before hanging up.

And indeed, Lynn had always been a good friend. They'd met in Pep Club and also had had an art class together. When they discovered they lived in the same neighborhood, they began hanging out and becoming friends and confidants. They'd even had slumber parties at each other's houses. Donna was glad she could always count on Lynn. Now she prepared to make herself beautiful.

Angie didn't allow her to wear makeup to mass, so Donna was starting with a fresh palette, as it were. She put on eyeliner and mascara, dark eye shadow under her soft brown eyes, and bright red lipstick on her full shaped lips. She brushed her thick, shoulder length black hair, parting it in the middle, so it framed her olive hued face in an oval shape before adding a little hair spray to hold it. She put on her glasses, so she could better scrutinize herself in the mirror. She was envious of girls who wore contacts. But the idea of placing something onto her eyeballs with her finger creeped her out, so she stayed with the glasses. Now, for the frosting on the cake, she sprayed a little Wind Song perfume in her hair and on her neck. Finally, she changed into a white summer blouse, black Capris, and black flats. She made a final inspection and was pleased to find herself attractive again, ready to rejoin the world, if only for the day.

Soon, the doorbell rang and there stood Lynn in the doorway, wearing a big smile, shorts, and makeup, which she used conservatively. Presently, they were off and running in Lynn's graduation present, a green 1960 Ford Falcon she'd dubbed The Beast.

On the way to Coronado Island, Lynn chatted breezily, trying to cheer Donna up and succeeding somewhat. They strolled into the Hotel Coronado trying to blend in, but secretly feeling out of place. Lynn pointed to a well-dressed man who appeared to be in his mid-twenties, hands behind his back, looking out the window. Lynn nudged Donna.

"Whadda ya think?" she whispered.

"Cute."

"Cute?" she said in a louder but still muted voice. "He's gorgeous. Oh, God, please let him be single!"

They strolled past him purposefully, trying to draw his attention, but his eyes were focused on a beautiful young woman who now entered the room. He walked over to her, they embraced, and walked off together arm-in-arm. Lynn and Donna looked at each other.

"All the good ones are taken," said Donna.

Lynn shrugged. "Ain't no big thang."

After a few more minutes of this, Lynn and Donna decided they weren't going to find any millionaires or movie stars at Coronado this day, so they'd fall back on the old stand by, O.B.

They drove out to Ocean Beach and concurred that it was a much better idea. The weather was perfect and the surf was up, which meant there were cute surfer guys to watch. They parked The Beast in the lot and strolled over to a hamburger stand. After ordering, they sat at a picnic table sipping Cokes, and checking out all the guys walking by on the beach, and the bronzed surfers shooting the curls. Donna regretted not bringing her sunglasses so she could stare at the guys more discreetly. After a while she said, "Maybe we should've brought our suits and towels."

"Ain't no big thang Don. Let's go check out Belmont Park."

And so they drove off in the direction of Mission Bay, toward the amusement park. As they cruised along, Lynn noticed a Grumman Goose of Catalina Vegas Airlines lifting off from Lindbergh Field and taking to the air. Suddenly, Lynn shouted, "Donna, I've got it!"

"Got what?"

"A brilliant flash! A plan. A way out of a humdrum boring summer around this old sailor town."

"What are you talking about, you nut?"

"With this brilliant mind," she said, tapping her skull, "I've found us a way to adventure, romance, freedom, and maybe a summer fling or two."

"Okay," said Donna, "spill it. What's the brilliant idea?"

"Catalina Island. We can go to Avalon, and you can forget all about that yucky Chucky, the sleaze."

"Catalina? Now I know you're crazy. My evil stepfather would never go for that. Unlike you, I'm still underage."

"Oh, screw Carl, that creep. What's he going to do, ground you for two weeks till you turn eighteen? Listen, I'll work on my mom, and I'll have her work on yours. It'll be a cinch."

"But what about money? And what about our jobs?"

"We'll get new jobs," said Lynn. "I'm not planning on a career with the Broadway, and I'm sure your restaurant can get along fine without you. I'm talking about Catalina, girl. The Island of Romance! We're young, single, and attractive. The world is our oyster. Let's do it! What do you say?"

"I say yes. I'd just as soon be pregnant somewhere else than here."

As it turned out, though, Donna wasn't pregnant. The red tide washed in two days later, and the following Monday they were landing in Avalon Bay and taxiing up to the seaplane ramp at Pebbly Beach.

By early afternoon, they were settled into a room on the second floor of the Hotel Atwater, and Donna had cheered up considerably, feeling like she'd been given a second chance at life and love. Since this was the first time either of them had been away from home since Girl Scout Camp, the first thing they did was to call their mothers. Only then did they unpack and set out to sightsee Avalon. Donna picked up a job application from the adjacent coffee shop and dropped it off at their room, to fill it out later. Then they went off down Avalon's busy streets. Lynn noticed a HELP WANTED sign in a gift shop window and made a mental note to check it out later. Right now they wanted to catch up with the day before it slipped away. They remarked to each other that Avalon certainly wasn't a Navy town, like San Diego. Lynn said she would've named it Vacationland. "Because," she said, "it looks like everyone is on vacation, and it's as busy a place as Disneyland."

They scanned the throngs of people, and noticed their ranks filled with college-age kids. Something else that impressed them was the absence of cars. They spent the rest of the day wandering around, checking out guys, window shopping, and seeing all the sights that interested them before having dinner at a little place with a nice view of the bay. They settled into their room that night, eagerly anticipating a new day in a new town, and feeling hopeful about finding employment.

The following morning, after breakfast at Sally's Waffle Shop, they went job hunting. Donna took her application over to the Skipper's Galley, while Lynn checked in at Molly's Gifts and Souvenirs. She was outfitted in one of only two skirts she'd brought along, the conservative long one, and a button-up-the-front off-white blouse, and a pair of flats. She wore just a hint of lipstick and a little mascara. She had put her short, honey colored and very straight hair up in curlers the night before, so that it had a little flip to it where it broke at the neckline. Molly, the owner, looked at Lynn's fresh, shining face, and remembered that she had been young once too. Now she was pushing forty, tended toward plumpness, and was draped in a full length, loose fitting floral print dress. She had her eyeglasses hanging from a chain around her neck as she sized up Lynn, and decided to forego the written application, and cut right to the interview. She asked Lynn to join her in the cramped back office and stock room, and offered her a folding chair next to the cluttered desk.

"Well, Miss Robinson," she said, "tell me a little about yourself, what job experiences you've had, why you'd like to work here, and why you're in Avalon."

Lynn was surprised to be feeling at ease, but maybe it was because Molly seemed so motherly.

"Okay, let's see. I just graduated from high school, and I'm going to college in the fall. I worked part time as a sales clerk at the Broadway, in the children's clothing department. I love people, and waiting on them and helping them. And I guess the main reason I'm here is because my best friend Donna's boyfriend dumped her, and I thought a summer in Avalon would cheer her up. You know, give her a change of scenery and a chance for a carefree summer. And I also thought it would be fun for me too, to meet new people and see new sights."

"If you want to meet people," said Molly, "you've come to the right place. Tell me, did you ever take inventory at the Broadway?"

"Yes, a couple of times."

"And you know your way around a cash register?"

"I sure do, and I make very few mistakes."

"Well," said Molly cheerfully, "I think I know enough about you now. I like you, and I think you'll fit right in here, enough to give you a chance anyway. Can you start today?"

"Sure," said Lynn, taken by surprise, "I guess so. When?"

"How about now? I'll have you fill out some paperwork and then we may as well start training you. I'll introduce you to Brenda. You'll be working together."

"Thank you," said Lynn. "I'm kind of stunned. I mean I hadn't expected to land a job so quickly."

"Your timing was just right. We only put the sign in the window yesterday. By the way, where are you staying?"

"Donna and I have a room at the Hotel Atwater. But it's a little expensive."

"The reason I ask, is because my husband and I have a basement apartment we rent out for the summer, usually to a single girl. It hasn't been taken yet. It's completely furnished and the utilities are included in the rent."

"Is it expensive?"

"No, it's very reasonable."

"Could Donna stay there too?"

"Well, I hadn't thought about renting to two people. It's small, really only meant for one. But I suppose if you're good friends and don't mind sharing a bed, why, of course she could stay too. You could split the rent."

"Gosh, I don't know what to say. It all sounds too good to be true. Thank you so much."

"As I said, Lynn, your timing is good. Our house is up the hill on Whitley. I'll take you there after we close."

Meanwhile, over at the Skipper's Galley, Donna was also interviewing for a job, with Sam O'Hara, the Skipper's wife.

"I see you were a bus girl on the mainland," said the wiry, middle-age woman examining Donna with hawk-like eyes. "We only employ bus boys here. Our girls either work as waitress or hostess. The position we have available is for a waitress. However, the job isn't much different from bussing tables. You wait on customers, and you need to be good at making change. If you come up short at the end of your shift, it comes out of your tips. Are you good with math?"

"Yes, I am," said Donna.

"Good. We pay minimum wage, but you get to keep your tips, provided your tickets balance. We ask you to give ten percent of your tips to your bus boy. You get one meal per shift worked. Do you still want the job?"

"Yes, I do."

"Good. You can start this afternoon at three-thirty. You'll need to get some comfortable shoes, preferably tennis shoes."

"Yes, ma'am."

"One more thing, young lady. Do you smoke?"

"Yes," admitted Donna, "I do."

"That's alright, I do too. But there's no smoking on duty. You'll get a break sometime during your shift, and you can step outside to smoke. Now, if you don't have any questions, I'll be off. We have to get ready for the lunch rush."

Sam pushed her chair away and stood to signal the interview was over. "Be here at three o'clock to fill out some paperwork. My daughter Marilyn will see to it that you're outfitted and trained. Once you get up to speed and Marilyn thinks you're ready, we'll put you on the day shift."

Then the tight lipped, compact woman with too much makeup, and graying hair tied in a bun, on top of which was pinned a tiny waitress cap, turned on her heel and walked off.

That night Lynn Robinson moved her things up steep Whitley Avenue and into the house that was perched on the side of a bluff. She liked the downstairs apartment with its own entrance. It was much more homey than the hotel room. In fact, it was quaint. Around midnight, Donna joined her, suitcase in hand, worn out from the steep climb and the long day on her feet. She unpacked, took a hot shower, put on her pajamas, and crawled into bed feeling tired, but content.

As she drifted off to sleep, she was thinking about how she looked forward to the Fourth of July, and then her eighteenth birthday. She wasn't aware of it, but this was the first night in weeks that her thoughts weren't troubled by memories of Chuck Belton.

CHAPTER 7

▼

FIREWORKS AND FRIENDSHIPS

"I wish they all could be California girls...."

"Hey, Hullabalooers! I'm Dave Hull, with you until six, and that was Hawthorne's own local Beach Boys with their latest song, which has been climbing the charts with a bullet. We're starting off your Fourth of July weekend here at KRLA with a beautiful seventy-eight degrees outside, and we've got more hits coming your way, right after this little message from Clearasil."

Jimmy Fontana and Waxie Shein were doing more at the moment than listening to the Beach Boys rave about California girls. As their sandal clad feet made tracks in the soft warm golden sand, their eyes were wide with the panoramic sight of beautifully bronzed and sunburned California girls on Crescent Beach this Friday afternoon. It was as if life was imitating art.

"I think we could be in the new Garden of Eden," said Jimmy.

"Watch out for snakes," said Waxie.

The smell of Coppertone and baby oil mixed with the smell of sand and ocean and fast foods frying on the Pleasure Pier as they navigated a maze of beach towels and bodies, looking for a place to land. The beach was crowded, so there weren't many open spots left. But then Jimmy spied a familiar face in an unfamiliar setting. She was out of her waitress uniform, wearing a two-piece bathing suit and sunglasses, but there was no mistaking the trim, curvaceous form of Donna Forte. Jimmy also recognized her by her full red lips, and the way her thick black hair fell around her face in an oval shape. He stopped in his tracks and then dropped to the hot sand beside her. Waxie took his cue and knelt down beside Donna's friend, who lay on her stomach, head turned to the side.

"Hello, stranger," Jimmy said with a smile.

Donna looked up, removed her sunglasses, and blinked at the brightness of the sun. She had to focus for a moment before she recognized the face that went with the voice.

"Oh, hi Jimmy. So you come down here after work, too?"

"Yeah, here we are. This is my friend Waxie," he said. The other girl had turned over and was now sitting up, watching.

"Nice to meet you, Waxie," said Donna. "This is my friend Lynn. Lynn--Waxie and Jimmy."

"Charmed, I'm sure," said Lynn. "Pull up some sand and join us. What kind of a name is Waxie, anyway?" she asked, as the guys spread out their towels and lounged on them.

"Oh, just a nickname," Waxie said.

"I figured that," said Lynn. "But what's it short for?"

"It's not short for anything. It's just a name."

"Come on, Waxie, spill it," she demanded. "My curiosity is piqued to no end."

"Well," said Waxie, with an embarrassed smile, "it's kind of a long story."

Lynn removed her sunglasses, gave him an insistent look, and said, "Come on, spill it. We haven't got all day."

Waxie laughed. "Okay. When I was thirteen, I got a crew cut and started using Butch Wax on my hair. Some wise guy called me Waxie, and pretty soon everyone else did too. Stuff like, 'look at Waxie's shine', and 'hey, kid, you got a waxy shine'. See, my last name is Shein, spelled with an e-i-n Get it? Anyway, it went from being a joke to my nickname."

"That's awful," said Lynn. "Why did you put up with it?"

"Oh, I don't know. I just kind of went along with it for a while, and then got used to it. I don't mind anymore."

"Well, I would," said Lynn. "You're too old to have a name like that. What's your real name?"

"David."

"That's much better," she said. "But somehow, that doesn't seem to fit either. Too formal. You look more like a Dave to me. Mind if I call you Dave?"

"Not at all. Call me anything you like. Just don't call me late for dinner."

Lynn looked at Donna, and they both groaned.

Donna changed the subject. "Jimmy's a cook where I work," she said to Lynn. "We're both on the day shift."

"How do you like your job?" Lynn asked Jimmy.

"It's okay for a summer job. How about you? Working anywhere?"

"I'm selling tourist trinkets at Molly's Gifts."

"I know Molly and Ben," Waxie interjected. "They're friends with my folks."

"Your folks?" said Lynn.

"Yeah," said Jimmy, "they own the Travel On Inn. Waxie works there. He's a real Islander, not just a summer one like us."

"Where are you girls staying?" asked Waxie.

"With Molly. Donna and I share the downstairs room."

"I know the place," said Waxie. "Long walk up a steep hill."

"Tell us about it," groaned Donna. "What about you guys? Where're you staying?"

"Well, Waxie lives at home, at the Travel On Inn, and Bob Silenski and I just moved from there to the Hotel Glenmore."

"Isn't that kind of expensive?" said Donna.

"Probably for tourists. But they rent out rooms on the fourth floor to us at a special rate. Phil told Sil about it, and the Skipper put in a good word for us."

"The Skipper," said Donna with a little laugh. "What's with him anyway, with all that nautical stuff? Did he used to be a sea captain or something?"

"From what I've heard," said Jimmy, "the only boat he's ever been on is the *S.S Catalina*. Sometimes he and Sam ride it over to San Pedro and back, and never leave the ship's bar."

"Then why all that sailor stuff?"

"Okay, here's what I heard from Phil. The place used to be called Jack's Place, and before his daughter worked there, he had his son, Will, there as a cook. He was planning to keep the kid on, teach him the trade, and have him take over someday, to keep it in the family, you know?"

"I know," said Waxie. "Believe me, I know."

"Anyway, Will had different ideas, wanted to be a fisherman, get off the island. They used to argue about it all the time. One day they had a big blowout, Will moved up to Monterrey and became a commercial fisherman, and the Skipper blew his stack. 'I have no son,' all that. Well, long story short, they made up, Jack changed his name to the Skipper, changed the name of the coffee shop, and became this full -blown Popeye character. Anyway, that's what Phil tells me."

"He sounds like a nutcase," said Lynn.

"He is a little odd," agreed Donna.

"The old guy drinks a lot," explained Jimmy. "Maybe his brains are a little scrambled."

"Oh," said Donna in sudden recollection, "that would explain the bottle of rum I saw in his office when I was filling out my W-2 form."

"Yeah," said Jimmy," that was probably his. He chugs a whole six-pack of beer during the lunch rush. Keeps 'em in the reach-in."

"Lunch rush is stressful," said Donna. "Sometimes I feel completely overwhelmed."

"You seem to be getting the hang of it," said Jimmy.

"Thanks, but give me a couple more weeks to catch up with the pace."

"Hey," said Waxie, changing the subject, "what're you girls doing Sunday night?"

"Watching fireworks, of course," said Lynn. "It's the Fourth of July."

"Are you going to the concert first?" asked Waxie.

"What concert?" the girls said in unison.

"The Dick Clark Caravan of Stars! It's in the Casino's ballroom," said Waxie.

"Who's on the bill?" asked Lynn.

"Several acts, including Ian Whitcomb, Peter and Gordon, and Jackie DeShannon. The show starts at seven-thirty, and it'll be over just in time for the fireworks display. They planned it that way," said Jimmy.

"Yeah," added Waxie, "and the Casino is the best place to watch fireworks. They set them off in the bay, behind the Casino"

"Would you girls like to go with us?" asked Jimmy. "We'll take care of your tickets."

The girls looked at each other, nodded in agreement, and Lynn said, "Sure, we'd love to. Thanks for asking."

"I know where you live," said Waxie, "so we'll pick you up around seven."

There was a lull in the conversation, before Lynn said, "Would you do me a favor, Dave, and rub some lotion on my back? I can't quite reach, and I burn easily. That's the problem with being fair-skinned."

"My pleasure," said Waxie as he took the bottle of Coppertone from her, smeared some of the cream in the palm of his hand, and then began working it into her back. Her skin felt soft and warm to the touch, and his skin nearly tingled with what felt like electrical current emanating from her. Or maybe it was just that he was getting turned on. Lynn felt Waxie's hands on her back and wondered why she'd asked such a request of him, because she usually felt self-conscious about her body. She felt she was too skinny, with no hips and a flat chest. Not very womanly, like Donna. But she guessed she just felt comfortable around this boy, Dave. He seemed so genuine and friendly, and well, innocent.

Over at the Skipper's Galley, Dan and Phil were busy filling orders. In the dining room Sil, who had already finished his meal, was hanging around drinking coffee and flirting with Shelly. She was flirting back, in between waiting on customers. Sil had asked her out to the Dick Clark concert and she'd said yes. She'd had to trade nights off with another girl who had no Fourth of July plans, and didn't mind helping Shelly our in the romance department.

J.T. had finished his shift at the post office, in the Atwater Arcade, just down the street from the Skipper's Galley. He'd been in luck the day he'd picked up the job application. There had been an opening for a part-time summer mail sorter, and he'd been hired. Even though the job was only part-time, it paid much more than washing dishes did, so he was able to move his things back to the Travel On Inn. He was relieved to be out of the Annex. Being there had depressed him. The new job required wearing a uniform, but he didn't mind, because he was working for the government, which leant more dignity to the position. He felt as if his work was something important, something that mattered much more than washing dirty dishes. He'd pissed the Skipper off, though, when he'd quit after two days. The Skipper had sworn and told J.T. not to bother coming by for his paycheck. He'd have Sil deliver it, and as far as he was concerned, if he ever saw J.T. again, it would be too soon. The Skipper put the HELP WANTED sign back in the window and coerced Hector into working double shifts at the dishwashing machine until he could fill the position with someone new.

"That ain't my problem," thought J.T. A new James Brown song came into his mind as he made the short walk up the street to his hotel. "Well, papa, he's in the groove," he sang to himself as he snapped his fingers and strutted along. "Yeah, papa's in the groove, alright," he thought. "And he may as well hang around Avalon a little while longer and see what happens. This job could be a stepping stone to a career for ol' Jay Tee."

The moon rose early on Independence Day, while the sun was still hanging just over the hills, and the day and the night were sharing spaces. The full setting sun and the full rising moon were giving their blessings to the crowds in the streets. And down these narrow streets rode Waxie Shein and Jimmy Fontana on a shiny new Vespa. They wore summer slacks and starched shirts and shined shoes, and were freshly showered and reeking of English Leather. The Vespa climbed the steep Whitley Avenue and Waxie brought it to a stop in front of a green and white wood frame house. The back of the house rested on stilts and hung precariously over a bluff. Waxie knocked at the door of the downstairs apartment and Donna opened it, all smiles. She looked radiant in a summer blouse and short skirt, and just the right touch of makeup. Lynn was wearing a short top, with bell-bottoms and sandals. She also wore light makeup. When she heard the knock at the door, she grabbed her bag from the bedroom and followed Donna out to the porch. She looked past the guys and saw the Vespa.

"Whose scooter?" she asked.

"Mine," said Waxie, smiling proudly.

"We can't all fit on that," she said.

"No, but you and I can. Jimmy and Donna can walk. Or we all can. It's all downhill, anyway."

"You go ahead,' said Donna. "Jimmy and I don't mind walking, do we, Jimmy?"

"Not at all," Jimmy agreed. "Save us a place in line, and we'll meet you down there."

And so they were off. Donna and Lynn didn't bother to lock their door. That was one of the advantages of living in a small town like Avalon. No real crime problem.

As Jimmy and Donna started down the hill, Jimmy complemented Donna on her attire, and also her perfume.

"You like it?" she said. "It's called Wind Song." Then she added, "Thanks again for asking me out."

"Thanks for accepting," he said. Then, after a pause, he added, "This is the first date I've been on in months, since my ex-girlfriend and I split up."

"You too?" said Donna. "Welcome to the club. I just recently got dumped by my old boyfriend." She now took Jimmy's hand. "I wonder what else we have in common."

And so, as they walked down Whitley, they talked a little about themselves and their backgrounds. By the time they reached the Via Casino and began strolling along the path by the breakwater, they were talking about their futures, about how Donna was going off to San Diego City College in the fall.

"What about you, Jimmy?"

"I'm going in the Navy," he said.

"The Navy! Why? Can you get out of it?"

"No, I'm already enlisted. I report end of September. Anchors aweigh. Why are you so concerned?"

"Oh, it's nothing. I'm just surprised. I live in a Navy town, and sailors are kind of looked down on. As a matter of fact, nice girls aren't supposed to go out with them." Then as an after thought, she added quietly, "But I guess that doesn't matter any more."

"What's that?" asked Jimmy.

"Oh, nothing. Just thinking out loud. Well, here we are," she said, as they reached the Casino. "There's Lynn." She pointed to the couple up ahead in line, joined them, and received harsh looks from the couple they'd cut ahead of. The line formed to the left of the theater's box office, and the girls marveled at the art deco frescoes that decorated the archways and alcoves of the entryway.

"That's nothing," said Waxie. "You should see the murals in the theater. The ballroom where we're going is pretty spectacular, too. You'll see."

After a very short wait, the doors opened and the line was allowed to snake inside and up a wide, winding ramp that led three stories up to the ballroom. The ballroom itself was huge and circular, with windows all around the outside, and doors leading to a wide balcony that spanned the circumference of the building. Donna pointed to the chandeliers in the ceiling. "Look there," she said. "How beautiful!"

"What did I tell you," said Waxie. "This room could hold twice the entire winter population of the island. It was meant to hold fifteen hundred couples back in the Big Band days."

The two couples moved up close to the stage. They chose to stand rather than sit on the beautifully polished dance floor, so they could have a better view. In a few minutes, the backing band appeared onstage and took their places behind music stands. The guitar player, who also held the positions of band leader and Master of Ceremonies, led the band in a couple of warm-up songs before bringing out the first act.

"Ladies and gentlemen," he announced, "let's give a big Avalon welcome to Freddie 'Boom Boom' Cannon!"

The slender, highly charged singer ran through his old hits, "Tallahassee Lassie," "Way Down Yonder in New Orleans," "Palisades Park," and finished with his most recent hit, "Action." A transition song by the band preceded the next act, Ian Whitcomb; who although he was introduced as being from London, was actually from Ireland. He sang a handful of songs, including his hits, "This Sporting Life," and "You Turn Me On." Near the middle of the dance floor, Sil sang the salacious lyrics to Shelly. *"Come on now baby, you know you really turn me on…"*

Jimmy caught a sideways glance at Donna, who was also happily singing along. The next performers, Peter and Gordon, actually were from London. They sang the obligatory hits: "A World Without Love," "I Go To Pieces," and "True Love Ways," and left the stage with great bows and smiles. The band ran through a couple more instrumentals, and then the emcee built the crowd up for the headliner.

"Is everybody ready for Jackie DeShannon?" he shouted. "I can't hear you! Come on, Avalon, let's give it up for the loveliest, most exciting and talented performer to have ever hailed from Kentucky. Ladies and gentlemen- ---JACKIE DeSHANNON!!!"

The crowd roared its approval, and the petite, blond haired songstress took the stage and made love to the microphone, breezing through her hits: "You Won't Forget Me," "Needles and Pins," and "When You Walk In The Room," before finishing with her current hit, which was still high on the charts. When she reached the chorus, she invited the audience to sing along.

"What the world need now is love, sweet love…."

Jimmy glanced at Donna as she sang along. He smiled deeply and joined in on the chorus. She looked at him, took his hand and squeezed it, then turned her gaze back to the stage.

All too soon, the concert was over. The house lights came up, the crowd filed out of the ballroom and three flights down the ramp to the outside world. Waxie led his friends to the back of the building where the water washed up against the big rocks, and there was an excellent view of the town and the harbor. The moon was shining a white gold out over Avalon Bay, boats were wearing their running lights like jewelry, and then came the rocket's red glare and bombs bursting in air. The big sky was lit with brilliant explosions of color. Star shells followed by fountain cascades and reds, whites, and blues streaking out, seeming to fall into the ocean. The crowd applauded and gasped with each new burst of sound and color. Jimmy nudged up against Donna, smelling her perfume, feeling her warmth and the brush of her hair on a sudden puff of breeze. Then came the grand finale, and the whole bay was lit up in a massive orgasm of explosions and colors. The crowd roared their approval. Donna threw her arms around Jimmy and gave him a hug.

"That was wonderful!" she exclaimed, wide-eyed and smiling. "The perfect ending to the evening."

"Ah, but the night is still young," said Jimmy. "Do you have to go right in?"

"No," said Donna, "I don't. What did you have in mind?"

"Well, how about if we let the crowd thin out a little, then take a walk over to the Pleasure Pier?"

And they did so, while Waxie and Lynn climbed aboard the Vespa and went on a moonlight ride of Mt. Ada Road for the view, and down to Pebbly Beach for the atmosphere. Eventually, they wound up back at the house on Whitley, where they hugged goodnight. Lynn stepped inside, and noticed that Donna was still out. Like a mother she began to worry, as she got ready for bed. However, she soon heard voices outside on the porch, sighed, and closed her eyes to sleep.

"Thanks again, Jimmy," said Donna on the porch. "I had a great time. This ought to hold me until next weekend."

"What's next weekend?" asked Jimmy.

"My eighteenth birthday," she said.

"Congratulations," he said. "I'll be nineteen in September."

"Isn't it nice to be this age?" said Donna. "We're not kids anymore, but not yet grown-ups with all those responsibilities."

"I suppose," said Jimmy. "But pretty soon, this carefree life will end, and it's off to the Navy."

"But at least you've got a whole summer ahead of you to enjoy," she said.

"True. I know one thing I've already enjoyed, and that's your company, and I'd really like to see you again."

"You will," she said. Then she kissed him goodnight. All the way down the hill and back to the Glenmore, Jimmy savored the feel of that kiss, and felt as if his feet never even touched the ground.

Meanwhile, Bob Silenski had taken Shelly Green up to the Chimes Tower to show her the view and to watch fireworks. During the display's climax, he took her in his arms and gave her a kiss that took her breath away. It stirred up deep feelings within her. As they walked along the waterfront later, Shelly heard a song playing on someone's radio, one by Barbara Mason, which crystallized these feelings in her heart.

"I'm ready to learn to fall in love, to fall in love right now."

She linked her arm with Sil's as he walked her home, and as they passed the Bamboo Lounge, Sil noticed "Pearly Shells" playing on the jukebox inside. He stopped, looked into her eyes, and said, "Would you like to see my new place?"

"Okay," she said, "but only for a minute."

Sil led her across the street to the Glenmore and into the hotel's lobby, where he seated her in an overstuffed chair.

"I'll be right back," he said.

The desk clerk, a young man about his own age, eyed Sil suspiciously as he approached. Sil leaned across the counter, pulled a ten-dollar bill from his pocket, and slipped it to the clerk, who held it in his hand and studied it. It was almost as much money as he would make per shift worked.

"Don't you have to check on something in the office?" said Sil.

"Uhm, yeah. Yeah, I have to check on something," he said, pocketing the bill and disappearing out of sight. Sil turned, smiling, and waved Shelly over, as he walked to the elevator and pressed a button. The doors opened and they stepped inside. They rode up to the fourth floor in silence. When the doors opened again, Sil stepped into the hallway and motioned Shelly to follow. He unlocked the room and opened the door, switched on the light, and said, "Check out this view."

He pulled the curtain aside to reveal a view of the street below, and a little of the beach and the boats in the harbor.

"It's beautiful," she said softly, as he placed his arm around her waist and kissed her hair.

She shivered at his touch.

"Are you cold?" he asked.

"No," she said, tuning into him and placing her head against his chest. "It feels good, being in your arms, that is."

He kissed her on the mouth, and then led her over to the bed.

"Have a seat," he said, as he walked over to the dresser and turned on the record player he'd borrowed from Jimmy. He put the needle in the groove of the record he had borrowed from Phil. The sultry sound of John Coltrane's saxophone floated through the little room. He lit the candle atop the dresser, switched off the overhead light, and sat next to Shelly, taking her hand.

"I shouldn't stay," she said without conviction.

"Just a little while," he whispered, putting his arm around her shoulder.

She looked deeply into his blue eyes, seeing the candlelight reflected in them, and closed her own eyes, surrendering to his long kiss. She felt his tongue on hers and felt as if she were melting. He laid her down on the bed and scooted her up to the pillow, where he held her close as she buried her head in his neck.

"I remember the first time I saw you out on the floor in the Skipper's Galley. I couldn't take my eyes off you. And now here we are."

"Yes," she said, "here we are. But where are we going?"

"Let's find out," he whispered in her ear.

"I really should be leaving now," she said feebly.

"Soon," he said, kissing her again. Her head was spinning. She laid her head on the pillow and let him kiss and caress her, felt him unbutton her blouse, and fumble with the hooks on her bra. She reached around and undid it for him. He slipped it off then removed his shirt. He pulled her against him, her bare breasts against his muscular chest. Her nipples were hard, and Sil began kissing and caressing them, as well as her neck and shoulder and cheek. She felt herself getting wet. She knew she should stop, but couldn't bring herself to do so. She had the feeling of being paralyzed. But when he began fumbling with the zipper on her Capris, she awoke suddenly from her dream-like state, and grabbed his hand with hers.

"Please don't," she said weakly.

He moved his hand down to the space between her legs.

"Hanky panky—no, no, no?" he teased.

"Please, Sil," she said breathlessly, "I'm not ready for this. You're going too fast for me."

"Sorry," he said, looking into her eyes. "It's just that you really turn me on."

"I'm sorry too," she said. "Would you mind taking me home now? Please."

"Well, okay," he said, disappointed, removing his hand and putting his shirt back on. Shelly likewise got dressed, pulled a hairbrush from her bag and began brushing her hair. Sil shut off the record player, blew out the candle, and switched the light back on. It's sudden glare made him squint. Shelly straightened herself out in front of the mirror, and soon they were down the elevator, through the lobby, and into the cool night air. They strolled arm in arm up to the little house on Beacon Street with the white picket fence, through the gate, and up to the front door. Shelly had walked in silence all the way, but now apologized again for not having sex with Sil.

"It's okay," he said dismissively. "Don't worry about it."

"I really did have a good time tonight, Sil," she said as they lingered on the doorstep. He cupped his hand under her chin and lifted her face to his as he leaned over to kiss her goodnight. She wrapped her arms around him and held him close, then turned away. He wasn't sure, but it seemed as if there were tears welling up in her eyes.

"Goodnight," she said, walking through the doorway. "Thanks again. I'll see you tomorrow."

Shelly closed the door and walked into her darkened room. Overcome by emotions, she wrapped her arms around herself and sobbed quietly.

Sil walked briskly back to the Glenmore and up to his room. In the glow of the streetlight pouring through his open window, he slipped out of his clothes, and under the covers.

"I was almost there," he thought. "Well, maybe next time. There's still a lot of summer left. I can afford to invest a little more time in her. But if it doesn't pan out, well, the island is crawling with chicks."

Then Bob "Never in Love, Only in Heat" Silenski quietly masturbated and fell off into a deep sleep.

CHAPTER 8

▼

THE BIRTHDAY PARTY

"You're listening to KRLA, and I'm Dick Biondi seeing you through this groovy summer night. And speaking of summer nights, here's Marianne Faithful with a song that's new this week."

"Winter's almost gone, oh how I've waited so long for summer nights...."

Jimmy and Donna were vaguely aware of the song coming out of the radio held by a passer-by on Crescent Avenue, just outside the window by the table where they were seated in a cute little Italian café, where they enjoyed a nice view of the palm lined street and the boat lined bay. There was a twilight glow outside the window and a candlelight glow inside. Donna was looking out the window and Jimmy was looking at Donna, captivated by her beauty, her charm, her nearness.

"Thank you again for bringing me here," she smiled, turning to look him in the eyes. She reached across the red and white-checkered tablecloth and squeezed his hand. "How did you guess that my favorite food was Italian?"

"Maybe because your last name is Forte," he said. "That's a pretty good hint. By the way, I've studied music a little, so I know what forte means."

"I know too," she said. "Loud."

"Yes, but the name doesn't really suit you. You're neither loud nor brash. You're more like mezzo-piano. But that's not exactly true either," he added. "There's no musical expression for just right, but that's the way you are."

"Thank you," she said. "That's very sweet. But you haven't seen my moods."

"Bring 'em on," he said. "I dare you."

The waiter arrived, they ordered from the menu, and then Jimmy said, "How's your birthday so far?"

"Wonderful" she gushed. "I got a card from my mom and brother and some birthday money too. I'll have to spend it in Lynn's shop. Oh, and look what Lynn gave me. It's a Lucrezia Borgia ring."

"What kind of ring?" he said as she held out her hand for inspection.

"Lucrezia Borgia. She was the sister of Cesare Borgia in Renaissance Italy. She used to poison her lovers. See," she said, opening the secret compartment on the ring, "here's where she kept the poison."

"Remind me not do order any drinks around you," he joked.

"I wouldn't poison you," she laughed. "You're too nice to me."

"Well," he said, reaching into his pocket and pulling out a little box, "I don't know if these will go with that fancy ring, but here's another gift for you."

As he handed her the box, he noted the look of surprise and joy that swept over her face.

"You shouldn't have," she said, opening the box and removing the jade earrings. "Oh, they're beautiful! I'll put them on right now," she said, removing her plain silver ones and putting the new through her ear lobes. "How do I look?"

"Ravishing," he said.

She leaned across the little table and kissed him on the cheek. "Thank you," she said.

"Happy birthday. So you heard from your mom and brother," he said. "What about your dad?"

"He doesn't live with us," she said. "I only see him a couple times a year."

"So, it's just the three of you?"

"No," she said hesitantly. Her voice now took on a far away tone as she continued. "There's my evil stepfather, too. But I don't want to talk about him."

"Okay," said Jimmy agreeably.

Their food arrived, and they ate quietly and contentedly. When they had finished, and the plates were removed, Donna fished a pack of Newports out of her handbag and extracted one. Jimmy lit it for her, and lit a Marlboro for himself.

"Now that you're eighteen," he said, "you can buy your own cigarettes. You can stay out past curfew, too."

"As if I never did before, huh?" she laughed. Then she said, "Tell me a little more about this party we're going to."

"It's just a little get together over at Phil's. An artsy crowd, I guess. Wine and cheese and all that. Pretty low key."

"Sounds like fun," she said. "Thanks for asking me. I have a good time with you."

"Likewise," he said.

As they stood up to leave, Donna said, "Don't forget to tip your waiter."

"It's already taken care of."

On the way to the party, they stopped by the Glenmore, and Donna waited in the lobby while Jimmy picked up his guitar.

"Can't go to a party without my music maker," he explained as they continued on their way. They arrived at Phil's little place on Catalina Avenue and knocked on the door.

"Who dat?" a voice called out from behind the door.

"Jimmy and Donna."

The door opened a few inches. Phil stuck his head out and said in a serious voice, "Who sent ya?"

"The Skipper," said Jimmy.

"Well, in that case, welcome to the pad, dad," said Phil with a smile as he opened the door wide. Other than the goatee, they hardly recognized him out of uniform. His hair was long, thick and black, and he was dressed in Levis, sandals, and a short sleeve sweatshirt.

"Where's everyone else?" asked Donna, looking around.

Phil let out a whistle and suddenly the doors to the kitchen and bedroom flew open, and bodies poured forth shouting in unison, "SURPRISE!"

Donna was flabbergasted. She stood in shock, her mouth agape, and then began laughing as everyone circled her, hugged her, and congratulated her. Jimmy brought out his guitar, strummed a chord, and said, "Ready, everybody?" They all sang "Happy Birthday" to Donna, and "For She's a Jolly Good Fellow." While this was going on, Lynn waltzed out of the kitchen with a cake, set it down on the coffee table, and Phil lit the candles on top. Donna was still in a state of semi-shock as she looked around at the faces before her. It seemed as if everyone from the Skipper's Galley had showed up. Sil and Dan Burton and Dan's girlfriend Vickie, plus an assortment of waitresses, bus boys, a dishwasher, and a hostess. J.T. and Waxie were there as well.

"Thanks, to all of you," Donna stammered. "Not only am I totally surprised, but this may just be the best birthday I've ever had."

"It was all Jimmy's idea," said Phil.

"Yeah, but it's your pad," said Jimmy. "Let's hear it for Phil."

At this, everyone whooped and clapped. Lynn said, "Hey, Don, ain't no big thang. Here, make a wish and blow out the candles."

She blew them out in one big breath, and then Bob Silenski said, "Donna's legal now. No more jail bait. Hanky panky---YES!"

"Shut up, Sil," groaned J.T. as he pulled the tab on a can of beer and took a swallow.

"Can I fix you a gin and tonic?" offered Sil.

"No thanks," said Donna. "Where's Shelly?" she asked, looking around.

"She's working," said Sil. "But she'll be here later."

The party was going full throttle now, Donna the center of attention, while Jimmy played his guitar and sang. For the first time in months, they weren't sad songs. Then, unable to make himself be heard above the din of noise and chatter, he put the guitar away. Phil put a John Coltrane record on the phonograph. Jimmy brought Donna a glass of wine, and they sat on the couch, conversing. When the Coltrane record had finished playing. Phil put it back in its jacket, and made an announcement.

"Okay, dig this, all you squares. I'm going to hip you to the groove of one far out, gone cat by the name of Bob Dylan."

He dropped the needle into the groove, and out of the speakers came a thin, raspy voice, accompanied by acoustic guitar, harmonica, bass, and an understated electric guitar. The music flowed along in an oddly hypnotic way, as the singer wove poetic images about a "tambourine man", and a "jingle jangle morning." While Phil nodded his head in time to the music, stating emphatically, "Dig it man, hip me to the truth," in through the front door breezed Shelly Green, out of breath and all smiles.

"Hi everybody!" she exclaimed. Then she added, "Happy birthday, Donna," as she handed a card to the birthday girl.

Sil snuck up behind Shelly and placed his hands over her eyes. "Guess who?" he said.

"Um, the Skipper?"

Sil removed his hands, Shelly turned her head and as she did, he kissed her and said, "You're off early."

"Yeah, it was a little slow, so Marilyn cut me some slack."

"Can I make you a gin and tonic?" he asked.

"Yes. Thank you."

While Sil was in the kitchen fixing drinks, Donna walked in, opened the refrigerator door, and removed a bottle of white wine. She was searching for a glass when Sil spoke up.

"Here, allow me," he said, taking the bottle from her hand. He brought out a glass from the cupboard and poured the wine. Their eyes met. There was a pause as they studied each other. Then Donna said, "Mind if I ask you something?"

"Shoot."

"Did you play football in high school?"

"Yeah, I was on the varsity team."

"Were you a quarterback?"

"No, tight end. Why?"

"Oh, nothing. Maybe you remind me of someone."

"Is that good or bad?"

"Maybe both," she said, excusing herself to return to the noisy living room.

Just before midnight, the law arrived in the form of Deputy Doug Martin. He was dressed in the green and khaki of the Los Angeles County Sheriff's Department, and from his utility belt hung the tools of his trade: flashlight, nightstick, two-way radio, and sidearm. He marched up the sidewalk, up to the door, and knocked loudly.

"Who dat?" came a voice from within.

"Open up, Phil. This ain't no social call."

Phil opened the door a little and exclaimed, "Deputy Doug! Why, this is a surprise. Sorry you didn't get an invitation. Come on in and have a beer."

"Like I said, this ain't no social call. Got a complaint about the noise. You'll have to break it up."

"It would groove me the most, daddy-o, but I just wanna make the late scene with the cats I dig the most, then we'll cool it."

"Got any underage drinkers here?"

"Ain't no squares in this scene, daddy-o."

"Didn't think so. You got ten minutes to clear it out. Sorry, but that's the deal."

"I'm hip to your patter and I dig the scene, loud and clear. I'll glim you in the early bright."

Doug Martin wasn't much older than most of the partygoers, and would rather be at the party than breaking it up. But it was his job, and a plum one at that. It beat the hell out of riding a patrol car in L.A., where he worked in the winter months. In Avalon, there was very little crime, and violent crime was nearly non-existent. He walked out to the sidewalk and down the street, hoping he wouldn't have to return to Phil's later. His shift was nearly over, and he just wanted to clock out. Phil shut off the stereo, and thanked everyone for coming. "But now it's time to get real gone again. Like splitsville, cats and kitties."

Sil walked Shelly home, kissed her goodnight, then returned to Phil's to look for J.T., who was still there, as were Donna, Lynn, and Jimmy. The stereo was turned way down low, and the lights were all off, save a solitary candle that glowed and flickered on the coffee table. Phil sat on the couch, rolling a thin cigarette. Lynn and Donna sat on either side of him, while Jimmy and J.T. sat on the floor facing them. Sil dropped down next to J.T.

"Ever get high, man?" Phil asked of Sil.

"Yeah, a couple of times."

"Groovy, man. This hipster J.T. is a head, too. But these other squares here… well, it's time to turn them on."

"Hanky panky, no, no, no!" said Sil.

"Shut up, Sil," said J.T.

Phil sealed the thin joint with his tongue, as one would an envelope, and said, "This here is some Acapulco Gold, and it is righteous."

He lit it, took a deep drag, holding it in his lungs, and passed it to J.T. Jay hit on it and passed it to Sil, who did the same before handing it off to Jimmy. Jimmy took a drag, coughed loudly, expelling the smoke as he did. He handed it off to Donna, but she declined, as did Lynn. So it went back to Phil and the ritual played out again. This time, when it got back to Phil it was burned down to a roach, which he snuffed out with his fingers, and then dropped into the ashtray.

"How're you trippin' now daddy-o? You stoned?" said Phil.

"I dunno. I feel a little weird. Light headed," said Jimmy.

"Stoned, alright. You are now officially a pothead. Congratulations."

Bob Dylan was singing about "the gates of Eden", and Phil said, "What did I tell you about Dylan, huh? The cat is heavy."

While Jimmy listened to the music, it seemed to climb inside his head and swirl around. He began to feel like he was floating. It was an odd, but not unpleasant feeling. Donna became aware of Sil's eyes on her. They were glassy, red rimmed, and burned with an intensity that made her want to look away, but he also wore a lopsided grin that drew her in.

"There are no truths outside the gates of Eden...." sang Bob Dylan.

But here was a truth, outside the gates of Eden. The truth that Donna now realized was that Sil did remind her of Chuck Bolton. The very same Chuck she'd thought she was over. Maybe she was, in fact, over him, but the way Sil stared at her made her want Chuck again. Or was it really Sil she wanted? She didn't know anything, except that her pulse was racing and her head was spinning.

"It's late," she found herself saying. "Lynn and I had better be going."

"I'll walk you home," said Jimmy.

"If you can stand up," said J.T., and then he began giggling.

"Guppy!" said Sil.

"Puma head!" said J.T.

"Long as my arm, hard as my fist, and up to here," said Sil.

J.T was now laughing uncontrollably as he rolled around on the floor, trying to catch his breath. Donna and Lynn looked at the two guys like they were crazy. With great effort, Jimmy pushed himself off the floor and stood up, shakily at first. He picked up his guitar, which now felt heavy, and opened the door for the girls. "Goodnight, and thanks," he slurred to Phil in parting.

As he walked with the girls down the street, Jimmy felt as if his feet were just gliding along, and his senses were sharper. He was aware of the smell of the salty air and Donna's perfume in the midnight hour. He gazed through the window of the Skipper's Galley as he passed by, and it seemed as if he were looking into a fishbowl. As he walked along the harbor on Crescent, he could hear and feel their footsteps on the cobblestones, mingling with the muted sounds of boats bobbing at anchor. He felt his heart swell when he snuck a glimpse of Donna walking alongside him. He took her hand, and thrilled at her warmth. When he kissed her goodnight, her touch was electrifying, and the feeling stayed with him up to the moment he drifted off to sleep back in his room, feeling detached from his body.

Bob Silenski was too stoned to turn in, so he wandered out to the steamer dock and walked to its end. He watched the horizon for while, and thought about the surf over on the mainland. Then he turned and studied the town. It looked beautiful to him. Everything twinkled and glowed, and the sound the waves made were mesmerizing, as they lapped against the pilings and rocks and sand. Then he thought about Donna Forte. Her face came to his mind in perfect detail. Her brown eyes, her full lips, her warm smile. Even the glasses she wore made her look intriguing. Then his thoughts turned to Shelly. She was pretty hot too. But what if things didn't work out with her? He dismissed the thought, and began walking back down the pier, still digging the beauty of Avalon, and a cool summer night.

CHAPTER 9

▼

FRIENDS AND LOVERS

"All I really want to do, is baby be friends with you...."

"That was Cher climbing up the charts with a Bob Dylan song, and I'm Bob Eubanks on KRLA, where it's a quarter past seven in the City of the Angels."

The radio sat on the nightstand in their little bedroom, but the music wafted into the tiny kitchen where Lynn and Donna were preparing dinner.

"You know," said Lynn as she sliced tomatoes for the salad, "I can really relate to that song. That's how I feel about Dave. He's cute, and we have fun together, but I really just want to be friends. I don't know if he feels the same, though. I don't want to lead him on."

"Why?" asked Donna, as she stirred the spaghetti sauce. "Is he getting serious? He's not pressuring you is he?"

"About what?"

"Oh, you know---sex."

"Ha! Dave? He's hardly even kissed me. Hey, ain't no big thang. We just have fun, that's all. But what about you and Jimmy?" she said suggestively. "Do I detect a little romance in the air?"

"Oh, I wouldn't say that," said Donna, tasting the sauce and adding a little pepper. "I think he thinks there's something between us."

"You mean there's not?"

"All I really want to do," sang Donna, "is baby, be friends with you."

"I don't get it, Donna. I thought the whole idea of coming over here was for romance, and now you act like you don't care. I thought you two had a date for Friday night."

"We do. We're going to see the new James Bond movie. But after that... who knows?"

"I don't understand. What's wrong with Jimmy? I think he's really nice. For that matter, what's wrong with you?"

"Oh... nothing."

"Hey, Donna, what's going on? Is there someone else? Come on... spill it. Who is he?"

"Bob Silenski," she answered with a coy smile. "You remember him, the guy at the party."

"The big blond guy? The loudmouth?"

"He's not a loudmouth," she said defensively. "He's just outgoing and sure of himself."

"What? You're kidding! I don't get it. What's the attraction?"

"Oh, you know. He's tall, masculine, good looking. And I guess he reminds me of Chuck."

"Yucky Chucky? That sleazebag? But I thought you were over him."

"I was, I mean, I am. I think."

"Well, this is sure a big surprise. What am I going to do with you, girlfriend?"

"Hey, Lynn, ain't no big thang. Remember, this is the island of romance."

Over at The Laundromat, Jimmy Fontana cradled his guitar and sang while his clothes spun in the dryer. *"Hey, Mister Tambourine, play a song for me,"* he sang. He'd learned the Byrds' version of the song from the single he'd picked up at the local record shop. The tune had been haunting him since he'd heard Bob Dylan's version at Phil's party. Then he'd heard it again, this time by the Byrds, one day while he was listening to KRLA, and he simply had to have the record, and had to learn the song. He dug the song on the flip side, also, "I Knew I'd Want You." The lyrics reminded him of the way he felt toward Donna. He wasn't exactly in love with her, not yet. But she had helped him get over Diane. It struck him as a wondrous thing how quickly a heart can heal when you're around the right person. It was as if his heart had been poisoned, and now the poison was gone. His heart was now able to feel something besides pain, and he thought it was almost ready to feel love again. Jimmy had almost forgotten about his date with the United States Navy, as well. His thoughts were more in the moment. He was here, now, in Avalon. He held a guitar in his arms, and Donna in his heart. And the summer seemed to be without end. He accepted these gifts gratefully as he closed his eyes and sang about a jingle jangle morning while his clothes continued to spin.

Monday was Lynn's day off, and Waxie had gotten permission to quit early in order to take her on a special excursion. Shortly after noon, when the guests were all checked in and attended to at the Travel On Inn, Waxie kicked over the starter on the Vespa and drove over to Lynn's apartment on Whitley. She hopped on the back and they motored off, Lynn leaning in to Waxie, her arms around his waist. He'd told her to bring walking shoes, so her tennis shoes now gripped the little foot rests on the back of the scooter.

They rode up Sumner Avenue until it ended, hooked left onto palm-lined Avalon Canyon Road, and continued uphill through the canyon as it narrowed, past the golf course, stables, Avalon School, and the bird park, leaving the town behind. The canyon dead-ended in a cove of steep hills and a memorial garden, in the very center of which there stood a great edifice, looking like a cathedral wearing a crown. It was similar in shape to the Chimes Tower, but much more majestic, gleaming white in the sun, its eighty-foot tower topped with red Spanish tile. At its base, near the long winding staircase, Waxie parked the Vespa and killed the engine.

"What is it?" asked an awestruck Lynn, as she climbed off the back seat.

"Wrigley's Memorial. Come on, I'll show you around."

They climbed the wide, round-stepped staircase to the lookout tower that was finished in marble with art deco designs of colored tile.

"It's beautiful," said Lynn.

"Check out the view," said Waxie.

They gazed out at a landscape of steep hills falling away to the little crescent shape of Avalon Bay with tiny houses nestled tightly together, and the huge Casino now the size of a thumbnail. The San Pedro Channel spread out beyond that with dots for boats leaving slivers of white wakes as they sailed cross-channel.

"Wow!" said Lynn. "Avalon seems like a dreamscape. It's like we're on top of the world."

"Not really, not yet. Wait till we climb to the top of the divide. You can see both sides of the island."

He slipped his arm around her waist, and she slipped away from his touch and sat on a marble ledge that was just a little high to be a bench, but now served the same purpose. Waxie sat next to her, again placing his arm around her, and leaned in to kiss her, but she turned her head away.

"What's wrong?" he said, sounding hurt.

"I'm not your girlfriend, Dave, and I don't want to give you the wrong idea." She turned to face him, looking him in the eyes.

"What about?" he asked.

"About us. We're not lovers, we're only friends. I don't want to hurt you by building up your expectations. I'm not an Islander, just a girl who's over here for the summer. Then I'm going back home to San Diego."

"I know that," he said sadly. "It's the story of my life. I meet someone I like, and then she's gone. So what? There's still half the summer left before you have to go. And that's enough time to get to know each other better. I really like you, Lynn, and I don't care if we're only friends. I'll take things as they come."

Feeling relieved, Lynn took his hand and said, "Thank you." Then changing the subject, she asked, "So what's the story with this monument? And who is this Wrigley, anyway?"

"William Wrigley," said Waxie. "You know, chewing gum."

"Oh yeah," she said in recognition, "Wrigley's Spearmint Gum."

"He also owned the Chicago Cubs and most of Avalon and Catalina Island. This monument was a gift from the people of Avalon and the Santa Catalina Island Company as a tribute for all he'd done for us. They entombed his body here when he died."

"Really, where?" she asked, looking around.

"You're sitting on him."

"Oh my God!" she shrieked, jumping up.

"I'm just kidding," laughed Waxie. "They moved his body right after World War Two."

Lynn punched him on the bicep. "Very funny! That nearly creeped me out," she said without humor.

"Shall we go on a hike?" Waxie asked.

"Yeah, let's get out of here. I don't want to think about sitting on bodies."

They followed a steep trail, which branched off the side of the building, Waxie leading the way. It was a long, grueling hike, offering little or no shade from the flanking scrub oak, cacti, and sage, but when they finally reached the summit, they were treated to a magnificent view. To the leeward side,

Avalon seemed even smaller, the *S.S. Catalina* a toy boat at its dock. To the windward side, the vast Pacific rolled away to the western horizon. Another island rose out of its expanse.

"That's San Clemente Island," Waxie pointed out. "It's one of the Channel Islands, as is Catalina. The Navy uses it as a target and bombing range. What a waste of real estate."

"I'm beginning to understand what it must be like to live on an island," Lynn said quietly. "When you're surrounded by water this way, it makes you feel small."

"You don't know the half of it," he said. "We call the island The Rock. Sooner or later you go stir crazy and look forward to going over town for any reason, just for a change of scenery. Don't get me wrong, I love living here, but sometimes it's such a small world I wonder what else is out there."

"Why don't you find out?" she said.

"Well, for one thing, I just got out of high school. And for another, I have responsibilities. Family business, family tradition."

"But what do you want to do?"

"I don't know. I haven't thought much about it. Besides, it's not what I want, it's what's expected of me."

"Well, you'd better start thinking about your future," she said seriously. "You're draft-age now, and in case you hadn't noticed, there's a war going on and President Johnson just called up another fifty thousand troops. And this war in Vietnam doesn't look like it's going to end anytime soon."

"There's nothing I can do about that. If they draft me, I have to go. It's my duty."

"What duty?" Lynn asked pointedly.

"To protect my country."

"Protect it from what---a bunch of poor Vietnamese farmers fighting a civil war in their own country? How are they threatening us? I would certainly care if you were killed or maimed fighting halfway around the world for reasons that aren't clear to me, or to a lot of others either. You know, Dave, you could give me cause to worry about you."

Then Lynn did a very unusual thing, something that surprised the both of them. She put her arms around his neck and kissed him. He put his arms around her and returned her kiss. They held each other close, her head resting on his shoulder, and the only sounds they heard outside of their own breathing was the sigh of a soft breeze, and the wings of a pair of ravens soaring overhead.

In the Atwater Arcade on Sumner Avenue, Joshua Taylor was just finishing up his shift at the post office. After clocking out, he made the short trek up to the Skipper's Galley and entered through the doorway, nodded to the hostess, and seated himself in Shelly's section. His eyes swept the room discreetly until they found Shelly, who was busy at something by the wait station, between the counter and the order window. Her back was to him, and he admired the sweep her neck made when she wore her hair up, and how her trim figure looked so cute in that waitress outfit with the apron tied in the back. Phil set two plates in the window and did not bother with the microphone.

"Yours, babe," he said, pulling the ticket.

Shelly's back was still toward J.T., so he didn't see her smile, but he could imagine it. She turned quickly on her heel and began walking his way, flashed a quick smile of recognition, and then set the plates down two tables away. She exchanged some pleasantries with her customers, and then moved toward him. His heart leapt.

"Well hi, J.T. Long time, no see. Hey, I made a rhyme. If you're looking for Sil, you just missed him. Sorry."

"Oh, that's okay," he said. "I'll catch up with him later. Besides, I really came in to see you. After all, you're my favorite waitress."

"Well, thank you," she smiled. "That's sweet. What can I get you?" she said, pulling out her little ticket book and a pencil.

"Oh, how 'bout a grilled cheese with fries and coffee. And I like my coffee like my women—hot and black."

She laughed and he thought to himself that it had been a stupid remark, and untrue. He liked his women like her—honest and kind.

"Comin' right up," she said cheerfully, while he slumped back in his chair and pondered the unfairness of life. He thought about how Sil didn't appreciate this treasure of a girl, and how she was destined for a broken heart. Shit, Sil was probably down at the beach right now, hustling someone new. J.T. had given up the idea of finding a woman of his own. He'd concluded that there weren't any black Islanders, and the colored girls who arrived from the mainland usually came as a set… either with a boyfriend, or with a girl friend. He'd escorted two ladies around one night, one on each arm, but he wasn't able to be alone with either one, and ended up walking back to his room empty hearted. Now as he watched Shelly walk gracefully away, he felt a deep longing and shame. For he wished, just for the moment, that he was Caucasian.

Along the sand of Crescent Beach, Bob Silenski strolled purposefully along, dressed in baggies, sandals, and wide striped surfer tee shirt. A towel was draped around his neck, and he carried his transistor radio, tuned to KRLA.

"Do you believe in magic, in a young girl's heart…." sang the Lovin' Spoonful.

J.T. had been correct, in a way. Sil was out trolling for chicks, but today he wasn't just fishing for some cute little thing. He was searching for someone special. He scanned the crowd deliberately and moved on, seeking out Donna Forte.

CHAPTER 10

▼

TRUTHS AND CONSEQUENCES

"Do you believe in magic, in a young girl's heart?"

The morning kitchen clatter of the Skipper's Galley competed with the little radio at the dishwasher's station for Jimmy's attention, when he heard his current favorite song being played on KRLA. But try as he might, the sound was just too faint to pick out any lyrics. He could barely make out the tune. So, he let it go and surrendered to the sounds of bacon sizzling on the grill, the swishing and humming of the dishwashing machine, and shouted orders. His attention was on his work, but when he could, he'd sneak glances at Donna Forte, who was busy out on the dining room floor.

He remembered the night before, when he and Donna had seen *Thunderball* at the Casino Theater, and he had cared less about watching the movie than about being with her. Sitting next to her, feeling the warmth of her nearness had been thrilling. Before the movie began, they sat and chatted and enjoyed the beautiful ornate frescoes and murals on the walls, and the gold leaf stars winking above in the domed ceiling, surrounded by silver leaf patterns. It had been very special.

Later, as he walked her home, she'd seemed moody and distant. There had been no passion in her goodnight kiss. She'd complained of feeling tired and wanting to turn in early. He'd dismissed it with the thought that maybe she was just on her period. But today meant another beginning, and he was glad they worked together, so he could steal glances at her, and speak a word to her now and then. Maybe tonight they'd be alone together again.

Although every morning was busy, weekends were the worst. Jimmy and Sil were a constant blur of motion. At the moment, they were putting together an order of Pigs in a Blanket, French toast, and a poached egg on the side. The Skipper had retreated to the sanctuary of his office, presumably to catch up on paperwork. But weekends were not for calling in supply orders to the mainland. That was reserved for Tuesdays, as the freight would arrive by air on Wednesdays. So they could only presume he was getting an early start to his drinking before the lunch rush kicked in.

Sil picked up the microphone and purred in his bedroom voice, "Donna, order up."

She soon appeared at the window and Jimmy thought he saw Sil flirt with her. Or was it only his imagination? After all, Sil tended to flirt with all the women. Shortly, Donna walked off the floor, past the office and into the kitchen, heading toward the walk-in. She needed to re-stock her station with butter. Jimmy didn't notice her pass, but Sil did.

"Take over for a minute," he said to Jimmy. "I need something from the walk-in."

He set his spatula aside, and padded casually but quickly around the dishwasher, and to the back room. He stepped inside the walk-in and closed the door from the inside. Donna looked up, startled. But the surprised look on her face tuned to one of happy recognition. Sil leaned her back against the shelves and kissed her on the mouth. She pulled away.

"What are you doing?" she said.

"Hanky, panky—no, no, no," he said with a sly smile.

"Someone will see us," she complained.

"How about tonight, then?" he asked. "Meet me on the Pleasure Pier around seven."

"Okay," she agreed.

He kissed her again, and grabbed a flat of eggs from a shelf, slapping her on the butt as he left.

The Skipper showed up for the lunch rush accompanied by a six-pack of beer. He was in a foul mood, and stumbled his way through the rush, barking out orders, making everyone uptight. When the rush ended and he left, Sil turned to Jimmy and squawked, "Batten down the hatches, ye lubbers, and furl the mains'l, or I'll have the lot of ye keelhauled! Yarrr!" They both laughed and began cleaning up.

That evening at seven, Bob Silenski stood at the end of the green Pleasure Pier, looking alternately out to the bay and then toward town, watching couples stroll along the sidewalk lining the beach, and past the restaurants, bars, and shops of Crescent Avenue. He listened to boats rocking gently at their moorings, the lapping of waves, and a mixture of music, voices, and laughter coming from the waterfront area. Then he saw her walk out of the shadow of storefronts and into the late evening sun. She crossed the street and strolled onto the boardwalk of the pier, her thick black hair falling around her shoulders, her shapely legs accented by the short dress she wore. Donna spotted Sil as soon as she was abreast the fast food stand, and a smile lit up her face as she quickened her pace. Sil sauntered toward her, and they met about half way, by the ticket stand for the glass bottom boat. They embraced, and Sil spoke first.

"You look familiar. Haven't we met before?"

"We have, but not here," she answered.

"Hmmm. I must say the atmosphere here is better than at the Skipper's place. I'm glad you came."

"I've been looking forward to seeing you," she said. "Especially away from work."

"Work is a four letter word," said Sil.

"So is play," she countered.

"True. Well, what would you like to do?"

"You decide," she said.

"Okay. Let's take a walk to Lovers Cove, and then go to the dance at El Encanto. Then maybe we could head over to the Saint Catherine Hotel, or a quiet café. The dance is for teenagers. I hope you don't mind."

"Not at all," she said agreeably. "I'm still a teenager."

Donna had cold feet, however, when they walked through the arched entry to El Encanto. She'd turned down a date with Jimmy for tonight, and she was worried he'd spot her there. As it turned out, he wasn't there, and neither were Lynn or Waxie. So she relaxed, and let herself go. She became enraptured with Sil, who was very attentive to her, which made her feel special.

They danced, talked, held hands, and kissed playfully, and Donna was filled with joy. Later, they walked over to the Casino and Hotel Saint

Catherine at Descanso Bay. As they strolled back to town and along Crescent, Sil suggested that they stop by the Glenmore, so she could see his room. She felt very uneasy about this, but found herself going along with the idea.

"Okay," she said nervously, "but only for a moment."

Sil was surprised she'd agreed to go up to his room on their first date. He hadn't planned on her saying yes, but was eager to take advantage of this opportunity. He navigated her past the night clerk, and up the elevator to the fourth floor. He wished he'd borrowed the record player again, and some mood music as well, but he would make do. He killed the overhead light, lit the candle, and turned the radio on low volume.

They kissed and petted for a while, and then Sil began removing Donna's clothing. She stiffened, and then began shaking a little. She felt a sense of panic wash over her, as her thoughts ran wild. "He'll know I'm not a virgin. But what does that matter? I'm damaged goods now, so I may as well give in to him. That's all that guys want. If I say no, I might lose him." While her mind ran away in confusion, she watched herself become naked in the candlelight, and felt Bob's muscular naked body against hers. He slipped on a condom and entered her. They made love while the Righteous Brothers sang "Unchained Melody" in the background. Donna felt afraid and vulnerable and watched their lovemaking as if detached from her body. But she felt safer with Sil than she had with Chuck, although at times both their faces appeared before her and seemed to merge. Sil groaned, and Donna faked an orgasm to please him. Afterward, they lay together quietly, arms around each other.

"That was great," said Sil

"Uh, huh," said Donna. But somehow she felt empty.

Sil glanced at his watch and said, "It's after midnight. Maybe we should be going. I'll walk you home."

"That would be nice," she said quietly.

He blew out the candle and they got dressed in the dark. There was enough light streaming in from the window from the street below to see by. He opened the door for her, and they stepped out into the hallway, and headed for the elevator.

At the end of the hall, Jimmy Fontana was just stepping out of one of the shared bathrooms, holding a wet towel from his shower. He caught a sudden glimpse of Sil and Donna together just before the elevator doors closed on them. He stopped dead in his tracks, and for a moment refused to believe what his eyes had just witnessed. Then he felt a stabbing pain in his stomach, as if he had been kicked, and a sinking feeling in his heart. Now his heart raced as he rushed to the window at the other end of the hall facing Sumner Avenue. He watched anxiously until they emerged on the sidewalk below, hand-in-hand in the streetlight, and stared as they rounded the corner and disappeared out of sight. He shuffled to his room as if in a trance, completely stunned. He laid in bed for a long time, unable to sleep, feeling betrayed, and replaying the scene in his mind. He remembered how Diane had dumped him, and began crying. He finally fell into a fitful sleep, tossing and turning, and disturbed by dreams about first Diane, then Donna.

After saying goodnight to Donna, Sil made the long, steep hike up to the Chimes Tower and gazed out over Avalon. He let out a long Tarzan yell, but it seemed the town was asleep, and no one heard him.

Jimmy didn't show up for work that Sunday morning, but when he returned on Monday, Sil noted that he seemed sullen and morose. Then near the end of the lunch rush, he exhibited strange behavior. Sil watched as Jimmy flipped a burger high in the air. On the way down, it missed the broiler altogether and hit the dirty slats on the floor. Jimmy scooped it up with the dustpan and tossed it back on the broiler. Moments later, he scraped it off the broiler with the dustpan and put it in the little Chili Size boat, and ladled some chili over the patty. He placed the boat in the window, pulled the ticket, and called Francie over.

"That," laughed Sil in disbelief, "is an abortion." Jimmy ignored him. Soon, Francie returned to the window, Chili Size in hand.

"The customer says the patty isn't done. Could you cook it a little longer?"

Jimmy took the boat without comment, dug the patty out, tossed it on the broiler, and placed a weight on top of it. When it began smoking, he slid it back in the boat, and sent it out. Again, it was returned.

"The customer says it's burned, the chili is cold, and he's not paying for it. So just cancel the order."

"Where is he?" Jimmy said, tight-lipped.

Francie pointed him out, a middle-aged man seated at the counter. Jimmy picked up a French knife and a steel, and stormed out to the counter. He took up a position behind the man and began sharpening the knife on the steel, first one side and then the other.

"So you don't like the our food, and you're not going to pay?" Jimmy said menacingly, watching the look of horror wash over the man's face. Just then, Sil appeared.

"He's just kidding, sir," he said, taking Jimmy by the arm. "Always the jokester, yes. Actually, we came out to tell you how sorry we are that you're unhappy with the service, and we'd like to make things right. Can we offer you a meal on us?"

"Forget it," said the man tersely. "I'm leaving this greasy spoon, and taking my business elsewhere."

"Yes, sir," said Sil. "Again, our apologies. If you change your mind, the free meal offer still goes."

The man cleared his throat and left in a huff, and Sil took Jimmy aside in the kitchen.

"Hey, pal," he said, "that was very un-cool. What the hell's your problem, anyway?"

Jimmy shot Sil an intense look of hatred. Then he took an egg from the carton by the grill, dropped it into the pocket on Sil's cook's coat, and smashed it with his hand.

"That," he said angrily, "is an abortion."

Sil looked down at the mess in his pocket, then back to Jimmy. "Okay," he said knowingly, "I get it. This is about me and Donna, isn't it? Well, pal, let's discuss it later. Right now, though, the orders are backing up and we need to get on 'em."

"Fuck you, Silenski. I'm clocking out."

Jimmy removed his apron and stomped off, leaving Sil to fend for himself. He punched the time clock, and then banged on the office door.

"What is it?" shouted an irritated Skipper, opening the door and glaring at Jimmy.

"I want off the day shift," said Jimmy. "Can I work nights?"

"What's this all about?" demanded the Skipper, chomping on his cigar as Jimmy stepped inside, uninvited.

"I want off the day shift. I'm not working with that asshole Silenski anymore."

"Oh, I see," said the Skipper, returning to his chair to glance up at Jimmy. "Well, why don't you try to work things out, try to get along. The season's half over for Chris-sake, and I need you both where you are."

"Can't do it," said Jimmy, emphatically. "Either I get another shift, or you get another cook."

"Okay, Goddamn it," said the Skipper, removing the cigar from his mouth and pointing it at Jimmy for emphasis, "you're off the day shift. But I can't give you the swing shift, because I want Phil and Dan there, and that's where they want to be. And graveyard is out of the question, because Pete can't hack any other shift. So the only thing I've got left is relief cook. I'll ask Manny. He'd probably like to switch shifts. But I'm warning you right now you won't like it. You'll work two daytime shifts, two swings, and two graveyard shifts. Your sleep pattern gets all screwed up. And you'll still end up working one day with Bob."

"I can put up with that asshole for one day a week," said Jimmy. "I'll take it."

And so it came to pass that Jimmy Fontana became relief cook for the Skipper's Galley, and Manny ended up on the day shift, working alongside Sil.

Shelly Green took the news about Sil and Donna more or less in stride. Marilyn, the O'Haras' daughter, and the Galley's number one gossip, dished her the dirt. Marilyn could be quite catty at times, but she liked Shelly, so she didn't gain much satisfaction in being the bearer of bad tidings this time.

"I think you ought to know your man's been two-timing you with that slut Donna," she said. "I'm sorry, Shelly, but you're better off without him. He thinks he's God's gift to women, but he's really just a heel. Let me know if I can do anything for you."

Shelly had already suspected as much, and answered in a quiet, steady voice.

"It's okay, really. We were just dating, nothing serious. He didn't make any promises. I'll be just fine, thanks." Then she added, "I just wish he'd been more truthful and forthcoming."

Although she didn't show it, Shelly was deeply hurt. After all, she'd thought she was in love with Sil, and that he felt the same way toward her. She forced herself to wear a smile during the rest of her shift, but later at home, when she was alone, she fell apart. A song on the radio triggered a crying jag.

"You've got your troubles, I've got mine...." sang the Fortunes.

J.T. began to drop by the coffee shop in the afternoons and evenings to visit Shelly and joke around, trying to cheer her up.

"You gotta understand something about Sil," he said. "He's a ladies' man. He likes the ladies, and the ladies like him. He never gets serious, though. I guess it's 'cause he's got so much college left to do, and he don't want to get tied down to one woman. He don't mean to hurt nobody, he just don't think ahead. Don't take it too personal. You're a real boss chick, and you'll find somebody who's good for you."

"Thanks, J.T. I appreciate your concern. But I'll be alright, really."

J.T. continued to drop in, and one night he stopped by late, and hung around until Shelly got off work. He offered to walk her home and she accepted. They kidded each other as they walked, and she shook his hand when they said goodnight at the door. One day he talked her into going out on her night off. They saw the comedy *Cat Ballou* at the Casino Theater, and when it was over she said, "Thanks, Jay. I needed a good laugh." And then she kissed him on the cheek.

J.T. tried to play things cool around her, as though he only liked her as a friend, but he knew he was living a lie. He was falling in love, and he couldn't tell anyone, much less her. As he walked alone back to the Travel On Inn after their date, he heard a song coming from somewhere, one that he was familiar with. Only this time, the words to "Down In The Boondocks" cut him deeply."

"I don't fit in her society...." sang Billy Joe Royal.

"Jay Tee" he said under his breath, "you one messed up muthafucka."

CHAPTER 11

▼

THE ACTRESS

The sign over the door of the small, nondescript office on Sunset Boulevard read SOLOMON FINE AGENCY, and underneath, the phrase "Home Of Fine Talent." Outside, in the summer heat, traffic snarled and tempers flared on the "Boulevard of Broken Dreams." The smog had settled in like a brown fog bank, and pedestrians shuffling along the sidewalk felt it sting their eyes and lungs. Inside the cramped waiting room the air conditioner hummed. It was one of the few luxuries Sol Fine allowed, and it was for the benefit of his clients, not himself. His clients consisted chiefly of models and actors, or more accurately, would-be stars. One of them, twenty-two-year-old Candice Lovelace, renamed Candy Love by Sol himself, sat in the outer office on a well-worn sofa, perusing a copy of *Variety* she'd picked up off the lamp table. The intercom buzzed, and a disembodied voice said, "Send her in."

"Mister Fine will see you now, Miss Love,' announced the plump, frowsy matron seated at the reception desk.

Candy strode confidently through the doorway that led to Sol's inner sanctum. He rose to greet her.

"Candy baby, please be seated." He motioned her to the chair facing his desk. She sat deliberately, crossing her legs, while Sol returned to his perch on the wide, padded swivel chair. In the center of the desk was an appointment calendar surrounded by a telephone, intercom, overflowing ashtray, in and out baskets filled with papers, a half-filled water glass, and a half-empty bottle of Maalox tablets. In a corner of the cramped room was a filing cabinet, and hanging in frames on the wall behind him were displayed his license, an award of some kind, and 8"x10" glossies of some of his more successful clients. Candy's photo was not among them.

Sol leaned back in his chair, his hands folded into the shape of a tent against his stomach. He was a small, balding, moon-faced man with a sallow complexion. He wore a short-sleeved white shirt, and in Hollywood circles, a very un-hip bow tie. Sol was a man who'd been around, and had seen the rise and fall of careers, and felt no need to change with the times. Consequently, his business volume remained about the same, neither growing nor shrinking. It was just enough to keep this unimpressive office and to employ Martha, an un-ambitious woman who filled the multiple roles of secretary, bookkeeper, and office manager. She'd been with him nearly the entire twenty years he'd had the agency. He now cleared his throat.

"Candy baby, have I got news for you. I have not one, but two assignments, back-to-back. Wonderful opportunities, both of them."

"Modeling work?" she asked hopefully.

"Much better than that, sweetheart. Acting jobs."

"Real parts, Solly, with lines, or is it just extra work?"

"Both, baby, and both of them location shoots on—are you ready for this---Catalina Island!"

"Fill me in Solly. Give me the particulars."

He picked up a sheet of paper, put on his glasses, and studied it. Then he said, "The first job, the extra work, begins shooting next week in Avalon. Should be three or four days' work, pays scale, and it's a big budget production. Major studio, MGM, and names like Doris Day and Rod Taylor. The working title is 'The Glass Bottom Boat.' You might get some close-up shots, get noticed. Could be a break. Remember how Tony Curtis got discovered?"

"What about the other film?" asked Candy.

"This you will like," he said, revealing a smile. "A speaking role. Only one or two lines, maybe, but enough to get a SAG Card. It's an independent production, Executive Pictures. But again, some names: Del Lord, Tommy Kirk. This could be your big break, kid."

"A Screen Actors Guild card," said Candy, wide eyed. "That's great! How can I ever thank you?"

"By working hard and making it big. Then my fifteen percent commission will amount to something. Now as far as wardrobe, you'll have to provide your own. Beachwear. Two-piece swim suits. And some nice evening wear. You get the picture?"

Candy got the picture, all right. And she understood why there had been no audition. She had been picked on the basis of her portfolio, which made this a glorified modeling job, in a way. She had the look that was currently in demand, the golden California beach look. No matter that she'd only been in California just shy of four years. Candy was tall, tanned, and statuesque. She was a natural blonde with deep blue eyes, and had the wholesome, natural beauty that didn't need make-up to enhance it. She had the California Look.

"The second film is 'Catalina Caper', Sol continued, after a pause to review his notes. "There'll be a few days' work in Avalon, and then you'll head over to Malibu for the other scenes. There will be a couple weeks down time between productions, so you might just want to hang out in Avalon. Take a little vacation. Work on that suntan, kid."

There were papers to sign and instructions for Sol to impart, but twenty minutes later Candy was slipping the key into the ignition and pulling her Sunbeam Alpine away from the curb. She would head back to her bungalow in West L.A. and begin making preparations for her upcoming movies, like choosing her wardrobe, for instance. Later, she would drive into Hollywood to her job slinging cocktails at the Palms Lounge. Tonight, she decided, she would tender her resignation.

As she navigated the traffic on Sunset, she contemplated the implications of a speaking role in a movie, and that after spending four years in Hollywood, she would finally get a Screen Actors Guild Card, which would open doors for her professionally. It was as if she'd just graduated from the University of Tinseltown, and would now receive her diploma, so she could go out into the real world of acting. She reminisced on how far she'd come to get to this point in her life. She shivered at the thought of those dreadfully long, dreary, frigid winters in Minneapolis. Then she smiled at the palm trees that lined the street as she turned onto the freeway onramp.

Like herself, Candy's mother, Britta, was a natural beauty of Scandinavian descent. When she was just eighteen, Britta had married her high school sweetheart, Ken Lovelace. But a world war was going on and Ken was soon drafted. He shipped out to Europe with the 99th Infantry Division. When he returned in 1945, he had a Purple Heart from wounds received during the Battle of the Bulge. He also had a bad case of nerves. Doctors diagnosed it simply as "battle fatigue." By the time of his discharge from the Army, his daughter, Candice, was beginning to walk and talk, and she added a new word to her vocabulary—daddy.

Ken Lovelace adjusted to civilian life by taking the first job to come along, in construction, and working hard. "Putting my nose to the grindstone," he called it. Soon, a second daughter came along, whom they named Constance. Not long after that came the insomnia, and Ken began taking a drink or two at night as a sleep inducement. But when he finally nodded off, he'd be haunted by vivid nightmares. The one that came most often was like a scene out of Dante's Inferno, with fire and shelling all around. He would find himself in a foxhole in the midst of this hell, alone, cut off from his squad and the rest of the company. He would scream into the radio, trying to raise help, and awaken in his bed in the middle of a stifled scream, drenched in cold sweat. So Ken took to keeping a night light on, working harder, and drinking more. When he succeeded in getting his contractor's license, he moved the family from St. Paul to the suburbs of South Minneapolis and started his own business. He continued to work hard and pay down the mortgage on his home, but the nightmares still plagued him. To combat this, he drank even more, and the evening nightcap became an evening bottle.

One winter night, when it was thirty degrees below zero, with a wind chill factor of minus fifty degrees, and snow drifts so high they crept halfway up the front door, Ken's supply of sleep inducement ran dry. He'd been home bound for days, unable to work, and going stir-crazy. Schools were closed, and roads impassable. He ordered his wife Britta to go out and buy him some more vodka.

"Are you kidding?" she asked in an annoyed tone of voice, "We're snowed in, and nobody's going anywhere."

"Don't give me no lip, woman," he slurred angrily as he backhanded her across the face. "Do as I tell you!"

She backed away from him, her cheek stinging red, surprise and shock registering in her eyes. She ran into the bedroom and slammed the door. When Ken sobered up, he was remorseful and begged forgiveness, which Britta gave him. But it did not stop the abuse. It was only the opening act of a drama that would be played out for years.

On one occasion while Ken was beating Britta, little Candy ran over to her mother, and grabbed onto her. "Don't hurt mommy!" she screamed. But as she was in harm's way, she got smacked too. That was a turning point in her fragile life. After that experience, Candy became withdrawn, and retreated into a fantasy world of her own. She would pretend that a handsome prince would come along to rescue her and make her his princess.

When she reached puberty, Candy read all about the marriage of Grace Kelly to Prince Rainier of Monaco, and a seed of thought was planted in her mind that movie stars can become real life princesses. Then when she saw *A Star Is Born* on television, she decided that she could become a movie star, with a little talent mixed with luck. And she devised a formula for herself—talent plus luck plus Hollywood equals princess and happiness.

By the time Candy Lovelace was in high school, she was obsessed with becoming a movie star, and felt that it was her destiny. She read the movie magazines religiously, and took drama classes throughout high school. She studied diligently and worked hard at becoming an actress. She auditioned for school plays, and won a role in all of them. And as her father didn't allow her to date until she was seventeen, the theater became her social outlet as well. When she wasn't busying herself with acting, she would be going out to the movies. Marilyn Monroe was her favorite actress, and she saw as many of her movies as she could. The highlight of her senior year was landing the lead role of Cherie in the play *Bus Stop*. It was the role that had gone to Marilyn Monroe in the movie version. In *Bus Stop*, Cherie is an aspiring actress who is trying to get to Hollywood to become a star. Her plans are altered when she ends up on a bus with the cowboy, Bo, headed for Montana. Candy was adamant, however, that nothing would detour her plans of stardom.

The other highlight of Candy's high school days was the Senior Prom, for which she begged her father's permission to attend. Her date was a popular young man whom she was quite fond of. The evening of the prom began very romantically, and would've been a perfect night, had her date not brought her home ten minutes past her curfew. Ken had been waiting up, drunk as usual, and a very ugly scene ensued. He yelled and cursed, and threatened the hapless boy.

"You are never to see my daughter again, and if I ever see your face around here again, I'll kick your worthless ass all the way to Saint Paul!" He then ordered Candy inside, slapped her across the face and called her a whore, then sent her to her room. "You're grounded, young lady,' were his stinging words.

This was another important turning point in Candy's life, for she swore that night to leave home in August on the day she turned eighteen. She had been saving up for over a year now, mostly from modeling jobs, the money going into a college fund account. It was planned that she would go to college in the fall to major in Theater Arts. Ken agreed to this plan, not because he wanted her to be an actress, but because it seemed like a good way to meet a potential husband. But Candy had different plans. She was going to Hollywood. Nothing and nobody could stop her.

On August 16th, Candy bought a one-way bus ticket to California. Her mother and her sister Connie saw her off at the station. Ken refused to come. He didn't want to take the time off from his work. "Besides," he said, "she'll be back when the money runs out. She doesn't realize how good she has it here. She needs to learn some gratitude."

As Candy boarded the westbound Greyhound, Britta handed her a sack lunch, kissed her, and said, "Good luck, honey. How I envy you. I wish I had the guts to leave. I'll be praying for you."

"Goodbye, little sis," Candy said to Connie. "Come visit me anytime." Then she stepped aboard the bus, and it rolled out into traffic and down the road.

It was in the pre-dawn hour, three days later, when Candy stepped off the bus at the station on Cahuenga Boulevard near Hollywood Boulevard. Fatigued from the long trip, she hauled her suitcase out to the sidewalk in the quiet gray morning. There was little traffic on the street, and no pedestrians to be seen, save for a wino passed out in front of the station. The air smelled of stale exhaust fumes, cigarette butts, and oil stains on asphalt. She could detect the scent of coffee brewing at an all night café, and the aroma of an old garbage can nearby. Down the block, a street sweeper fought a losing battle against debris, and parked in front of her was a taxi cab, its engine idling. Candy approached it slowly, cautiously.

"Need a lift, miss?" asked the cabbie.

"Yes, please," said Candy. The cab driver got out, opened the trunk, and placed her suitcase inside. Then he opened the passenger door for her. "Where to, miss?" he asked as he turned on the meter.

"I don't know," she said. "A motel, I suppose."

"First time in Hollywood?" asked the cabbie.

"Yes," she answered.

"You an actress?" he said, looking her over in the rearview mirror.

"Yes, how did you know?"

"Lucky guess, but mainly because you look like a movie star." Then he said, "I know just the place for you. It's nothing to brag home about, but it's clean, safe, and centrally located. Best of all, it's inexpensive."

"Thank you," she said, as he pulled away from the curb.

He deposited her in front of an older motel, collected his fare and tip, and wished her luck. "See you in the movies," he said. For a moment, Candy felt all alone in the world, and vulnerable, and had second thoughts about leaving home. But after a nap and shower, she was revitalized, and eagerly set out to see the sights. She lunched at the Brown Derby, and marveled at photos of movie stars who had been there. Then she went to Grauman's Chinese Theater on Hollywood Boulevard and slipped her hands into the handprints of Marilyn Monroe encased in cement. She was surprised that Marilyn was so small. She'd appeared so large on the silver screen. It would have been a big shock for her to know that Marilyn would be dead within a year from a drug overdose. Candy spent the rest of the day walking around Hollywood in a daze, amazed that she was finally here. Now she needed only to make her dreams of stardom come true.

Regardless of Ken Lovelace's predictions, Candy did not return to Minneapolis. Instead, she began the long, slow process of developing her career.

Within a week, Candy had found a job waiting tables at Denny's. Soon after, she moved in with another waitress, who was also an aspiring actress, to a studio apartment off Western Avenue. Later, after she hooked up with the Fine Agency, she got her own place, a converted garage apartment on Bundy in West L.A. Over the next few years she would hold many jobs, including modeling, working as a go-go dancer, a brief stint as a topless dancer, and a series of acting gigs in small theatre productions. When she turned twenty-one, she was able to work as a cocktail waitress, a job she found as lucrative as the modeling assignments Sol Fine sent her on. She had yet to break into the movies, other than extra work. But she took acting classes and workshops, and made contacts in the business. And she waited.

Candy took on several lovers after moving to Hollywood. The first one was Martin. He was a photographer, and did the first series of shots for her portfolio. He was several years older, and she had hooked up with him mainly because she was lonely in the first months she'd been away from home. When that ended, she'd been with Lee, a lifeguard at Santa Monica Beach. The beach was near her bungalow, and she liked spending time there, working on her tan and studying scripts. She met him soon after Martin, when she'd been looking for the company of someone her own age. They began dating, and Lee would squire her around to see movies at prestigious theaters like Grauman's, the Egyptian, and the Pantages in Hollywood, and the Regency in Westwood. Lee even managed to wrangle tickets to a movie premiere in Hollywood, and

Candy was thrilled to be mingling with genuine movie stars in the lobby. This was something about Lee that impressed her, that he was in tune with her needs and he made her feel special. They had fun together, she felt safe with him, but she knew she didn't love him, not like in the movies. She knew she hadn't found her prince yet. So when he pressured her for a commitment, she broke it off with him. Her current boyfriend, Stan, was a bartender at the Palms Lounge, where up until today she'd been working. Stan didn't know it yet, but she was about to leave him as well. She had never even considered him prince material. It had been merely a relationship of convenience.

On the Sunday morning of July 25th, 1965, Stan drove her down to the steamer pier in San Pedro, and carried her suitcases to the landing of the *S.S Catalina,* where a stevedore tagged and took charge of them. Stan kissed Candy goodbye at the foot of the gangway.

"So long, honey," he said. "See you soon. Have fun."

Candy blew him a kiss from the main deck railing as the ship, its anchor weighed and lines cast off, chugged away from the dock. She moved forward, toward the bow, where she could feel the fresh breeze against her skin. Her long hair was tucked up under a wide straw hat. She paid no attention to Los Angeles Harbor, receding off the fantail as she squinted ahead, hoping to catch a glimpse of dolphins and flying fish. As Santa Catalina Island rose out of the deep blue water, she watched intently as it grew larger on the horizon, as if she were watching her future approach as well. From where she stood on the rolling deck, Candy Love, everyone's idea of what a California girl was, could see her future was a beautiful sight.

CHAPTER 12

▼

HIGH HOPES AND GLASS BOTTOM BOATS

Candy Love checked into the Hotel Atwater where some of the film crew were holed up. She reported to a production assistant, who gave her a list of instructions. She was to report to the make-up trailer, parked down at the Cabrillo Mole, at 5:00 AM, outfitted in a two-piece swimsuit. Candy returned to her room, 252, unpacked, showered, and changed. Then feeling hungry, she wandered down to the adjacent coffee shop. The hostess handed her a menu and seated her, while the bus boy brought a glass of water. Candy glanced over the menu and made her decision. Then she gazed out the window facing the street. She imagined it a movie screen on which the passers-by were actors in a drama unfolding before her. The window was a view into a world that held myriad stories. "There are eight million stories in the Naked City," she thought, quoting the closing lines of the television show of the same name. Then she turned her chair and her head to watch the cooks behind the order window, working away in a ballet of sorts. One cook was stocky and sported a goatee, while the other was taller and younger looking. Candy sensed the waitress approaching, and turned to face her.

"Good afternoon," said the smiling, attractive young woman with a pencil in one hand, and a ticket book in the other. "Ready to order?"

"Yes, Shelly, I am."

"How did you know my name?"

"Your name tag gave you away."

"Oh, that," laughed Shelly. "Of course. For a moment, I thought you were a mind reader."

Shelly took the order and returned a short time later with a Chef's Salad and a glass of iced tea.

"Now that you know my name," said Shelly, "what's yours?"

"Candy Love."

"Really? That's a wonderful name. Makes you sound like a movie star." Then a curious look came over Shelly's face. "You aren't by chance in that movie they're filming here?"

"Now you're the mind reader. Tell me, how did you guess?"

"Just a hunch. But you're very pretty, like a movie star. And we had some of the film crew in earlier, including Doris Day's stand-in. You must be excited."

"It's just a job," said Candy modestly.

"Well, it's a more glamorous job than waiting tables. I think it's exciting, and I'll look forward to seeing you in the movie."

"So will I," Candy agreed.

The next morning before dawn, Candy waited in the alcove of a shop on Crescent, wearing a two-piece swimsuit and a terry cloth robe. Shooting was to commence as soon as there was enough light for the cameras to work with. A group of extras milled about with gaffers, grips, best boys, and other technicians. Cameras, booms, and lights were set up, and a sound truck was parked nearby. Trailers, which had been brought over by barge, were clustered at the Mole, a short walk away. The crew had positioned a yellow speedboat on Crescent Avenue at the edge of the beach, as if it had run aground. A few cars had been strategically placed in camera view for the scene. Candy's orders were to rush up to the boat as soon as the ACTION command was given, then to stand by the boat looking concerned until the director commanded, "CUT!"

As the sun rose to the east, over the mainland, Doris Day was escorted to the set, and positions were taken. A make-up person attended to Miss Day as she sat in the boat, lights and microphone levels were adjusted, and the command was given, "Places, everyone."

"Quiet on the set!" yelled the second unit director. Then, "Roll camera. ACTION! Background---ACTION!"

Candy and other extras ran to the boat on cue and surrounded it. An actor dressed as a Los Angeles County sheriff's deputy strode up to the boat, pulled a pen and ticket book out of his pocket, and began writing a parking ticket.

"CUT!" said the assistant director. Then, "Places, everyone. Let's run through it again."

The scene had taken only a minute to film, but the actors and crew ran through it again, then again, and yet again. It was late morning before they had a finished take, and by then quite a crowd of onlookers had arrived, milling around just outside camera range. The extras were finally told to wrap for the day, while the principals would move to another location to shoot another scene. The second unit director instructed Candy and the other extras to report back the following morning, same time and place, for a similar scene.

By the time Candy returned to her room, showered and changed, it was nearly noon and she was famished, having had nothing to eat since 5:00 AM, when the Extras had been given coffee and donuts. She hurried down to the Skipper's Galley for lunch. Candy saw an open seat at the counter, and decided to take it, rather than take up a table in the dining room. A waitress wearing the nametag Donna took her order, and while she waited, she watched the cooks behind the order window. She noticed that one of them, the tall, good-looking guy, was staring at her. In fact, she felt as if his eyes were boring a hole through her. She imagined that at any moment now he would start panting and drooling like a dog. She couldn't help but laugh at the image, which he must have interpreted as a flirtatious smile. He smiled back, and a scowling, red-faced, middle-aged cook wearing a sailor hat upbraided him. The young cook's smile vanished as he looked away and continued about his business.

Candy's order arrived, and as she ate, she felt the young cook's eyes on her again. She smiled to herself, thinking that she was getting a preview of what fame must be like: strangers staring at her, wanting her, or wanting to be her. Perhaps fame held a special power. If it was a power that would bring her security and the opportunity to rescue her mom and her sister from Ken Lovelace, then she wanted it. But the rest of the trappings were superfluous.

Tuesday's shoot went pretty much the same as Monday's. It was the boat scene again, except with a twist, in that Rod Taylor was seated next to Doris Day, and the extras were to run up to the boat this time from the direction of the water. Again, the short scene took hours to set up for and film until the director was finally able to say, "CUT! Print it, that's a wrap."

Candy was finished for the day, and told to report tomorrow for a night shoot on the steamer pier. This was to be the scene where she'd wear an evening dress. After a light lunch at the Skipper's Galley, Candy walked over to the Casino, then to Descanso Beach, where she watched the filming of the speedboat in the bay, while they were using stunt people and a camera boat. She found the mechanics of movie making fascinating. It was so different from live theater. In live theater, everything happened sequentially, in real time. In movie making, scenes were done multiple times until they were right, shot out of sequence. Then they were edited and pasted together so that the finished product looked seamless.

On Wednesday morning Candy rose early and strolled down to the Mole, where she hung out, watching scenes being filmed in Lovers Cove with Doris Day, Rod Taylor, and Arthur Godfrey, on the glass bottom boat *Nautilus*. She'd hoped to meet some of the actors, but was only able to watch from a distance. When the cast and crew broke for lunch, Candy did as well. In what was becoming a routine, she dropped by the Skipper's Galley. The lunch rush had slowed, and she found a table in the dining room. She noticed the good-looking cook staring again, so she blew him a little kiss. He blew one back, and the middle-aged cook hit him across the back with his sailor hat.

Later in the afternoon, Candy returned to the same beach where she had been working the past couple of days. Now, instead of movie people, it held only sunbathers. She found a spot on the sand, slathered her body in baby oil, and sat on a beach towel she'd just purchased. Tucked inside the bag she'd bought at the same tourist shop, was a script for *Catalina Caper*. She would look it over, but first she would catch some sun. She put on her sunglasses and lay back on the towel. She was contemplating how to tell Stan that things were over between the two of them, when a shadow fell over her and lingered. She sat bolt upright and blinked. The blond young cook from the coffee shop stood over her, dressed in jams and sandals, with a towel and tee shirt draped over his shoulder. He had a rich tan, and flashed a wide smile.

"Hey, sugarpie honeybunch!" he said. "You're a sight for sore eyes."

"I beg your pardon," she said coolly.

"Mind if I join you." It was a statement, rather than a question. He placed his towel next to hers and sat.

"I'm sorry," she said, "but have we met?"

"I'm the cook at the Skipper's Galley," he said. "The one you blew a kiss to, remember?"

"Yes, I remember."

"My name is Bob, but my friends call me Sil."

"In that case," she said, "I'll call you Robert, because I don't see us getting any chummier than that."

"Ouch," he said, placing his hand over his heart. "You really know how to hurt a guy."

Candy laughed. "There's line I've never heard before. Where'd you get it, from a song?"

"As a matter of fact, I did," he replied. "It's a Jan and Dean song. Have you heard it?"

"Can't say that I have. But then, I don't keep up with pop music."

"That's a drag, I mean that's too bad. But as I said, I'm Sil, and you are---?"

"Candy. Candy Love."

Now it was Sil's turn to laugh. "You're putting me on," he said.

"I am not. That's my name."

"Sounds like a stripper's name," he teased.

"I was a stripper once. Actually, a topless dancer, but same difference."

"What do you do now?" he said.

"I'm an actress. And actually, Candy Love is my stage name. My real name is Lovelace. Candice Lovelace."

"You here for the movie they're shooting."

"Robert, you're so perceptive."

"I am? Actress, huh? Sounds exciting."

"You mean, as opposed to being a short-order cook?"

"Oh, that's just a summer job," he said defensively. "I'm actually a college student. Pre-Med."

"So you can play doctor?"

"Yeah, gynecologist," he said, holding up his index and middle fingers to illustrate.

"What a surprise," she said. "I'll bet you're a frat boy, too."

"Delta Chi," he affirmed. "Ever been in a sorority?"

"Hardly. I haven't been to college. I got my education at the school of hard knocks. I've had courses in acting, modeling, dancing, waiting tables, and slinging cocktails, just to name a few. I've even done a topless photo shoot for a men's magazine."

"Which one?" he asked with interest.

"Wouldn't you like to know?" she said slyly.

"So, do you get any time off from your movie making?"

"What do you think?" she said, removing her sunglasses, revealing her deep blue eyes.

"Yeah," he said. "Dumb question, huh?"

"You said it, not me."

"Ouch," he said.

"No you don't," she said. "You already tried that line already."

"What line?"

"You really know how to hurt a guy."

"Oh yeah, sorry. Well, since you have some time off, how about going out tonight?"

"I'm busy."

"Okay, how about tomorrow?"

"Look, Robert, you seem like a nice guy, but you're wasting your time here. You're not my type, and anyway, you couldn't afford me."

"How do you know I can't?"

"Because I'm a gold digger, and I'm looking for a sugar daddy to take care of me. When I was younger, I wanted a prince, but now I'm more realistic. And let's say hypothetically you were out of school and a practicing doctor. It still wouldn't work. You'd be busy with your career, and I with mine, to have a relationship, let alone be married. As I said, you're not my type, and frankly, I'm a little out of your league. Sorry to be so blunt, but I hate to waste your time."

"Oh, I have plenty of time," said Sil, taken aback, but regaining his composure.

"Well, I haven't. My plate is full. But look on the bright side—you're a personable and good looking young guy, and not a bit shy, and the beach is filled with available women. Why don't you just run along and find one, okay?"

"Okay," said Sil, "I get the picture. You're busy. But I'll see you later."

"Ciao," she said. "That's Italian for goodbye." She put her sunglasses back on, and lay on the towel on her stomach.

Sil reluctantly picked up his towel and walked away. Then he turned and looked upon her form, and said to himself, "Cute little thing! She shall be mine. Yes, she shall indeed."

That night, Bob Silenski and Donna Forte emerged from the Casino Theater after the early show. Donna said, "Let's go for a walk," so they strolled toward the Pleasure Pier, along the Via Casino. As they passed the Tuna Club, they noticed a crowd gathered at the steamer pier, which was all lit up.

"What's going on, I wonder," said Donna.

"Maybe they're filming a movie scene," said Sil.

"Let's take a look!' said Donna enthusiastically.

They joined the crowd of on-lookers at the foot of the steamer pier A helicopter sat atop the pier, surrounded by the film crew, and the usual lights, booms, and motion picture camera and dolly. The director, Frank Tashlin, was giving directions to Rod Taylor and Doris Day, who stood nearby. "QUIET ON THE SET!" a voice sang out. Then, "Places, everyone. Let's do a take." Then more commands. "Roll cameras. ACTION! Background---ACTION!" Sil and Donna watched with the rest of the crowd as they ran through the scene. When the director yelled, "CUT!" Donna turned to Sil and remarked, "See that tall blond girl in the long black dress, the really pretty one?"

"Yeah," said Sil, as he spotted Candy Love.

"I waited on her today."

"Really?"

"Yes, I'm sure of it. How about that? I waited on a movie actress."

"Well, that's something to write home about."

"Do you think she's beautiful?" asked Donna.

"No," he lied. "Not compared to you, anyway. No one can hold a candle to you."

"Donna threw her arms around him and gave him a kiss. "That's one of the things I love about you, Sil. You know just what to say to a girl."

The couple watched the crew and actors run through the scene again, and then Donna said, "Well, this is where we came in, and it's starting to get boring. How about walking me home? We have to work in the morning."

"Your wish is my command," said Sil gallantly. But as they turned to go, he snuck another glance at Candy, and was stunned at how beautiful she looked in her evening gown. She was on the arm of another actor, and for a moment Sil imagined himself in the actor's place. She was the most beautiful and desirable creature he'd ever seen. He hoped she would return to the Skipper's Galley soon.

The film crew worked late into the night on the helicopter scene, and it was after midnight when Candy was told to wrap. She made the short walk to her room at the Hotel Atwater, and stayed up a couple more hours, too wound up to sleep. This had been her last scene in *The Glass Bottom Boat*, and now she felt empty. The next crew would arrive in Avalon in a couple of weeks to begin work on *Catalina Caper*, but until then, she'd be in a sort of limbo. She was finished with the Palms Lounge, and things were over with

Stan as well. There was nothing calling her back to her little place on Bundy in West L.A., so she felt temporarily adrift. Why not just stay on in Avalon, as Sol had suggested? But how would she fill her time? She drifted off to sleep with these matters weighing heavily on her mind.

Candy awoke late in the morning on Friday. After leisurely dressing, showering, and getting ready for the day, she traipsed down the stairs, through the hotel lobby, and out to the sidewalk. The desk clerk told her there was a bank of pay phones in the Atwater Arcade, just around the corner. She made a call to Stan, who worked nights, and so would just be getting up for the day. She told him she'd decided to stay over in Avalon for a while, and encouraged him to start dating other women. She now walked over to the Skipper's Galley for either a late breakfast or early lunch. She hadn't yet decided which. As she passed through the front door, she noticed a HELP WANTED sign in the window. She sat at the counter, and Donna handed her a menu.

"You're in the Glass Bottom Boat, aren't you?" said Donna. Before Candy could answer, Donna added, "We saw you filming a scene last night. It's an honor to wait on you."

"Well, thanks for saying that, Donna. Tell me, are you still serving breakfast?"

"Yes, I think so. What would you like?"

"Coffee, small orange juice, two poached eggs with wheat toast. I also wanted to ask about the sign in the window. What kind of help are you looking for?"

"A hostess. One just quit, so we're short-handed. Do you know someone who's interested?"

"Yes. I may be."

"You're kidding," said Donna. "You're an actress. Why on earth would you want to work here?"

"Because my work on the Glass Bottom Boat is finished, and I've got a little down time before my next picture. I like to keep busy, and working in a restaurant allows me to study people, which is an essential trait for an actor. You might call it doing homework."

"You're serious, then?"

"Yes, I think so. Could you bring me an application?"

"You bet! Just as soon as I get your order in."

Within the hour, Candy had been interviewed by Sam O'Hara, and immediately hired. Sam was so impressed with Candy she hadn't even treated her condescendingly. "I think you'll be a real asset, Miss Love. We'd like you to start tomorrow morning, if it's alright with you." Candy said it would be fine. Having something to fill her time with took a load off her, but more so, she was happy to have an income for a while. She wouldn't have to dig into her savings while she waited for her paycheck from the extra work.

As she was leaving the Skipper's Galley, about the time the lunch rush was beginning, Candy turned in the doorway, and glanced toward the order window. The cute but annoying cook was staring at her. She smiled, winked, and waved to him, and watched as his jaw dropped. She walked out into the sunshine, thinking how she would like to spend the day on the beach, just relaxing. Then she remembered the day she'd boarded the Greyhound bus in long ago and far away Minneapolis, and felt a great sense of gratitude. And she thought how Avalon deserved to be named after a mythical kingdom. There seemed to be something magical about the place.

CHAPTER 13

▼

REFLECTIONS ON
A BLUE MOON

July gave way to August quietly, but not unceremoniously, as a second full moon climbed into the sky on the last day of the month. It was on the advent of this "blue moon" that a tour boat pulled away from its mooring at the green Pleasure Pier and chugged lazily through Avalon harbor, heading for deeper water. Long and low slung, it resembled a launch more than anything else. Its rows of backless wooden benches were filled with weekend tourists and at least one Islander couple. The boat had already made its daily run to Two Harbors, and was now underway for the Flying Fish Cruise, a favorite with lovers and other romantics.

The bow of the launch contained a covered area where the helmsman steered, and behind him facing aft, the tour guide stood, uniformed in a short-sleeved shirt, shorts, canvas shoes, and a yachtsman's cap. He was young, tanned, and outgoing, with a warm smile that put everyone at ease. Three rows back, on the port side, Waxie Shein sat upright, outfitted in a windbreaker, his arm around Lynn Robinson, whose sweater was draped around her shoulders. For although it was on the cusp of August, the night breeze sometimes kicked up choppy waves out in the deeper water, which could result in damp and chilled passengers. Tonight, however, the air was still, the water calm and glassy, and the moon seemed to smile down from its perch among the stars.

Although he knew the tour guide's talk would soon make his own words redundant, Waxie leaned in to explain some things to Lynn. He told her how the waters around his island were the only place in the world to see this particular flying fish. "And," he added, "they don't really fly. They propel themselves out of the water by moving their tails back and forth really fast, then spread out their long pairs of fins and use them to glide on."

"So why don't they just call them gliding fish?" asked Lynn.

"Because flying fish sounds cooler. Besides, they really do look like they're flying. You'll see."

The boat soon cruised past Descanso Cove, and the lights of Avalon and the Hotel Saint Catherine disappeared behind a bluff. The sky now appeared darker, the stars brighter, the moon more radiant. The young guide gave a brief talk about flying fish, repeating what Waxie had told Lynn, cracked a few jokes, and promised the chances very excellent this night for spotting the fish. He turned on the vintage 1914 searchlight, originally from a battleship, and swept its light across the dark water. The launch was cutting through the smooth ocean just off the coast, the dark mass of land jutting up sharply off the port side, when suddenly a sleek blue and silver fish broke the surface. It glided just above the water for about a dozen yards, and then splashed back under and out of sight. A current of excitement and expectation ran through the group of passengers like a jolt of electricity.

"Look!" a voice cried out.

"Where?" yelled another.

"There!" shouted a third. But the elusive fish had already vanished. Then another one popped out of the water, leaping and gliding farther than the other, its path traced by the powerful searchlight. The launch continued on a northerly course, following the outline of the island, while the exotic fish put on a show, leaping, gliding, and splashing in a unique aerial display. Some of the fish climbed nearly as high as a house, and flew for over a hundred feet. Suddenly, one of them banged head first into the side of the boat, just below the searchlight, and bounced off. Gasps, shrieks, and nervous laughter ran through the boat. Lynn was enthralled, craning her neck to follow the light's path. She smiled broadly, and Waxie in turn smiled at her obvious pleasure. The boat passed by several coves and small beaches, accessible only by water, before rounding Long Point. Now a breeze caught the waves, making for a choppy ride. Spray began to spill over the gunwales, and Lynn drew the sweater around her tightly. However, it was here that the boat changed direction, putting about, to place the wind to their backs.

With the turn-around at Long Point, the wind and waves subsided and the launch began its homeward run to Avalon. The searchlight continued to sweep the water and draw in fish, for they were attracted to the light. But when they reached the boats anchored offshore, near the entrance to Avalon harbor, the light winked out, and the tour guide invited everyone to just quietly enjoy the rest of the trip. All too soon, they rounded the bluff that revealed the lights of Avalon, and the running lights of boats at anchor. Lynn shifted her gaze from the blue moon to the waterfront to Waxie's brown eyes, which also glowed. She studied his soft, open face for a moment, and then squeezed his hand and held it with both of hers.

"Thank you," she said, "for one of the most wonderful evenings I've ever enjoyed." Then she kissed him.

"My pleasure," he said. "But it's still early. I hope you're not ready to go home yet."

"No, not yet," she said.

"Good."

The boat glided up to its dock at the Pleasure Pier, everyone disembarked, and the guide said goodnight as he assisted the couple onto the dock. Waxie took Lynn by the hand and led her up the ramp and on to the pier.

"Let's go for a walk," he suggested, to which she agreed.

They walked to the end of the pier, and then turned left down Crescent along the beach past the Mole, and down the road that led to Pebbly Beach. At Lovers Cove they found a bench perched on a bluff overlooking the ocean. The lights of town were hidden from view, and the moon and stars bathed the clear, calm water in a soft light. Waves lapped gently at the rocks below them as they seated themselves and gazed out at the mainland.

"It's such a lovely night," said Lynn.

"Sure is," Waxie agreed.

"I can't imagine what I'd be doing in San Diego tonight. I know it wouldn't be this peaceful or romantic. The big world with all its hustle and bustle and stress seems so far away. I feel safe here. It's like a paradise, our own little Shangri-La."

"You wouldn't say that if you were an Islander. It gets pretty boring in the winter."

After a long pause, Lynn said, "I'll be leaving soon."

"I know," said Waxie. "College."

"Why don't you come with me?" she said hopefully.

"I can't. You know that. Pop wants me to stick around and help out. I'll be taking over the business someday."

"Why can't your sister do that?"

"What, run things? She's too young. Besides, I think it's the sort of thing you pass along to the oldest son."

"If that's really what you really want to do with your life, you could take some business classes at City College. Bookkeeping and things like that. It couldn't hurt." Then she added, "And you could get a student deferment."

"You mean from the draft? Come on, I'm not afraid of being drafted. Pop served his country, and when the time comes, I will too."

"Dave," she said in carefully measured words, "World War Two was very different. It was right to defend your country then. It was a noble thing to do, defending the world for democracy. But this war in Vietnam worries me. I don't think we have any business being there. It seems to be a civil war between the north and the south. The Vietnamese aren't threatening to invade us. Why should American boys be dying on the other side of the world? You tell me."

"What about Communist aggression and the Domino Theory?" argued Waxie.

"You mean if the two parts of Vietnam are united, the whole world is going to succumb to Communism? I don't believe that for a minute. I don't think the government is telling us the whole truth."

"Maybe you're a commie yourself," teased Waxie.

"Far from it," said Lynn. "But I am a Quaker, and we have pretty strong feelings about killing and wars. Jesus said, 'blessed are the peacemakers, for they shall see the Kingdom of God.'"

"I'm Jewish," Waxie said matter-of-factly.

"I know that," said Lynn. "I don't care about that. A lot of Jewish people oppose this war too, you know. I really care about you, Dave. I care about your future and your well being. I don't want to see you go to war for no good reason. Won't you please just consider college, for me?"

"Okay," Waxie said after a pause, "I'll think about it."

"Thank you," she said. "That's all I ask." Then she kissed him warmly, and buried her head in his chest. He could feel her sobbing quietly, and it bothered him. They sat still for some moments, no words expressed. Then a gull cried out and landed on the ground beside them. It turned its head sideways, as if studying them. That broke the ice. They looked at the bird, then each other, and laughed. Then they sat back on the bench and watched the night sky together, not saying anything for a long while.

Over at the Skipper's Galley, Phil Munday and Jimmy Fontana, who was giving Dan a night off, were finishing their shift, and cleaning their work area.

""Hey, hep cat," said Phil, "like what's shakin' after we split this nowhere scene?"

"I don't know. Guess I'll just go to my room and read for a while."

"Man, don't be a square. Live a little. Drop by the pad, dad, and we'll smoke some reefer and groove to the new Coltrane album I scored. It's called 'Impressions', and it'll blow your mind."

"Okay, why not? I'll clean up a little first."

"Groovy."

A little later, with candlelight and the sounds of Coltrane's sax swirling around in their heads, Phil and Jimmy passed a slender joint between them until it was burned down to a roach. The song "India" had just finished, and Phil said, "Dig it. Is that cat the most?"

"He's the grooviest," agreed Jimmy.

"You know," said Phil, "it's a real bummer you goin' in the Navy. You could've split up to Frisco with me and had some real kicks. Not in North Beach, though. That's like Squaresville now. Tourists and topless bars. No, daddy-o, the scene has moved to the Haight-Ashbury. That's what I'm told, anyway. Cheap rent, good vibes. Some young cats making a new scene. They call themselves hippies, like junior hipsters, you dig? This cat I know told me he saw Allen Ginsburg hangin' out with Ken Kesey and Neal Cassady. He says they got some new dope up there, LSD. Supposed to be better than pot, and it's legal."

"When're you leaving?" asked Jimmy, nodding his head in time with the music.

"After Labor Day, when the season's over. The Skipper won't dig me splittin', though. He'll be bugged about it."

"Why do you owe the Skipper anything?" asked Jimmy. "He doesn't give a shit about us, that's for sure. No paycheck this week, and nobody knows where he is. Off on a drunk over town is the best guess."

"Don't let it bug you," said Phil. "We'll get our bread. I've never known the Skip to stiff anyone before. He's been hitting the sauce pretty heavy, though, I'll give you that. But life ain't just about the bread, you dig. If it were, I wouldn't be an artist. I'd be just another work-a-daddy square. What about you—what turns you on? What's your future look like, after the Navy, that is?"

"I haven't thought that far ahead," said Jimmy. "It'll be a long time before I'll get to be a civilian again."

"Time will fly, trust me. Sometimes it all seems like a dream, time does. Or it's like the bass line in this song," he said, with a nod toward the stereo. "You just get in the groove with it, and then it's over, and you're on to something else. Look at me. I came over to the island three years ago, and now it seems like yesterday. One day you wake up and you're pushin' thirty, and you think--man, what's it all about? Well, I'm movin' on to a hipper scene, where the cats will dig my real work, not just that hash slingin'. You gotta look ahead, too, man. Can't get where you're going without a road map."

"Were you ever in the military, Phil?"

"No, man, I beat that rap. To the mutual benefit of myself and Uncle Sam, I might add."

"How did you manage that?"

"Back in the Fifties, during the so-called Cold War, the draft was breathing down my neck. I heard a married man could get a deferment, and at the time I was shacked up with this little chick in North Beach. She worked at a coffee house where I hung out, that's where we met. Anyway, we tied the knot, partly to beat the draft, partly to make her folks less uptight. It worked out for about a year. Then we got one of those Mexican divorces. I neglected to notify the draft board, of course, and they never asked me about it. So I never got my notice."

"Why'd you get divorced?" asked Jimmy.

"Well, there's this thing with chicks, see. When they get married, they expect the man to support them. I mean, like before we were married, she was cool with my lifestyle and my art, you dig? But after the ring, she got hung up on bread, security, having kids, having a nice pad, and I wasn't in the same bag. But I don't hold it against her. Women are born to be that way. We split up on good terms, though. No hard feelings."

"So you understand women, then. I sure don't."

"No, man. I don't think I'll ever really understand them. I just dig them, like a lot of other cats do. It seems like when creative people fall in love—I'm talkin' writers, musicians, painters, they put that feeling into their art. They get inspired and create stuff that transcends and lasts. And you hear about some cats that are too sensitive to love that deeply. They get messed up. I'm talkin' winos, suicides, basket cases. Can't deal with all the beauty and pain in their psyches."

"Wow, Phil, that's heavy."

"Nah, man, don't mean shit. Just the reefer talkin'."

Phil got up from the couch, and took the album that had just finished, off the turntable. Then he put on another record.

"Now I know you're gonna dig this cat, cause I already hipped you to him." He dropped the needle in the groove, and Bob Dylan's nasally voice, accompanied by electrified instruments, rasped through the speakers.

"How does it feel," he whined, *"how does it feel...."*

"Like a rolling stone," Phil replied. "Yeah, man, feels just like a rolling stone."

Jimmy Fontana closed his eyes and let the music take him away for a while, to a place where he could forget about Donna, and Sil, his tardy paycheck, and the U.S. Navy. He just grooved along.

Over on Whitley Avenue, Donna Forte ran her right hand over Bob Silenski's bare chest and let it rest there. She lay on her side on the bed, leaning on her left elbow, and gazed down into Sil's blue eyes, which twinkled in the candlelight. His face was slightly flushed and his smile seemed a little lop-sided, but these were things that endeared him to Donna. She moved her hand to his mouth and traced its outline with her soft, warm fingers.

"I love your mouth," she said.

"And I, yours," he said. "It fits mine perfectly."

She smiled contentedly and leaned in to kiss him. His tongue found hers as they connected.

"Will you still respect me in the morning?" she teased, as she slowly disengaged from him.

"I'll always respect you," he lied smoothly. "And anyway, it already is morning. And now it's August as well. Summer has peaked, and now we're in the pipeline, and I'm stoked. And time is slipping away like the outgoing surf during the winter heavies."

"I like the way you express yourself, Sil. In fact, I like everything about you."

"The feeling is mutual," he lied again. "In fact, I'm flat-out stoked." The words seemed hollow to him.

"I'd like to keep this moment forever," she said. "I'd like to put it in a locket, and wear it next to my heart. Then when I'm feeling down, I could open the locket and feel the happiness of this moment again."

She ran her fingers through his long blond hair, sighed, then reached around to her purse and pulled out the pack of Newports. She extracted one, lit it on the candle flame, and took a drag. She knew Sil didn't smoke, but she didn't know how much it bothered him that she did. He disliked the smell of stale smoke on her breath, and in her thick hair. He wondered if Candy Love smoked. He didn't think so. At least he hadn't seen her smoke.

"I just love this song," said Donna, turning the radio up.

"I think I just love you cause roses and rainbows are you," warbled Danny Hutton.

Donna now sat up in bed, and the covers slipped down to reveal her breasts. Sil stared at them, admiring their shape and beauty in the soft light, and how the nipples stood out proudly. Then he found himself thinking about Candy again. He wondered what her breasts looked like, and how they felt.

"When's your roommate due back?" Sil asked suddenly, glancing at his watch.

"Any time now," said Donna. "Waxie usually brings her home by midnight."

"It's after midnight now," said Sil, fluffing up a pillow to lean his head on. "I'd better get going soon."

"So, trying to get rid of me, huh? You men are all alike. Wham, bam, thank you ma'am."

"No, it isn't that," Sil said. "It's just that I don't want to traumatize Lynn, by having her see us in bed together. Then we'd have to explain to her all about the birds and the bees."

"Hah! A lot you know about it," she teased. "We girls learn about these things long before you boys do."

"That may be so. But I'm glad you know a few things about how to please a man, because baby, you're the greatest."

"Thank you, sweetheart," she said, leaning over to kiss him on the forehead, while she kept the cigarette at arm's length. But secretly, she felt a wave of anxiety and guilt suddenly wash over her from somewhere deep inside. She stuffed the feelings back down, and snuffed the cigarette out.

Sil felt uncomfortable, like an animal cornered. He looked for a way out, an "open door." An open door to a surfer is a wave that breaks in such a way that the surfer can ride away from the peak, out of the hook. His thoughts kept returning to Candy Love. He couldn't wait to get back to work at the

Skipper's Galley, so he could see her again. Donna would be off work today, so he could stare at Candy and talk to her without having to look over his shoulder. Sil cleared his throat.

"Well, it's been a real blast being with you," he said, "but the witching hour is upon us, and I gotta make like Willie Mays and slide on outta here." He pushed the covers aside and jumped out of bed to get dressed. He turned his back to Donna as he hitched up his jeans.

"Will I see you later?" asked Donna, suddenly feeling needy.

"Sure, why not?" he replied vaguely.

"When?" she pressed.

"After work, I guess. I'll be down at the beach. You can meet me there." But he secretly hoped she wouldn't.

They kissed goodnight, held each other for a few moments, and then Sil walked out of the room, through the living room and out the front door. He hurried down the steep hill until the harbor came into view, looking beautiful as always. That was something he could always count on. Now that he was safely away from Donna, he began to feel carefree again. He remembered how he felt the first night in Avalon. It was like being on a green back, an outside swell that hasn't yet broken, with the drop still ahead of him. Now he felt as if he were in the soup, the swash, and the ride was about over. And yet half the summer still lay ahead. What was missing? When he thought about Candy, though, it was like that first night again. Excitement. Anticipation.

Sil reached the bottom of the hill, and strolled along the waterfront toward his hotel. There were fewer people out on the streets at this hour. He knew some were in the bars, because he could hear voices and music spilling out the doorways. When he reached the Bamboo Lounge, he stepped inside, dropped a coin into the jukebox, searched for a song selection, and punched up the number. Then he took a seat at the bar as Burl Ives began singing "Pearly Shells." He ordered a gin and tonic, and wished J.T. were with him, so he could order a beer as well. He thought about J.T. for a moment, and then realized something that made him uneasy. He discovered that he was lonely.

CHAPTER 14

▼

THE SUMMERTIME BLUES

"But there ain't no cure for the summertime blues...."

"That was Eddie Cochran with 'Summertime Blues,' his biggest hit, which entered the Top Ten this month in 1958. Tragically, Eddie was killed in a car crash in England less than three years later at the age of twenty-three, a crash that badly injured his friend Gene Vincent, who had a number one hit in 1956 with 'Be Bop A Lula.' You're tuned to the Casey Kasem show on KRLA. We've got lots more music coming up, including this week's Top Ten countdown, right after these messages."

Luis the dishwasher was grooving to the radio over the sounds of his machine, and dirty dishes clattering around. Over in the cooks' area, however, Manny was barely listening, while Bob Silenski was oblivious to everything but the orders on the wheel, and a certain hostess out on the floor named Candy. The lunch rush was winding down, the Skipper was still AWOL, but nobody really seemed to care. In fact, Manny had remarked how things seemed to run smoother without him around, barking out orders, chugging beers, and putting everyone uptight. Sil didn't care one way or the other. He wanted only for this shift to end, so he could be alone with Candy Love.

Three-thirty finally rolled around, his shift ended, and Sil made a beeline for the time clock and the restroom. He cleaned up, then rushed over to the employees' table and waited for Marilyn to take his order. While he waited, his eyes swept the dining room for Candy, and found her seated in Shelly's section. He quickly excused himself, and made his way over to where she was, at the same time trying to summon up some self-confidence.

He approached her table, and standing over her asked, "Mind if I join you?"

She gave him an amused look, and said, "Oh, I don't see why not, now that we're co-workers."

He seated himself across from her and opened with, "So how do you like it here?" He heard the words leave his mouth and they sounded silly and superficial. Just then Shelly appeared with a menu, a glass of water, and a forced smile.

"Know what you want, Sil?" she asked, taking out her pencil and ticket book.

"Oh, hi Shel. Uh, yeah. Cheeseburger, fries, and a Coke." Then to Candy he added, "The all-American meal."

"Hmmm," she replied as Shelly walked off, "not very healthful sounding. But filling, I suppose." Then, changing the subject, she said, "Shelly and I were just talking about you."

"Really?" said Sil, his eyes wide with interest.

"She said you used to date her."

"We went out a couple of times," he said matter-of-factly.

"And now you're seeing Donna."

"Well, yeah, sort of."

Candy took a sip of iced tea, then said, "You certainly get around, don't you Robert? And now I'll bet you've come over here to ask me out."

"Well," he stammered, squirming in his chair, "now that you mention it---" He let the sentence trail off.

"Do you remember the conversation we had on the beach the other day when I told you that you weren't my type? Well, nothing's changed since then." She took another sip of iced tea.

"Yeah, I remember," he said. "But I thought we could still do something together."

"Oh really," she said with wide-eyed mock interest as she leaned forward in her chair and rested her chin on her hand. "And just what did you have in mind?"

"Well, how does this sound?" he said, the wheels in his mind spinning frantically, trying to come up with an idea. "You know the glass bottom boat? Not the movie, but the boat itself?"

"Yes, go on," she said, batting her eyelashes.

"Have you ever been on it, the boat that is?"

"No, can't say that I have. Why?"

"Well, I was thinking since you're in the movie, you should go on a glass bottom boat tour, so you'd know what it was like."

"And you'd be my tour guide?" she said.

"Yeah, that's it, I'd be your guide. What do you say?"

She sat back in her chair, took another sip of tea, and pondered the question for a moment. Then she answered. "I guess that would be okay," she said. "It qualifies as research, and I guess you're harmless enough."

"Great!" said Sil, his old confidence returning. "Then we could go out to dinner, have a drink, and then--."

"Whoa," she said. "Back up a bit. I only agreed to go on the boat ride with you. That's it. You're not only not my type, but I know you're seeing Donna, and I don't think she'd approve."

"Don't worry about her," he said. "We have an understanding."

"I'll bet you do," she said with a touch of sarcasm.

A little while later, Bob Silenski and Candy Love cruised over the undersea gardens in Lovers Cove on the glass bottom boat *Phoenix*. They gazed down through the glass floor to a lush kelp bed filled with lobster and many types of fish, including the large orange Garibaldi, a protected fish found only in these local waters.

It was the first time either of them had been on the tour, and they were both impressed with all the sights.

Meanwhile, Donna Forte was walking along Crescent Beach, looking for Sil, beach bag slung over her shoulder. At one point, she thought she'd spotted him, coming out of the water. She began clomping through the sand, toward him, her hand raised in greeting. But the smile on her face disappeared when the young man shaking water out of his long blond locks turned out to be a stranger, and the name on the edge of her lips was choked off. She continued looking for Sil. She searched the beach, Casino Point, Descanso Beach, and ended up at the end of the Pleasure Pier. She was remembering her meeting with Sil here a fortnight ago, when she had spotted a familiar form walking toward her on the planked pier. To her great disappointment, it wasn't Sil, but Jimmy Fontana. She was just looking for someplace to hide when he spotted her. Jimmy Fontana did not look any more pleased to see her than she to see him. Before he could find an avenue of retreat, they were within speaking distance. Donna lifted her hand in a half-hearted greeting.

"Hi, Jimmy," she said, trying to appear casual.

"Hi, Donna," he replied, expressionless.

"How've you been?" she asked, avoiding eye contact.

"Okay. You?"

"Just great!" she said with a forced smile. "I haven't seen much of you lately."

"It's the new shift," he said, jamming his hands into the front pockets of his jeans. "Relief cook. The hours are all over the place."

"Well, it's nice to see you again," she said, searching for something more meaningful to say, but coming up with nothing.

"Likewise," he mumbled.

Then she said, "You haven't seen Sil, have you? We were supposed to meet up."

"No," replied Jimmy coolly, "I haven't. But then, I'm not looking for him."

"Okay. Just thought I'd ask. Well, nice to see you."

"Yeah," said Jimmy. "See you around. Take it easy."

Jimmy walked past her to the end of the pier, while she went in the other direction. He turned his head once to watch her walk away, and then strode over to the railing overlooking the Catalina Airlines seaplane dock. It was empty at the moment, but Jimmy knew a Goose would be splashing down soon, then tying up and unloading passengers and freight. For a moment he wished he were catching the next flight out, back to the mainland. But he knew that outside of his family, there was nothing waiting there for him anymore, nothing of value, anyway. So he would just kill time in Avalon until it was time to go off to boot camp.

Jimmy Fontana walked back to the Hotel Glenmore, feeling in a blue funk. He wouldn't admit it to himself, but seeing Donna just now had really upset him. He chose to stuff the hurt feelings, so they were festering as quiet anger. As he walked down the narrow alleyway behind the Glenmore, he noticed a crowd walking toward him, almost as if a procession. At the head of the mob strode a mountain of a man, who was smiling, chatting, and signing autographs as he moved toward Jimmy. He suddenly realized the larger-than-life figure in front of the mob was John Wayne, come down from the Valhalla of the Silver Screen to mingle with mere mortals. As Wayne stepped closer, the two came face to face. The movie star nodded cordially, and Jimmy stepped aside to let him and the crowd pass. When they were gone, Jimmy continued onward, and by the time he stepped through the lobby of the Glenmore, far from being star-stuck, he found his anger toward Sil and Donna was being projected irrationally toward movie stars instead If there was such a thing as a mind grumbling to itself, Jimmy's would have been grousing something like this: "Big, cocky, strutting phonies. Think they're God's gift to the world. Women always go for flash over substance. Big deal. Who cares? Mutter, mutter, mutter." Later, on his shift at the coffee shop, during the bar rush, he was equally unimpressed when the waitress excitedly told him that John Wayne and his entourage were sitting at one of the tables. "Big deal," she heard him mutter, as he began cooking their orders.

Meanwhile, after Donna had left the Pleasure Pier, she walked along Crescent Avenue, still on the lookout for Sil. Unknown to her, Sil had just disembarked the glass bottom boat, Candy Love at his side. They walked off the Pleasure Pier and down Crescent. Candy was telling Sil how much she'd enjoyed the trip, and remarking how clear the water was, when Sil spotted Donna walking up ahead and panicked. As his eyes darted about, looking for an escape route, he spotted a lounge directly ahead. He took Candy by the arm and steered her toward it.

"Hey,' she protested, but Sil cut her off.

"Let's have a quick drink in here," he said hurriedly. "It looks like a cool spot."

"Let go of me," she protested, jerking her arm free.

"Just one drink," he pleaded. "Then we can split."

Candy studied his face, and was suddenly reminded of a puppy, begging to be petted, so she gave in. "Oh, alright," she said, allowing herself to be led inside the lounge, whose door stood open, allowing daylight to pour in. To her surprise, Sil led her to the back of the room, far from the door and picture window, and seated her at a table in a dark corner.

"What would you like?" he asked, standing over her.

"A Black Russian," she said.

"Done," he said, heading to the bar to order the drinks. Candy thought it strange that he hadn't let the cocktail waitress do that. But maybe that was just because she used to be a cocktail waitress. Now it dawned on her that she'd never have to sling cocktails again. She was an actress, and that's the only career she would have from now on. The thought made her glad. Sil returned now, drinks in hand, and set them on the table.

"What are you having?" she asked as Sil pulled out a chair and sat.

"Gin and tonic," he answered.

"Yuck," she said. "How can you stand the taste of gin? I had a martini once, and I found it to be highly over-rated."

"I like it this way," he said, taking a sip. "The tonic and lime give it just the right mix of sweet and bitter."

"Like life, eh?" she quipped.

"I find it refreshing. It makes me think of the tropics. I've never been, but I'd like to go to Hawaii sometime and catch the heavies."

"The heavies?" she said curiously.

"Yeah, the big surf on the North Shore."

"So you're a surfer too," she observed.

"Of course," he smiled. "But I haven't caught any waves in weeks. Avalon's on the wrong side of the island for surf. By the time I get back to surfing, people will think I'm a Gremmie."

"Gremmie?"

"Yeah, a fake surfer. A hodad, a kook."

"Colorful language," she said, sipping her drink. "We certainly inhabit different worlds. And as I've said, you are definitely not my type."

"I get it," he said. "But you are here with me, aren't you?"

"Yes," she laughed. "I admit I am. Maybe you amuse me. Or maybe I like your persistence. You know what you want and you go after that. I admire that in a person."

"Then I have a chance?" he asked hopefully.

"I sincerely doubt it," she answered. "But maybe we could be friends. That is, if Donna doesn't mind."

"Don't worry about that," he said. "We have an understanding."

She laughed at the emptiness in his words and said, "Of course you do. And another thing, Robert---I'm not going to sleep with you, so don't get your hopes up."

"Don't be so sure," he said suggestively. "After all, this is the Island of Romance."

Candy smiled and said, "You know, there's something else I like about you. You make the corniest remarks I've ever heard, but you don't seem to notice."

"Thank you," he said.

"That wasn't exactly a compliment," she said.

"To us," he said, lifting his glass.

"We have no future," she said. "But I'll drink to success. May you find what you're looking for, and may I achieve my dreams."

"Okay," he said, lifting his glass again, "to our success." Then he downed his drink in one long swill. Candy imagined him tossing the empty glass at an imaginary hearth. Then she realized another reason she was becoming drawn to him was because he sometimes seemed so theatrical, so dramatic. "You know," she found herself saying in measured tones, "I won't be staying in Avalon much longer."

"How long?" he asked, searching her eyes.

"A couple of weeks, give or take a few days. I'll be doing scenes for another movie here, then going back to the mainland to finish shooting. The crew will be here in ten days, and whenever we wrap here, I'll have to leave."

"Then I've really got my work cut out for me," he said.

"Good luck," she said, then lifted her glass. "To dreams," she toasted, and finished her cocktail.

On Friday, July 30, Joshua Taylor clocked out at the post office in the Atwater Arcade and walked up the street to the Travel On Inn, stopping along the way to visit with Shelly Green. Back in his room, he showered and changed his clothes, and packed a travel bag. For some time now, he had felt disconnected to the world, adrift and alone. Since Sil seemed always occupied with chasing the ladies, his own world had grown increasingly smaller. His life now consisted mainly of his job, his room, and his visits with Shelly, which usually only took place at the Skipper's Galley. Whether it was homesickness or loneliness J.T. was feeling, he wasn't sure. But he knew he felt isolated and devoid of a sense of purpose. He needed a weekend away from Avalon, so he decided to pay a visit to his hometown of Lynwood to clear out his head. After packing, he walked down to the green Pleasure Pier and caught a flight to Long Beach Airport. After landing and disembarking, he found a pay phone and called home. He spoke with his younger brother Levi, who was eighteen, and asked him for a ride.

That night, J.T. slept in his old room, in his old bed, where he had grown up, and it made him feel comfortable. After high school, he had lived at home for the better part of a year, holding down a series of part-time and minimum wage jobs, before the Army came calling. In a way, he had felt relief at being drafted. At least now he would have some structure to his life. Following his discharge, he had spent a couple of weeks back home with no sense of direction, when Sil appeared on the scene and presented him with a way out—a summer in Avalon. But now the plan had seemed to stall out, and here he was back at home, if only for a weekend. But it would give him a chance to think some things over. Should he stay at home until the fall semester began at L.A. City College, or finish out the summer in Avalon with the post office? He would sleep on it for now.

The next morning Levi, who had been taking care of J.T.'s old sleek Cadillac while he was away, handed him the car keys, and the pair went out cruising. Their first stop was Lynwood High, where both had graduated, and where J.T. now reminisced about his glory days on the football field. Somehow, the school seemed much smaller now, and empty, like a stage when the play is over and the actors have gone home. They got back in the Caddy and cruised some of J.T.'s old haunts, then headed over to 107th Street in neighboring Watts, to view the Watts Towers. J.T. remembered vividly the first time he'd been there, ten years earlier. His parents had brought them to see the folk-art towers, not long after they were built. They stood 55, 97, and 99 feet tall, respectively. The boys had stood in awe of the structures, while their father explained their significance. He told the boys the tale of how they had been constructed almost single-handedly by Simon Rodia, an Italian immigrant, who intended the towers to be a tribute to his adopted country. He went on to describe how it had taken Rodia thirty-three years, and how he'd made the structures out of discarded materials.

"He would get the children to help him find pieces of glass, pottery, shells, and tile from empty lots and along the railroad tracks. He made the framework from junk steel and chicken wire and cement. And now look," he'd exclaimed, his arms open wide to take in the wonder of the masterpiece, "it's the pride of Watts." Then he added with solemnity, "So let this be a lesson to both of you. You can accomplish anything in life if you put your mind to it, and keep at it, and never give up."

His first trip to the Watts Towers had been an impressionable moment in young J.T.'s life, one he hadn't forgotten. He'd valued that talk with his father much more than the later ones about how to fit into whitey's world. After a period of silence, J.T. spoke to Levi.

"You remember when dad first brought us down here?"

"Sure, Josh, I remember."

"Do you remember the towers being a lot bigger?"

"Yeah, I sure do."

"What happened?"

"I think we grew up, Josh."

They stood there in silence a little while longer, lost in personal memory. Then J.T. said, "Let's roll."

The brothers went back home for a while, played a little one-on-one basketball, and sat at dinner with their folks, before going out cruising again. While driving around Lynwood that night, J.T. spotted an old high school buddy, Leroy, hanging out on a street corner with a couple other guys from the neighborhood. J.T. pulled the Caddie to the curb, and he and Levi exited the car and walked over to them.

"Hey, lookie here. What do my eyes see but ol' Jay Tee his own self, and in the flesh." Leroy stepped up and slapped hands and butted fists with J.T. and Levi. Then he said, "Where you been keepin' yo' self, bro? I heard you was in the Army."

"You heard right, man. But I'm out now."

Leroy handed him a bottle of Thunderbird fortified wine, but J.T. waved it off.

"So tell me, bro, whassup with you?"

"I'm workin' for the post office over on Catalina Island."

"You shittin' me?" Leroy said suspiciously. "You workin" for the Man? You ain't no Oreo now is you?"

"Hell, no. Just got me a job, that's all. Government work. What ch'all up to?"

"Nothin'. Ain't no jobs 'round here. Just hangin' with the soul brothers." He nodded to the two guys next to him, who were giving J.T. and Levi hostile, sullen looks.

"So you workin' for da Man," said one of them contemptibly. "Well not me. I ain't axin' whitey fo' shit. If I want sumpin', I take it."

"Right on, bro," his friend opined. "Tell it like it is."

"You hear what the brother Malcom X say," said Leroy. "Got to arm yo'self against whitey, an' don't take no mo' shit."

"I don't take shit off nobody," said J.T. defensively, as he again waved off the Thunderbird.

"You packin' heat?" asked Leroy. "Brother Malcom say you should."

"Shee-it," said J.T. derisively, "that nigger's dead. And it wasn't whitey what cooled him, neither. His own people, the Black Muslims, done that brother in. Tell you what, man, I don't need no gun. My hands are weapons. I got me a Black Belt in karate while I was in the Army. Ain't nobody gonna mess with Jay Tee and walk away in one piece."

"Well, you can have yo' gook ju-jitsu shit. Me, I take a thirty-eight special or a fo'ty-fah magnum anytime."

The conversation continued along this course for a little longer, until J.T. grew bored with it. He also tired of the resentment he sensed from the street corner trio over his own seemingly successful lifestyle. He excused himself, saying he had "places to go and people to see," then he and Levi drove away. Lying in his old bed again that night, he realized that he felt as out-of-place in his own neighborhood as he did in Avalon. But at least in Avalon he had a job and an income.

Sunday morning the Taylor family attended the second service at the First Baptist Church in Lynwood. The pastor was pleased to see J.T. back among the fold as he pumped his hand vigorously, and held on to it for far too long, all the while beaming his brightest preacher smile. Afterwards, the family had their Sunday dinner together, and it was time for J.T. to leave. He had Levi drive him to the airport. J.T. had at least resolved some things that had been bothering him.

He'd come to the conclusion that his post office job could be a stepping-stone to something better in life, and he should keep it until the fall semester began. But he had another reason for returning to the island, something more personal, that he couldn't share with his brother, or anyone else. He had to see Shelly again. He missed her warm smile, her beauty, her grace and sincerity. It didn't matter that she wasn't interested in him, or that he could never possess her love. He was hung up on her, pure and simple as that, and he only wanted to be near her as long as he could.

A few days later, J.T. showed up at the Skipper's Galley in his postal service uniform, with a letter in his hand. He sat at a table in Shelly's section, and waited for her to take notice of him. When she did, she immediately came to him, armed with a menu and a smile.

"I have something for you," he said, handing her the letter.

"For me?" she said, curiously.

"I came across it while I was sorting. I spotted your name, and by the return address, I could tell it was from your brother. I could get in trouble for this, but I wanted to deliver it personally, because I thought it might be important."

She took the envelope, studied it, and smiled. "It's from John, alright," she said. "Thank you for delivering it. Don't worry, I won't tell anyone how I got it. I'd like to read it right now, but I've got customers to take care of first."

She stuffed the envelope into her apron pocket, and began walking away. Suddenly, she stopped, did an about-face, and returned with a sheepish grin.

"Gosh, I'm sorry,' she said. "I forgot to take your order."

"Just coffee, thanks," he said.

He was on his second cup when Shelly returned, sat down across from him, and fished out the letter. He studied her face as she read it, watching her smile evaporate. She frowned, and fought back the tears that were welling up in her eyes.

"Anything wrong?" he asked, handing her a napkin.

She stared at the napkin mutely, then dabbed at her eyes. "Thanks," she murmured.

"What is it?" he prodded.

"It's John. He finished his training at Fort Benning, and they gave him his orders. He has a two-week leave, so he can come home for a visit. Then he goes to Vietnam." She looked up at him with reddening eyes and sobbed. "He's going off to war."

"He'll be okay," said J.T., searching for something to say to comfort her. "Maybe they'll assign him to a rear echelon unit."

"He's in the infantry," she said angrily. "You know what that means."

J.T. could think of no reply to make. Then after a pause, he said, "I'm so sorry. Is there anything I can do to make you feel better?"

"No," she said, "nothing. I'll be okay. Thank you, though. You're always so thoughtful." She placed her hand on top of his and squeezed it. "I'd better get back to work before Marilyn says something."

J.T. left money on the table to cover the coffee, and also a generous tip. Then he walked out the door and onto the sidewalk. He did not go to his room at the Travel On Inn, but instead began walking toward the beach, then along it, and down the road that led to Pebbly Beach. He was confused, mixed-up, messed-up, jumbled-up, and blue. Here he had tried to do something nice for Shelly, only to have it backfire on both of them. He wanted to comfort her, take her in his arms, hold her, and kiss away her tears. But he knew that was impossible. He felt guilt at having been stationed in Germany while Shelly's brother had drawn Vietnam as his lot. And yet he was secretly relieved that he'd avoided the whole mess in Asia by a combination of good timing and blind luck. As he continued walking, J.T. wondered what the future would hold, after he and Sil and Shelly had all left the island. What would he major in at college, and was a degree really necessary? Could he ever find a black woman who made him feel as Shelly did? He wished he wasn't in love with her. Life would be so much easier.

J.T. heard the drone of twin Pratt and Whitney engines and looked into the sky. A blue and white Grumman Goose circled Avalon, then splashed down in the water, just outside the harbor. He suddenly wished he had wings like that plane, or the gulls that circled over his head. Then he would just take to the sky and land when he found a place where he felt he belonged.

Joshua Taylor kicked an empty beer can on the pavement in front of him, and continued walking alone along the road to Pebbly Beach.

CHAPTER 15

▼

THE NEXT IN LINE

It was not a good week for Donna Forte. Her insecurities bubbled to the surface, and doubts about her relationship with Sil nagged away at her. She remembered the old hurts caused by Chuck Belton, and doubted her worth as a woman. She'd grown more anxious since she'd been unable to find Sil at the beach, and sensed he was lying to her concerning his whereabouts on that day. "Oh," he'd explained innocently, "I was around, here and there. Just hanging out." Something about his explanation didn't ring true. But her suspicions were given more weight when Marilyn walked by her one afternoon, a smug smile on her face, singing *"Who'll be the next in line...."*

"What's that supposed to mean?" snapped Donna.

"Oh, nothing," Marilyn replied in a saccharine voice. "Just a song I heard on the radio."

Donna knew there was more to it than that. "Catty bitch," she muttered under her breath.

Then Sil emerged from the kitchen, having cleaned up at the end of his shift, and sat next to her at the employees' table. Her heart was troubled by a vague fear as she decided to test him.

"Let's do something special tomorrow night," she said, pouring on the charm. "Maybe we could go on a moonlight boat cruise."

"Hmmm---tomorrow night," he mused, as if searching his memory. "Let's see, tomorrow's Friday. Hmmm. I think I've got something going on then."

"What do you mean, something going on? What's going on?" she demanded.

"I mean I'm busy," he said, shrugging his shoulders and looking away.

"Are you seeing someone else?"

"Hanky panky---no, no, no," he joked awkwardly.

Donna glowered at him.

"Hey, I'm tied up," he said defensively. "Listen, Donna, we've been seeing a lot of each other lately, and it's been fun. But I need a little break, a little time out. You understand."

"Who is she? Who are you seeing?"

Sil looked out the corner of his eye and was aware that the table had now filled up with other employees, and he suddenly felt self-conscious. "Let's discuss it later," he said. "We'll go out Saturday night, okay? In the meantime, let's get some food. I'm starved."

Donna didn't answer, but with an angry and hurt look, pushed her chair away from the table and stood, eyeing first Sil, then everyone else before turning abruptly on her heel and storming away and out the door, holding back her tears.

"That didn't go so well," Sil thought as he watched her leave in a huff. Then he excused himself and went over to Shelly's section to sit with Candy.

The next evening, Robert "Never in Love, Only in Heat" Silenski pulled up to the curb in front of the Hotel Atwater and parked the golf cart he'd borrowed for the night from one of Phil's friends. The arrangement was that Sil would in turn introduce the friend to a "cute little thing" he knew who worked at one of the gift shops. The catch was that the cart had to be returned by midnight. "I feel just like Cinderella," Sil had quipped. He now strode across the sidewalk and into the lobby of the hotel, noting the wall clock behind the desk clerk.

"Five-fifty-nine," he said out loud. And then to himself, "Damn, I'm not only punctual, I'm one minute early."

He climbed the stairs to the second floor, and knocked on the door of room 252.

Candy appeared in the doorway, wearing the same strapless black evening dress she'd worn on the movie set. It accentuated not only her blue eyes and platinum blond hair, but also her feminine curves. Sil was struck nearly breathless by her beauty, and now felt under-dressed in his surfer shirt, powder blue Levis, and sneakers. For a brief moment, he had an urge to leave. Just then she spoke, and it was like music to his ears.

"Hello, Robert," she smiled, stepping into the hallway, closing and locking the door. She dropped the key into a slim bag hanging by a strap from her shoulder. "I'm ready," she said cheerfully.

Sil opened his mouth and began stammering self-consciously. "Wow! You look outta sight. I mean boss. No, I mean gorgeous."

"Thank you," she replied modestly.

Suddenly brought to his senses, and remembering where he was and why he was here, he said, "Your limo awaits you, my lady."

"A limo in Avalon?" she laughed. "I'll believe that when I see it."

They walked down the stairs, through the lobby, and Sil opened the front door for her, and followed behind.

"Your carriage," he announced, stepping over to the golf cart and holding out his hand.

"Robert, I am indeed impressed. Where on earth did you come by this?" she said, as she stepped into the passenger's seat.

"I have my ways," he said mysteriously.

"Yes, I can see that," she said.

Sil drove to a nearby restaurant along the waterfront, and they sat by a window overlooking the harbor and the Casino. When they had finished a leisurely meal, skipped desert, and Sil ordered a cup of coffee, he steered the conversation toward the movie business.

"Tell me about your next movie," he said.

"'Catalina Caper'?"

"Yeah. What's it about?"

"Well, as a matter of fact, I just finished reading the script," she said. "There doesn't seem to be much to it. My agent Sol describes it as being a beach party movie with a sub-plot about a stolen art treasure and art forgers. Lots of water, sand, and skin, with a chase scene thrown in. It's all being filmed on location, either here or in Malibu, I guess."

"What's your role in the movie?" asked Sil.

"It's a very small part, actually. My character is one of Charlie Moss's girlfriends. Charlie, in fact, is a lot like you," she said slyly.

"Like me?" said Sil, obviously flattered.

"Absolutely. He's tall, blond, and handsome. All the girls go for him. He's also shallow and conceited."

"Ouch!" said Sil, clutching at his chest. "You really know how to hurt a guy."

"Robert, Robert," she admonished. "You promised not to use that line on me anymore."

"Sorry," he said sheepishly, "I forgot."

"Okay, you're forgiven this time. Anyway, that's about all there is to the plot, except for some bands and dancing. I get to dance a couple of times." Then she added, "That's probably why I got the role in the first place. I used to be a go-go dancer at Gazzari's, on the Sunset Strip."

"Go-go dancer?"

"Sure. They had me in a little cage, like a trained monkey, suspended above the stage. I'd dance the Jerk and the Monkey and the Swim while the bands played. In a way, it was a pretty crummy job, but the pay was good, and I got lots of exercise."

"So what's next, after you finish this movie?" asked Sil.

"I suppose I collect my pay, and see Sol about doing another project. But this is an important movie for me, because I have an actual speaking role, I can get my SAG card, and that should open a lot of doors for me."

"What's a SAG card?"

"Screen Actors Guild. It's a union," she explained.

Sil glanced at his watch and said, "Speaking of movies and actors, we'd better hurry if we want to catch the early show."

The couple cruised along the waterfront and around the Via Casino, and parked in front of the Casino. Sil bought the tickets at the box office for *The Sound of Music*, starring Julie Andrews. Candy was quite impressed with the solid black walnut paneling in the lobby and its royal red arched ceiling. She was even more knocked out by the theater itself, with its art deco frescoes and murals, the actual gold and silver trim, and the stars set into the domed ceiling. The room's perfect acoustics also caught her attention.

"This is the most elegant theater I've ever been in," she whispered as the lights dimmed, the curtains parted, and the projector came on. "Even better than Sid Grauman's on Hollywood Boulevard."

After the movie, they strolled outside and around the back of the Casino and stood by the breakwater, where the sound of wavelets against the rocks broke the stillness of a soft summer night.

"That was a wonderful movie," Candy remarked as they looked out over the water. "I'm still taking it all in. Everything was first class, all the way. The sets and location shots, the costumes, the score and choreography. I would love to be in a musical some day, but I'm not a very good singer. That needs a lot more work."

"I'll bet you're just being modest. You're probably great. Sing something for me," he said.

"Oh, no," she said firmly. "I don't even sing in the shower, let alone where anyone could hear me. Still, I think it would be fun. I did a lot of plays in high school, and Community Theater back home in Minneapolis," she said, reminiscing. "And when I got to Hollywood, I did some plays as well. Also some acting workshops, and some work with the Freeway Circuit Theater around Southern California. But I was never in a musical. Funny, too, considering I'm a good dancer."

"Maybe you could take singing lessons," he suggested.

"I could," she agreed. "Maybe I will. Marilyn Monroe wasn't a very good singer, but she was in musicals. She even sang in The River of No Return, and that was a western. Marilyn started out with bit parts, just like me. And she became such a big star."

"Maybe you'll be a star, too," said Sil. Then he added, "I have to get this cart back by midnight, or it turns into a pumpkin or something. So what say we take a little drive? I'll give you a scenic tour of Avalon by night."

"Why not," she agreed, linking her arm in his. "You're only young once."

Sil made a roundabout circuit of Avalon in the cart, and then turned down Pebbly Beach Road, past Lovers Cove to Pebbly Beach, where they got out and strolled around. Then they took the golf cart up a steep, sharp switchback to Mt. Ada Road. They continued uphill until they reached a scenic overlook, 350 feet above Avalon. Sil pulled the cart over to the side, and switched off the key. They got out of the cart and stood side-by-side. Candy scanned the scene below, wide-eyed. The sparkling village lay beneath them, with its harbor extending out into the ocean. Everything seemed to be lit up-- the buildings, the boats, the streetlights, stars in the sky. She took in the panorama for a long time before speaking.

"It's beautiful." she sighed. "I had no idea Avalon could look this way at night."

"What way?"

"I don't know. Like Monaco, I suppose. I've never been there, but I've imagined it looking something like this since I was a young girl, and I've always wanted to go there. Maybe I'll get there someday, but if not, I can still have the memory of tonight."

"Why not just pretend we're in Monaco," said Sil.

"And that I'm Princess Grace?" she laughed. "No, I'm no princess, just a girl from the Midwest with her head in the clouds." Then she added, "And you're no prince, sorry."

"Yeah, I know," said Sil. "But I'm not going to say you really know how to hurt a guy."

"You just did," she laughed. Candy let her eyes sweep over the panorama below again, then turned to Sil and said, "You know, maybe it's true that first impressions can be deceiving. My first impression of you was that you were a jerk, and there was no way I'd ever go out with you. You seemed so full of yourself. But I was wrong. I've really had a good time tonight, and you've made me comfortable enough to open up a little and just be myself. You don't know how nice that feels. I guess we just got off on the wrong foot."

"Should we start all over?" he said.

"Let's," she agreed.

"Okay, how's this? Hi, I'm Bob, but my friends call me Sil."

"Nice to meet you, Sil," she said, shaking his hand. "I'm Candice, but my friends call me Candy."

"Does that feel better?" he asked.

"Yes, it does."

Candy continued to take in the surroundings, then said, "I wonder who owns that big house on the bluff behind us."

"Oh, that's Mt. Ada," said Sil. "It belonged to the Wrigleys, William and his wife Ada. He named the place after her."

"How very sweet," she said.

"Wrigley bought Catalina in 1919 and developed Avalon," Sil explained. "He also owned the Chicago cubs and Wrigley's chewing gum."

"Really?" she said. "Believe it or not, I recently did a photo shoot for Wrigley's Doublemint Gum. It was a modeling assignment for a print ad. They shot me on the front seat of a tandem bike, then on the back seat. They edited the two shots together, and presto---I'm twins. The slogan was 'double your pleasure, double your fun.' Doublemint Gum, get it?"

"Clever," said Sil. "I think I may have even seen that ad."

"It's in a bunch of magazines," she said.

They stood there a little longer, admiring the view, until Candy remarked how far the moon had traveled across the sky. Sil looked at his watch and exclaimed, "Holy cow!"

"What is it?" said Candy, startled.

"It's Cinderella Time," said Sil. "We'd better get going. It's past my curfew, so to speak."

They climbed back into the golf cart and were off. Sil took the direct route; down the hill, a jog at Tremont, and right onto Sumner. He pulled a u-turn in front of the Atwater and parked.

Candy took his hand and said, "Thanks, Sil, for a nice evening, and an educational one too. I had a good time, which I admit comes as a surprise."

"My pleasure," he said, stepping around the cart to help her out. Then he said, "Want to do something tomorrow?"

"Okay," she said. "Pick me up around seven. You won't need the limo," she laughed, "and you don't need to walk me to my door. I'm fine."

Then she said goodnight and kissed him on the cheek. He stood there on the sidewalk for a few moments, watching her as she walked through the lobby and up the stairs. Then he turned around and almost walked into the golf cart, so distracted had he been. "Get a grip, Silenski," he told himself. Then he almost forgot about returning the cart, as he began walking across the street to the Glenmore. He felt intoxicated.

The next morning, August 7, was a red-letter day of sorts. It was the day the Skipper and Sam returned to the Galley, and everyone finally got paid. But it was a mixed blessing, as it meant the Skipper was also at the helm in the kitchen, barking orders and chugging beers. For Sil, however, it was but a minor distraction, compared to the one that held his attention like the grip of a pit bull. His eyes kept seeking her out, the beautiful blond hostess, as she seated people, or stood by the door, smiling warmly. He tried to think of the old Four Seasons song, "Candy Girl," but couldn't remember the words. There was only room in his mind for the breakfast orders and watching her, although he managed to glance at the clock occasionally, and wonder why the time seemed to stand still. But as everything in the universe is in a state of motion, the hands on the clock did finally move, the breakfast rush became the lunch rush, and finally the shift ended. Sil and Jimmy ignored each other at the time clock, and Sil successfully eluded Donna as well, to join Candy in the dining room.

At half-past three, Sil hurried out of the Skipper's Galley, and nearly knocked J.T. over on the sidewalk outside.

"Sil, you slick muthafucka. Where you goin' in such a damn rush? I was just on my way to see your sorry self."

"Hey, J.T. you old hodad. Man, I'd love to hang out and catch up, but I gotta split. Got big plans."

"Let me guess," said J.T. in a disgusted tone, "I bet she's a cute little thing, huh?"

"Cute is not the word, she's way beyond that. She's a righteous babe."

"Well, good luck, Romeo. I hope you don't wipe out. Maybe I'll catch up with your ass later."

"Yeah, maybe. Gotta split."

That evening, Bob Silenski took his time getting ready to go out. He dressed up as best he could. He had a pair of slacks, which he broke out of the closet, and an Ivy League shirt to wear. He also had a pair of wingtip shoes, which he put on for the first time this summer. He hoped he would be presentable to Candy. So it came as a complete surprise to find Candy had dressed down for their Saturday night date. She wore tight-fitting Capris, a casual blouse, and flats. It was as if they were on different tracks. But, oh, did she look gorgeous to Sil.

"Where would you like to eat tonight?" he asked, expecting her to mention Italian food, or maybe a steakhouse. So it blew his mind when she suggested the fish and chips stand on the Pleasure Pier, and added that it would be her treat.

"But I thought you were a gold-digger," he said.

"I am," she said. "But your claim is about played out. So tonight, I'm buying. I think it's called Dutch treat."

"Gotta love those Dutch," said Sil. Then he added, "Are you Dutch?"

"No, Swedish and German, mostly. Some other things thrown in too, like most Americans."

After their fish and chips meal and a stroll along the pier, Sil asked Candy what she'd like to do next.

"I've heard there's a dance at El Encanto." she said. "We could go dancing."

"But it's for teenagers," said Sil.

"Even better," she said. "I'd love to be a teenager for a night." She took him by the arm and added, "I didn't get out much in my teens. I led a very sheltered life."

"That's hard to believe," said Sil.

"It's true. My father was very strict. He was more than that, though. He was a drunk and a wife beater, a very abusive man. So theater became my outlet, where I could escape my life and be another person. I didn't get to go to dances in high school, so we'll make up for that tonight," she said, as she led him down the Pleasure Pier and along the sidewalk that fronted Crescent Beach. As they neared the entrance to El Encanto, they began hearing music spilling out from inside the plaza. Sil recognized the song, "She's About a Mover," by the Sir Douglas Quintet. Candy began dancing around even before they reached the little horseshoe dance area, and she dragged Sil out into the center, with her purse still hanging off her shoulder, and danced until the song ended. Only then did she check her purse, then brought Sil back onto the floor to dance to a Beatles song. Sil noted that she seemed to dance with abandon, not noticing that everyone's eyes were on them, including those of Waxie, Lynn, and Jimmy Fontana. Jimmy soon slunk away and through the arched entryway. Then a slow song came over the speakers, and Sil felt his knees weaken as Candy held him close, swaying like a willow to the sound of violins. Then all too soon, it was over, as the deejay packed up his equipment, and the kids all filed out of the plaza.

"Where to now?" asked Sil.

"You decide," she deferred. "I'm not particular."

So they wound up at the Bamboo Lounge for a quiet drink. "Pearly Shells" was making another appearance on the jukebox, and Sil found that somehow comforting, like being with an old friend. They found a quiet booth and Sil ordered the drinks, a gin and tonic, and a white wine.

"Thanks again, Sil, for another fun-filled time," Candy said. "I really enjoyed the dancing. It made me feel free."

"I should thank you," he said. "It was fun for me, too. I'm really digging being with you."

"Just remember, I'm not going to sleep with you."

"Yes, I know."

"But I think we're becoming friends," she added.

"That's something, I guess," he said.

"You know, Robert, you're a study in contradictions. You're a surfer and a frat boy. But you're studying to become a gynecologist. Why? Why not go for something more suited to your free-wheeling spirit?"

"I like women." he stated, although it seemed almost a question.

"I gathered that. But I can't visualize you making that kind of a commitment to the medical profession. Frankly, I can't even see you making a commitment to one woman. So what is it that really motivates you?"

"Okay," he said after pausing to collect his thoughts, "I'll tell you something I haven't told anyone else, including my buddy J.T. Medical School is my ticket out of the draft. As long as I'm in school, I can get a student deferment. Medical school takes a long time, and even if the war in

Vietnam is still going on when I finish, I'll go in the Army as a doctor, not an infantryman."

"That seems like a lot of work just to avoid the Army," she said. "Funny, but among all your good and bad traits, I wouldn't have thought you a coward."

"I'm not," he argued. "You don't understand—I'm a lover, not a fighter. And I can assure you that if America were under attack from another country, I'd be the first to enlist. But no one has attacked us, and I don't see any future in fighting someone else's war. It's not my business. One of my fraternity brothers got drafted. He came back from Vietnam missing a leg, and he's not all there in his head anymore either. His surfing days are over. That's why I've decided to stay in college as long as I can."

There was silence between them for a long minute, while Candy swirled the liquid in her glass, and Sil watched the bartender fix drinks. Then Candy said, "I think I understand. My father was in World War Two. He's a combat veteran, and I'm sure it crippled him emotionally. Maybe that's why he drinks and why he was violent. So maybe you're right in not getting involved. But tell me this, if the draft wasn't an issue, what would you really want to do with your life?"

"Something that would allow me the time and access to the beach, so I could surf. I'd own a surf shop, or build boards."

"No money in that," she said. "I know exactly where I'm going. I'll be a successful film actress, make good money, live in a nice house, and raise a couple of healthy children in a safe and loving environment. That's why you and I have no future together, and our little fling, such as it is, will have to end soon."

"Here's to flings," said Sil, raising his glass. "But don't count me out just yet. Can I see you again tomorrow?"

"Why not," she said, taking his hand. "After all, you're only young once."

Meanwhile, up on Whitley Avenue, in a house set on stilts and hanging precariously over a bluff, Donna Forte was just getting in for the night. She'd been wandering aimlessly for hours. Earlier, she'd run into Lynn and Waxie, as they were just leaving El Encanto. Lynn had taken her aside and said, "Brace yourself, Don, it's better if you hear this now, from me. We just saw Bob Silenski and Candy Love together at the dance, and they looked pretty chummy. I'm really sorry."

Donna gave her a blank expression, and then said in a flat voice, "Hey, Lynn, ain't no big thang. This is the Island of Romance. Plenty more fish in the sea." Then she walked off, despite Lynn's insistence that she shouldn't be alone, and that she'd keep her company. But Donna had wandered off, in a state of shock, feeling numb.

Now she was home, her summer safe place, and she was alone, so alone. She stepped into the tiny bathroom and switched on the light. She studied her face in the mirror, noting the red-rimmed puffiness of her eyes. Maybe she wasn't pretty anymore, she told herself. Maybe she was no longer desirable. And God knows, she was no longer a virgin. She should just give up on men altogether. They were all alike—they only wanted one thing. She knew she could never compete with someone like Candy, anyway. Donna shuffled into the bedroom and sat on the edge of the bed. She picked up a copy of "Cosmopolitan" from the nightstand and scanned the articles on the cover. One caught her eye immediately. "How To Tell If He's Cheating." She tossed the magazine on the floor, and switched on the radio, which was tuned to KRLA. The We Five were singing "You Were On My Mind."

"I got troubles, I got worries, I got wounds to bind...."

She turned the dial to KFWB. Gene Weed was coming out of a Pepsi commercial and into the latest song by the Kinks.

"Who'll be the next in line, who'll be the next in line for heartaches...."

Donna shut the radio off, turned over on the bed, and buried her head into her pillow, sobbing uncontrollably.

CHAPTER 16

▼

NOWHERE TO HIDE

"And you tell me over and over and over again my friend, you don't believe we're on the eve of destruction...."

Barry McGuire's voice was being propelled out of a raspy speaker on a transistor radio dangling from the arm of a tourist on Sumner Avenue. The song found its way into the ears of one Joshua Taylor, who was sitting on a bench in front of the liquor store, eating an ice cream cone on a beautiful Sunday afternoon in the second week of August. He didn't pay much attention to the lyrics, as he was deep in other thoughts, but a corner of his mind perceived that the song was an angry one, and maybe an indictment of society. And in another area of Mr. Taylor's mind, there festered an un-named, un-focused anger that had yet to rise to the surface, but was seething patiently away, waiting its proper time of expression.

Preoccupied as he was with the taste and texture of the ice cream, and the swirling, random thoughts that buzzed in his brain, it took him a moment to notice the tennis shoe that anchored the foot and bare leg that had placed itself next to him on the bench. He slowly looked up the sunburned leg to a pair of Bermuda shorts, a yellow sport shirt, and a square-jawed face framed by close-cropped black hair and a pair of dark sunglasses. The form spoke.

"Hey, Taylor, how's it goin'?"

J.T. blinked and said, "You know me?"

"Of course I know you. It's my business to know people. You're the summer help at the post office. I'm Doug Martin," he said, offering his hand, which J.T. shook, but with a wary look on his face

"I'm just a summer worker here, myself," he explained. I'm with the L.A. County Sheriff's Department, off-duty, of course. You were at the party I rousted at Phil's place last month."

"Yeah, now I remember," said J.T.

"Mind if I join you?" asked Doug.

"It's a public bench."

Doug slid in next to J.T. "So how do you like our little post office?" he asked, fishing for conversation.

"It's okay," said J.T., taking a lick off the cone. "Part-time work. Mail boat don't show up till ten, an' I'm off by three-thirty. Weekends off too, except for sometimes on Saturday mornings. Why you askin'?"

"No reason, just curious."

J.T. looked him directly in the eye, and said, "You like bein' a cop?"

"The job has its ups and downs, I must admit. But all in all, I feel pretty good about working Avalon. I'm on nights, so I got my days free to hang out on the beach and meet women. It's pretty low-key over here. Not much crime to speak of in Avalon, just misdemeanor stuff like under-age drinking, some shoplifting, a fight now and then. Drunk in public is about the biggest concern we've got. After Labor Day, though, it's back to the mean streets of L.A., riding shotgun in a patrol car. Give me Avalon anytime. Nice thing about a small town is everyone knows you, and there's no place to hide. And it's even harder to hide on an island."

As if to underscore his point about under-age drinking, a teenage kid now approached them, looking a bit nervous. His eyes darted up and down the street before settling on J.T.

"Could, uh, one of you guys buy me some beer?" he asked tentatively.

"Not me, buddy," said J.T., waving him off. "Don't have my I.D. with me. Ask this guy," he pointed at Doug, "he got his on him."

"No dice, kid," said a tight-lipped Doug Martin.

"Aw, go ahead, man," prodded J.T., "show him you old enough to buy beer."

"Alright," said the deputy, pulling out his badge and Sheriff's Department I.D. "Take a good look."

The kid blanched as his eyes opened wide. He began to shake noticeably. Doug put his badge away, and said, "That's why I'm not buying you any beer. And that's why you'd better move along, and forget about drinking on my island. You just never know who your friends are here, so go party back on the mainland."

"Y-yes, sir" the kid stammered. "Thank you." Then he hurried along the sidewalk, not looking back.

"See what I mean?" said Doug. "Good thing for him I was off duty." Then Doug, who was now standing in front of J.T., said, "Well, I'd better get a move on myself, before the day gets away from me. See you around, Taylor. Keep your powder dry."

"Right," said J.T. Under his breath he added, "Whatever the hell that means. Keep your own goddamn powder dry, cracker." He watched disinterested as the deputy took long strides down Sumner toward the beach.

Shelly Green had taken two days off work to fly over to the mainland and visit her folks and her brother, who was home on leave. With Shelly gone, J.T. had no reason to visit the Skipper's Galley, other than to connect with Sil. But Sil had been growing increasingly harder to find, what with all his romantic entanglements. However, J.T. stopped by the coffee shop on Wednesday afternoon, mainly out of habit, found Sil hanging around, and joined him for a Coke.

"What's up?" asked J.T.

"Nothing much. Why—you wanna do something?"

"Yeah, sounds good," said J.T. "I got nothin' goin' on myself, and I don't hardly ever see your sorry ass 'round no more."

So the two went to their respective hotels to clean up and change clothes, and met up in beach wear at Wrigley Plaza at the end of Sumner Avenue. Sil suggested they rent a boat from the stand at the Pleasure Pier, and take it out. They cruised around the harbor and Lovers Cove, and then ate some fast food on the pier after returning the boat. Then they dropped by the Bamboo Lounge for a drink-- beer for J.T., and a gin and tonic for Sil. They tried to talk about old times, but soon ran out of stories. So they moved into the present tense, and J.T. realized that they were really living in different worlds, and that their friendship had already become a thing of the past. Their conversation seemed artificial, and J.T. noticed that Sil had changed in the past few weeks. He wasn't his usual talkative, bombastic self. He seemed more reserved, and his braggadocio about women had changed as well. It was obvious that he had only one woman on his mind, the blond hostess at the Galley. J.T.'s life had been changing as well, his world narrowing down to his job, his room at the Travel On Inn, and his encounters with Shelly, which always seemed to be too few and ended too soon. He hadn't made any new friends in Avalon, outside of Shelly, and had a hard time feeling like he fit in anywhere. And now he sensed Sil slipping out of his world, and it gave him a renewed sense of isolation.

"Damn you, Sil," he later thought to himself, as he stepped onto the porch of the Travel On Inn. "You self-centered muthafucka. You drag me over to this cracker town and give me all this jive about how cool it's gonna be here. Like a damn paradise for both of us, then you leave me hangin' while you off chasin' around like a dog in heat. Maybe you ain't no white trash honky bigot, and maybe you think you're a friend to everybody, but you don't see much past your own sorry self." Then he slammed shut the door to his room, picked up the new biography of Malcom X, and began reading it.

As if a bad omen, on the following afternoon J.T. ran into Doug Martin again, along the Via Casino. This time the deputy was in uniform. He stopped, smiled, and said, "Well, we meet again."

"Yeah, so we do," said J.T.

"Where did you say you were from, Taylor?"

"I didn't say. But it's Lynwood. Why?"

"Lynwood," the deputy repeated. "That's next door to Watts. Guess you're glad you're not there now, huh?"

"Say what?" said J.T.

"Haven't you heard about the riots?"

"What riots?"

"The race riots in Watts. You haven't heard? It's a big deal, Taylor. Mayor Sam is calling it a rebellion. A lot of people are dead and injured."

"You shittin' me," said J.T.

"I wish I was. It started yesterday. A couple of highway patrolmen tried to arrest a drunk driver in Watts, and the citizens didn't take too kindly to the idea, so the shit hit the fan. It's a big mess. Everyone in law enforcement is trying to keep a lid on it, but the thing is boiling over. Hope it doesn't spread to your neighborhood. Right now I'm glad I'm walking a beat in Avalon, or I'd surely be in the middle of it. Gotta move along now. You take care now, hear?"

"What did he mean by that?" thought J.T. Then he added under his breath, "Take care of your own damn business, cracker." J.T. decided he'd buy a newspaper to find out what was really going on. He looked around for an L.A. Times or a Herald Express, but all the news racks were empty, and the shops were sold out as well. He glanced at his watch and figured if he hurried, he could catch the evening news. There was no television at the Travel On Inn, but J.T. knew there was one in the lobby of the Hotel Glenmore, so he hurried on over there. He walked through the lobby door, over to the set, and turned it on. As he turned the dial to channel five, he noticed the desk clerk staring at him, so he glared back. The clerk nervously looked away, and pretended to be busy.

The newscaster appeared on the screen with a sheaf of papers on the desk before him. He put on his reading glasses and his serious face.

"Good evening. This is George Putnam with the six-o'clock news. The race riots continue to grow in the Los Angeles suburb of Watts. We take you now live to the KTLA news copter hovering over the carnage at 103rd Street and Compton Avenue."

J.T. realized with a start that it was only a few blocks away from the Watts Towers. A scene appeared on the screen of burned-out rubble, resembling a war zone, and as the helicopter pulled up and away, the camera panned blocks of burning buildings and mobs milling about in the streets. Some were pushing shopping carts filled with appliances from looted stores. The camera was on Putnam again as he described how rioters were shouting "burn, baby, burn" as they torched buildings. He went on to say how thousands of young Negro men formed the ranks of the lawbreakers, and in the other camp were hundreds of law enforcement officers from the LAPD, sheriff's department, the highway patrol, and local firefighters. Those in the law enforcement camp were all engaged in an effort to quell the rioting and extinguish fires, but so far were making little progress.

"The latest word,' continued Putnam, "is that the area affected covers eleven square miles. Mayor Sam Yorty has called on Governor Brown to send in the National Guard, but as of yet, there has been no reply from the governor. Both Yorty and Police Chief Parker have made statements blaming Martin Luther King and other leftist elements for the violence, which so far has claimed at least a dozen lives. We will return with more news after these messages."

J.T. shut the television off in disgust. So Parker and Yorty were blaming all this on Dr. King? Well, that was bullshit. Everyone knew those two honkies were racists, and that was one of the problems with race relations in L.A. Furthermore, everyone knew Dr. King was a good, righteous leader, a man of peace. Maybe J.T. hadn't marched for civil rights down in the South, but he was no fool. He knew how the system worked. And he also knew that Martin

Luther King would never sanction rioting-- he'd always been a believer in non-violence, unlike Malcom X, who spread the doctrine of Negroes arming themselves for protection. J.T. was convinced that Yorty and Parker were hypocritical bigots, and had no business bad-mouthing Dr. King. Somebody ought to speak out against them.

As J.T. walked to the Travel On Inn, he was filled with troubling thoughts. He could see Watts in his mind, in its pre-riot days. He thought of his own Lynwood, and of the war that seemed to be taking place in those communities of the "haves" against the "have-nots", and black against white. It all seemed so senseless. And what was really the truth? Was it really just a case of a lawless mob gone berserk, or was it a larger issue of an oppressed minority rising up against injustice. Maybe it was a little of both. But why was any of this J.T.'s concern? He remembered his father's words, "You gotta lighten up, son, to make it in Whitey's world." But whose world did Joshua Taylor belong in?

J.T. considered Malcom X, and what he stood for. Was he really a proponent of violent agitation, as some suggested? Or did he instead stress the importance of self-respect and equality among the black race? J.T. was torn in his beliefs, and unsure of where he belonged in the big scheme of things. The images of violence he'd just seen on television had really disturbed him, and he didn't know whether he should condemn or condone such things. On the one hand, he felt removed from all the drama, a man apart. On the other hand, this was his neighborhood, and his neighbors who were killing each other. He was a man without a center, without a cause, without a course. And now he felt angry, but wasn't exactly sure where his anger was directed. He closed himself off in his room, chewing over these thoughts, and reading Malcom X's biography.

The next day was Friday the thirteenth, and the disturbing news from Watts continued. J.T. made a phone call home to check in on his family. They were okay, but his parents were worried. The rioting had escalated, with dozens now dead, and hundreds more wounded. They were afraid the rioting would spill over into outlying neighborhoods. People in the middle class white suburbs were arming themselves against the "black menace," so they now feared vigilante groups running amuck.

By Saturday, August 14th, the number of rioters numbered in the tens of thousands, mostly young black males, and Governor Brown had finally authorized the use of National Guard troops to quell the "rebellion", as it was now called. J.T. was nearly in a state of disbelief, but when he looked out on the horizon, he could see a pall of smoke clearly hanging over the south-central L.A. area. He also noticed tourists' eyes following him, darting nervously away when he returned their stares.

Saturday night, still troubled by the news from the mainland, J.T. walked into the Skipper's Galley to eat, and to perhaps to take some comfort in Shelly's presence and her heartwarming smiles. He took a table in her section, and gave a small wave. She hurried over to him with a menu, and a smile that was at odds with the sadness in her eyes.

"Hi, J.T. Know what you want? ".

"Sure enough, sweet thing. A Club Sandwich with fries, and a cuppa coffee."

"Comin' right up,' she said as she wrote it down in her ticket book. She returned a few minutes later, with the order.

"How was your trip?" he asked.

"Oh, okay I guess," she said half-heartedly. "I got to visit my brother John, but it was too short and too sad. I'll tell you all about it later. Right now, I have some orders up." She hurried off to the order window where Dan had pulled her ticket. J.T. watched as she delivered the plates to a couple seated near the front door. His eyes continued to follow as she walked to the wait station at the horseshoe-shaped counter, picked up a coffee pot and refilled the cups of two guys seated on stools, their backs to J.T. They were talking too loudly with the slurred speech of too much drink. As Shelly passed behind them on her way to refill J.T.'s coffee cup, one of them slapped her on the rear. "Hey, mama," the long-haired drunk in the surfer shirt said, "that's choice Grade A meat." The guy next to him, wearing jeans, a tee shirt, and sporting a crew cut, laughed uncontrollably. Shelly jumped, turned to face them, and said, "Watch it, buster!"

Shelly continued on, and muttered, "Assholes," as she poured coffee into J.T.'s cup. J.T. pushed back his chair, stood, and walked deliberately to the counter.

"What's wrong?" asked Shelly in a startled voice. J.T. did not answer, but stood over the longhaired guy, staring menacingly at him from behind. "I think you owe the young lady an apology," he said gruffly.

Long Hair turned to face J.T. Then he blurted out in a slurred voice, "What're ya gonna do about it Sambo, burn the place down?" Crew Cut began giggling. As Long Hair swiveled back in his stool to the counter, he suddenly felt himself being jerked to his feet, his arm pinned behind his back by a powerful force, with another arm lifting him under his chin. He cried out in pain and surprise as he heard an angry voice say, "Nobody calls me that, honky!"

"What's going on?" shouted a distressed Shelly as J.T. pushed the struggling guy toward the door.

"Get your black hands off me, nigger," he demanded as J.T. shoved him through the door and onto the sidewalk.

"Your ass is eighty-sixed from here, ofay," said J.T. He then moved on Crew Cut, who looked panicked and protested, "Hey, man, no problem. I'm just leaving." He tossed a couple of bills on the counter and backed around J.T. and out the door. J.T.'s intense eyes followed him every step of the way, his fists clenched into balls of powerful fury.

J.T.'s eyes now scanned the dining room of the Skipper's Galley, which had fallen strangely silent, everyone staring at him, as if waiting for the next outburst. Instead, he quietly returned to his table and sat, then lifted his eyes to Shelly, who was still standing there, like a statue, coffee pot still poised in her hand.

"What was that about?" she asked, accusingly.

"I was defending you," he said flatly, the anger now dissipated.

"Defending me?" she said, incredulously. "From what?"

"I was defending your honor," he said, running his hand through his short hair, and staring at his coffee cup.

There was a moment's silence as she digested this information before answering.

"Look, J.T., I'm sure you thought you were doing the right thing, but I don't need defending or protecting. I can take care of myself. Honestly, I don't know what got into you. If Sam had seen that, I might've lost my job over it. I may yet." Then she walked off and replaced the coffee pot to its station warmer.

J.T. looked around the room self-consciously, and picked at his food awhile, letting the coffee grow cold. He finally left, quietly, leaving enough money on the table to cover the meal, plus an over-generous tip. He slipped out the front door and turned toward the Travel On Inn, but only got as far as the adjoining parking lot, when three figures stepped out from the semi-darkness to accost him. It was Long Hair and Crew Cut, and they'd brought reinforcements in the form of a tall, lanky character wielding a baseball bat.

"Hey nigger," said Long Hair, making his move, "it's payback time!"

Joshua Taylor, who decided he'd taken enough shit for one day, went into a karate stance.

"You think you bad, muthafucka?" he shouted. "You think you bad? Let's see how bad you honkies are!"

As the trio closed in on him, J.T. launched into a series of movements and motions, and as the Bat Man swung at him, he kicked his leg out, sending the bat flying, then spun around and sent Bat Man flying as well. Then with swift kicks and karate chops, he laid Crew Cut out. Long hair was quick enough to punch J.T. from behind, but not quick enough to get out of the way of J.T.'s powerful arms and legs, which sent him sprawling. He lay on the ground, moaning, bleeding, doubled up, and clutching at his stomach. By now Crew Cut had stumbled to his feet, and taken off running across the street and through Island Plaza. Bat Man lay on the pavement, semi-conscious and moaning. J.T. stepped across his prone body and muttered, "You ain't so bad now, muthafucka." Then he stomped up the street to his hotel, feeling an uneasy satisfaction. It was the first and last time he would ever use his karate training in anger or self-defense.

The following morning, Joshua Taylor sat on a stool at a fast food stand on the Pleasure Pier. He was enjoying a breakfast of bacon and eggs, toast and coffee. He watched a gull drop down from the clear Sunday sky and land on a deck plank beside him. It cocked its head at J.T. as if sizing him up for a handout. J.T. broke off a piece of toast, and tossed it down. The gull snapped it up quickly and flew off. J.T. took a sip of coffee, then sensing a nearby presence, turned around to face a casually dressed Doug Martin.

"Mind if I join you?" asked Martin, as he took the neighboring stool. "Good thing I ran into you before one of my partners did," he added.

"Say what?" said J.T.

"There's a warrant out for your arrest. Those kids you roughed up last night filed a complaint. Assault and battery."

J.T. made no reply, but picked up a piece of bacon and started chewing it.

"I'm not here in an official capacity, Taylor. I'm not on duty now, which is a good thing for you."

"It was self-defense," said J.T., taking a sip of coffee.

"No doubt," said Martin. "I've had run-ins with that bunch before. They probably needed a good thumping. But they're locals, Islanders, and you're not. You're an outsider."

"Tell me something I don't know," said J.T., staring at his coffee cup.

"For what it's worth, I believe it was probably justified on your part. I like you, Taylor. And that's why I'm going to offer you some good advice. Leave town. Now."

"What about my job?"

"That's all over now," said the deputy. "You can't sort mail if you're in jail. But I'll try to square things with Herb. I'll say you had to leave suddenly due to an unforeseen emergency. It probably won't wash, though --news travels fast in a small town. And in a town like Avalon, there's no place to hide."

There was an uncomfortable silence while J.T. let the gravity of the situation sink in. Then he replied, "Okay, I'll go pack my things."

"I wouldn't do that. Your place is probably under surveillance, as is the Skipper's Galley. You can arrange to have your belongings shipped over later. This conversation, of course, is strictly off the record. If I were you, I'd get up right now, walk to the end of the pier, and catch the next plane out." He looked at his watch. "Should be here in about fifteen minutes."

J.T. finished his coffee. "Okay, I'm gone," he said.

"I don't think the warrant will follow you home," said Martin. "They just want you off the island." Then he stuck out his hand. "Good luck to you."

J.T. pumped the hand once, without making eye contact, muttered "Thanks," and shuffled away.

J.T. bought a one-way ticket to Long Beach, walked down the short ramp to the seaplane landing, and waited. Soon, a blue and white Grumman Goose splashed down outside the harbor, and taxied up to the platform. Dock boys helped the passengers out and retrieved their baggage. Someone turned on a transistor radio.

"Good Morgan, Boss Angeles! This is Robert W. Morgan with your Boss Radio weather report. Overcast now at the beaches, but expect it to burn off soon with a high of seventy-eight degrees. Expect a high in the city of eighty-five. Right now in Hollywood, it's a comfortable seventy-nine." The jingle singers announced," 93 KHJ Golden," and Martha and the Vandellas began singing.

"Nowhere to run now baby, nowhere to hide...."

The irony of the song was not lost on J.T. as he nervously waited to board. He impatiently asked a dock boy if he could be seated.

"Where's your bags?"

"Ain't got any," J.T. answered.

"Okay," said the dock boy, helping him through the doorway. J.T. watched as the plane was loaded, stealing glances at his watch. Finally, the door was locked shut, the Goose taxied out into open water, revved its engines, and began the long, bouncing takeoff. J.T. gave a long last look at Avalon as the plane circled, and climbed for the sky and the mainland.

As the plane approached Long Beach, Joshua Taylor noted the pall of smoke coming from the north and settling over the city ahead. It was a dark, ominous cloud, and he felt as if he were descending into the bowels of Hell. J.T. didn't know it at that moment in time, but he would never return to Avalon. And about a year from now he would change his name and join the Los Angeles chapter of the newly formed Black Panther Party.

CHAPTER 17

▼

CATALINA CAPERS

"It ain't me, babe, no, no, no, it ain't me babe, it ain't me you're lookin' for...."

A curious thing happened in during the second week of August in Avalon. Donna Forte and Shelly Green became friends. The gossip about Sil and Candy had made the rounds, and as Donna moped around the Skipper's Galley one day at the shift change, Shelly approached her and said, "I heard the news, Donna, and I want you to know I sympathize with you. We're in the same club now, the S-EX Club."

"Sex club?" said Donna, startled. "What sex club?"

"No," laughed Shelly, "not sex. S-EX. It stands for Sil's Exes."

The questioning look went out of Donna's eyes as she grasped the joke. "Oh, I get it," she said.

"Welcome to the club," said Shelly, extending her hand. "No hard feelings?"

"No hard feelings," Donna agreed, as she shook Shelly's hand and gave her a hug.

"Let's you and I go out some night and do something fun together," Shelly suggested.

"Okay," said Donna. "Maybe we could bring my friend Lynn along with us."

"Why not?"

And so it came to pass that a few nights later they did just that, and became friends.

Bob Silenski, meanwhile, was wrapped up tight in his new pursuit, that of Candy Love. He wasn't even aware of J.T.'s absence from the scene until the day Waxie took him aside and asked what he should do about J.T.'s belongings. Sil said he'd take care of it, and send them on, but so far he hadn't gotten around to it. He was quite preoccupied.

Sil had a vague strange feeling that something had gone haywire with him. He didn't seem to be in heat anymore, and thought he might be losing his touch. Take this weekend for instance. A sorority from Long Beach State, Alpha Phi, had taken over the first three floors of the Glenmore for a pre-semester party, unaware of the fact that there was a fourth floor, and that there were four males ensconced there. But as one was a senior citizen and over-the-hill, and another preferred the company of his own sex, that left only Sil and Jimmy Fontana to reap the benefits of this unexpected windfall. And since Jimmy had been burned twice lately in matters of love, he preferred to stay clear of women for now. This left Robert "Never in Love, Only in Heat" Silenski as the only rooster in the hen house. As a matter of fact, being alone with a whole sorority of scantily clothed young ladies was a fantasy that had floated around in the back of his mind for quite some time. And now, like a dream come true, as he walked down the stairs from the fourth floor, he was confronted by dozens of the aforementioned ladies parading around the hallways in various states of undress. While some of the girls shrieked and ran off, many more did not. In fact, some of them mobbed Sil as they said things like, "A man! Hey, where're you going?"

"C'mere, you!"

"Hey, handsome, what's your hurry?"

Yes, it seemed as if Sil had hit the proverbial jackpot. All he had to do to fulfill his wildest fantasy was to stop for a moment and say something like, "Hello, ladies. What sorority are you in? Really? Small world. I'm a Delta Chi myself. So what say in the interest of (ahem) inter-Greek relations, we all get together and party?" That is what Sil realized he should have done, after the opportunity had passed. What he said instead showed a clearly disturbed mind. For what he said was, "Excuse me, ladies, but I have a date."

A DATE???

Something was definitely wrong in the world of Silenski. He brushed past the high concentration of estrogen and hormones gone wild, and hurried down the stairs, and out the door, making a beeline for the Hotel Atwater, where he was meeting with Candy Love. As he strode happily across the street, he whistled a tune he'd been hearing on the radio lately, "A Walk in the Black Forest," his feet keeping time with the rhythm. He bounced through the hotel lobby and bounded up the stairs, his heart gripped by anticipation. He paused a moment to catch his breath before knocking on the door of room 252. When it opened, and she stood there statuesque before him, he felt as if he'd swallowed his heart. She smiled and he melted. When she spoke, he felt as if he'd left his own body, and was seeing himself as a stranger struggling with a response.

"Hello," he croaked, his voice cracking, as if he was going through puberty again. "You look---breathtaking." He had stumbled across the right word to describe how he felt.

"Hello, Sil," she said, with a smile as she kissed him on the cheek. "I'm ready. Where are we off to tonight?"

"How about a Dinner Cruise on the bay?"

"How very romantic," she said, closing the door, then taking his arm and leading him down the hallway.

They had been going out like this all week, as if trying to cram a year of living into a few nights. For they both knew that a film crew would be in on Monday next, and their relationship would end as Candy returned to acting. She'd already quit the hostess job, giving 48 hours notice. Everyone was surprised when "Old Hatchet Face" (as Sam O'Hara was called behind her back) hadn't flown into a rage over it. Instead, she had graciously accepted the notice with words like, "We're sorry to see you go. You've been a real asset to us. But I suppose if stardom beckons, one must heed the call." No one had ever heard Hatchet Face speak so deferentially to someone. But such was the power that beauty and fame, or in this case perceived fame, wielded. Candy was aware of this phenomenon, and looked forward to the future, when she could take advantage of the benefits of that kind of power. For now, though, being on a last date with Bob Silenski was something she looked forward to. Although they had no future together, she nevertheless had been enjoying his company. He'd been knocking himself out all week to show her a good time. They'd gone snorkeling at Casino Point, and he'd taken her on the Seal Rocks Cruise: out past Pebbly Beach, the PG&E plant and the rock quarry, to the east end of the island. They had spotted seals and sea lions sunning themselves on the rocks, a new experience for the girl from Minneapolis, and it delighted her. In Sil's company, Candy was beginning to understand why Catalina was called the Island Of Romance.

Romance was in the air on this Saturday night as she and Sil strolled along the beach and down the Pleasure Pier to the glass bottom boat, *Phoenix*, which was doing double duty tonight as the Sunset Buffet Cruise boat. During the cruise, the couple was treated to a nice meal, music, and in the moonless night a velvet sky filed with brilliant stars. They sipped wine, and Candy found Sil to be unusually quiet. And she noticed that he couldn't keep his eyes off her, which made her feel flattered, but also uncomfortable.

"Is anything wrong?" she asked.

"No," he answered. "In fact, things couldn't be better."

"We start shooting Monday," she said.

"Yeah, I know."

"Some of the crew are already here, and the rest of the cast and crew should be here by tomorrow."

"That gives us one more day," said Sil. "Why don't we get together one more time?"

"Alright," she conceded. "As long as I'm in early. Monday begins before dawn."

"I hate to see this all end," said Sil.

"It has been fun," Candy agreed.

"There's something else," he said, hesitantly.

"What's that?"

"I—I think I'm in love with you," he said, looking into her eyes.

Candy let out a little laugh, one that caused Sil to blush and drop his gaze.

"I'm sorry, Sil," she said, taking his hand. "I didn't mean to laugh at that. It's just that it took me by surprise, that's all."

"I'm serious," he complained.

"Don't look so hurt," she said. "Anyway, you're not in love, you only think you are. You're not in love, you're in heat."

Sil was stunned. He'd just heard his own line thrown at him, and it left him grappling for a way to respond.

"Maybe you're right," he said, looking down at his glass of wine and swirling the liquid around. Then he looked up at her again. "But I just feel on top of the world when we're together."

"You'll get over it," she said. "I warned you from the beginning that you weren't my type. I have my career to think of, and at the moment I'm in a good position to achieve a measure of success. I am not going to jeopardize that for a summer fling. You do understand, don't you?"

"Yes, I guess so," he said. Then he added, hopefully, "But we're still on for tomorrow, aren't we?"

"Of course we are," she said, taking his hand and placing it against her cheek.

The word went out that another film company, Executive Pictures, was in town to shoot the movie *Catalina Caper*. Candy Love reported to the set early Monday morning, to work as an extra in a crowd scene. She wore a two-piece swimsuit again, and the assistant director and cameraman were pleased with the way she filled it out. Candy wondered whether she was now typecast as a half-naked blond bimbo. The scene was finished by early afternoon, and she was told to take the boat to San Pedro and grab a nearby motel room. The film crew would be shooting some scenes on the fly as the morning boat sailed to Avalon. Executive Pictures had rented the *S.S. Catalina* for the day. Part of the ship would be closed off for filming, while passengers would have access to the rest of the ship. A few of the passengers would even be utilized as unpaid extras.

The first scene the following morning was filmed as passengers boarded the *S.S. Catalina*. Then the crew set up in the bow, which was a closed set, while the ship got underway. One scene involved Little Richard and the band The Cascades. Little Richard lip-synched to the music while stepping down the staircase that led to the top deck, as the Cascades mimed playing their instruments. The pre-recorded music boomed out of speaker boxes off-camera. Candy's job was to dance along with other extras, to the music. The next scene involved Tommy Kirk and other actors, also in the bow. Candy was in the background of the scene, sitting on a bench, wearing a blouse and Capris, with a scarf around her head. This scene was filmed as the ship pulled into port. A final scene took place while a second crew on the steamer pier filmed the passengers disembarking with the actors. Candy mingled with the crowd leaving the boat. Her work was now finished for the day, and it was only early afternoon. She was excused for the day, but was instructed to report early in the morning for another shoot.

Candy realized that if she hurried, and didn't bother to change clothes or remove make-up, she could still have lunch at the Skipper's Galley, before Sil left for the day. Immediately on entering the coffee shop, she was given the royal treatment by the new hostess and the waitress. She waved to Sil from her table as soon as he spotted her, and in a little while he had clocked out, and joined her, smiling broadly.

"What a surprise!" he said. "I am stoked to see you. How's the movie goin'?"

"Super," she said. "I've got a background scene to do tomorrow, and a final one here on Thursday. Next week we go over to the mainland to finish up. That's where they shoot the scene where I have dialogue."

"That's groovy," he said. "For you, anyway."

"How would you like to be in the movie with me?" she said.

"What do you mean?"

"The scene I'm doing Thursday is a crowd shot, with dancers. The assistant director said we could use more extras dancing in the background, and I told him I knew someone who could dance. He told me to bring you along. You won't get paid, but we'll get to be together on screen. Can you get the day off from work?"

"Be there or be square, huh? Listen, I'll be there if I have to kill the Skipper on the way out the door."

"Don't do anything that drastic," she laughed.

"I'll get Dan to cover for me," he said enthusiastically. "He owes me one. When and where do I have to be, and what should I wear?"

"Meet me at Wrigley Plaza at six a.m., and wear what you usually do. Look casual. I guess you'll get more instructions when you get there."

"I am so stoked," said Sil. "This will be more tubular than shooting the Huntington Beach pier."

"Oh, and by the way," said Candy, "I'm free tonight, in case you'd like to take me out to dinner."

"Anything your little heart desires," he said.

"You can't afford the things my heart desires," she teased.

Partly to celebrate her new status as an actress, Candy insisted on paying for the meal at the Italian restaurant that night, over Sil's protests. "It's my turn to treat," she said. "I'll be well paid for my work, and anyway, I just turned twenty-two yesterday, and I'm celebrating."

"Congratulations," he said, "and happy birthday. I wish you'd told me sooner, I'd have bought you a present."

"No need to," she said. "You've already done so much for me." She took his hand and gave it a squeeze.

After dinner, Sil walked Candy back to her room. As she unlocked the door, he fought back the urge to take her in his arms and profess his love for her. But he stood like a statue, watching her from behind, mesmerized by her long blond hair. She turned to him to say goodnight, but instead impulsively kissed him on the mouth and held him in an embrace for a few moments. Only then did she say goodnight, and stepped inside room 252, closing the door behind her. Sil walked downstairs and out into the street, his heart full. A funny sensation swept over him that he'd never felt before. He was light-headed and disoriented, and walked the length of the waterfront, past the Casino, and all the way to Descanso Beach, thinking of Candy. It was a long time before he came down enough to return to his hotel. Once there, he climbed into bed, but couldn't sleep. He kept thinking about Candy Love, seeing her face before him, feeling her kiss.

Thursday morning found Sil and Candy at Wrigley Plaza, on the set of *Catalina Caper*, surrounded by actors and extras, sound technicians and cameramen, and the Cascades, who were on a makeshift stage, their backs to the bay. And while the band mimed and lip-synched to music playing over loudspeakers, the couple danced and gyrated around the plaza. Sil had never danced so much in his life, and got quite a workout. He wondered if the director would ever say the magic words, "Print it. That's a take." Instead, he just kept saying, "Cut! Okay, let's do it again. Places." Finally, the director said, "Okay, that's a wrap." The crew struck the set, and Candy was dismissed for the rest of the day, while the crew set up for another scene in Avalon Harbor.

"Well," said Candy, "I hope you saved enough energy to go out dancing tonight."

"Dancing?" he said. "You've got to be kidding."

"I am," she said, with a laugh. "And if you believed me, then I must really be a pretty good actress."

"Very funny."

"But I think we ought to do something tonight, since it's our last night together. Don't you agree?"

"You know I want to see you again," he said. "Just tell me when and where."

"Why don't you pick me up at six-thirty, and we'll catch the early show at the Casino Theater."

"And then maybe the glass bottom boat night cruise?" he said.

"Sure, why not," she agreed. "After all, you're only young once."

The movie that night was a Jerry Lewis comedy. Sil didn't pay much attention to it though, as all of his focus was on Candy Love. He draped his arm around her shoulder and his heart around her presence. Afterwards, they took the glass bottom boat cruise, and as they glided over the undersea gardens on the *Nautilus*, Candy was captured by the sight of jellyfish, lobsters, octopi, and other creatures lit up by the boat's floodlights. Sil was more interested in watching Candy, and her reaction to the sights. He felt intoxicated, or as if he'd smoked some of Phil Munday's pot.

The pair ended their date with quiet drinks at the Bamboo Lounge, while the strains of "Pearly Shells" emanated from the jukebox. The bartender polished glasses behind the bar, and a couple danced closely in a corner of the room.

"I still don't understand your fondness for gin and tonics," Candy said, as she sipped her Black Russian.

"You don't understand surfing, either," Sil countered. "That's because you've never tried it. Someday I'll teach you how to catch a wave."

"I'm afraid that day will never come," she said. "I'll be leaving soon, and my future has no room in it for you. All we really have is this moment, right here and right now. Tomorrow all we'll have are memories. So let's make them good ones, shall we?"

"If only I had the power to stop time," said Sil. "This would be where it would stop, so we'd always have this moment."

"That would go against all the laws of physics," she said. "You ought to know that. After all, you're a college boy." Then she took his hand and examined his watch. "Our time has run out," she said. "Will you walk me back to my room?"

Sil accompanied her the short distance to her hotel, and his heart was heavy as he watched her slip the key into the lock of room 252. As she opened the door, she turned to him and said, "Would you like to come in for a minute?"

"Okay," he said, knowing that he was not the one in charge of this relationship, and never had been. He'd just been following her lead all along, and he knew he would follow her anywhere.

They stepped across the threshold, and rather than turning on the overhead light, Candy walked to the nightstand and switched on the lamp. Then she sat on the edge of the bed and patted the spot next to her.

"Have a seat, Sil. I promise I won't bite."

He did as she asked, and she put her arms around him. She began kissing him, running her fingers through his long hair, and the palm of her hand inside his shirt along his chest. She felt like Greta Garbo as she whispered huskily in his ear.

"Can you stay the night?"

He nodded.

"Then make love to me, Robert. Give me some good lovin'."

"I don't have a condom," he said as she began unbuttoning his shirt.

"Don't worry," she said, "I'm on the Pill."

She pulled his shirt off, then stood and began undressing. Sil followed her lead, clumsily pulling off his clothing, while his eyes were transfixed on the beauty of her form. Candy thought he looked a little like a deer caught in someone's headlights. Standing naked before him, she wrapped her arms around him and held him close, and he felt the warmth and softness of her skin against his, and his hardness against her femininity. Then they were lying in bed together, wrapped around each other, and Sil felt as if transported to another realm, beyond time and space. He gazed deeply into her Nordic blue eyes and they seemed to smolder.

"Make love to me, baby," she purred, before closing her eyes and surrendering to him.

Later, as she lay in his arms, her head resting on his chest, she broke the perfect silence by saying, "What time do you want to get up?"

"Six-thirty," he said, his eyes closed, as if dreaming.

Candy set the alarm, and turned out the light. In the darkness she confided, "I lied when I said I wasn't going to sleep with you, so I guess you win that bet."

"But I've lost my heart," he said.

"Don't be so dramatic," she said with a smile that he could sense rather than see. Then she rolled over to sleep.

In the morning, after Sil had left for work, Candy showered, dressed, and packed her bags. Then she put on make-up and walked down the stairs and into the adjoining coffee shop for breakfast. She waved to Sil as he slaved away behind the grill, and he in turn blew her a kiss. The Skipper whacked him across the shoulder with his sailor cap. Candy laughed, and then shrugged her shoulders. She finished her modest meal and left a large tip for Donna.

After collecting her bags and checking out of the hotel, Candy strolled down to the steamer pier and bought a one-way ticket for San Pedro, and checked her bags with the steamship company. She had a few hours to kill, so she strolled around town, did some window-shopping, bought a few souvenirs, and had a leisurely cup of coffee at a café overlooking the harbor. In the mid-afternoon, she boarded the *S.S. Catalina*, and stood by the fantail as it pulled out of the harbor and into the channel. As Avalon grew smaller, then disappeared into the island mass, she entered the ship's bar and made a request.

"Could I get a gin and tonic?"

"Certainly, miss," said the bartender as he reached for a bottle and a glass. He put ice into the glass, poured a shot of gin, added the tonic, then the lime.

Candy took a sip of the drink, noting the bitterness of the gin and the quinine. She took another sip and discovered the sweetness in the sugar and lime. She set the drink down, unfinished, and paid the bartender. "Thank you," she said. "That was very enlightening."

Candy Love walked to the bow of the ship, so she could watch as Los Angeles Harbor came into view, and maybe catch a glimpse of a passing porpoise or flying fish. She thought about Bob Silenski, and decided that if she ever wanted to call his memory to mind, she would find a quiet dim-lit bar that had the song "Pearly Shells" on the jukebox, and order a gin and tonic. Someday she would learn to appreciate the drink the way Sil had. And someday she would understand the drink as being a metaphor for life.

CHAPTER 18

▼

THE MUTINY

"Heart Full Of Soul" by the Yardbirds had reached number nine on the Top 40 survey for the week. But for Bob Silenski, it was not only number one, it was the only song that mattered. It went around and around in his mind, like an endless loop, especially the line about being in "dark despair," and "thinking one thought only, where is she, where---?" Where is she, indeed?

It had been less than twenty-four hours ago when this thought, perfectly mirrored in the song, had crossed his mind. He had a heart full of soul, for certain.

Yesterday afternoon, after getting off work, and changing his clothes, Sil had raced over to the Hotel Atwater, and bounded up the stairs to see Candy one last time. He just had to tell her that he loved her, even if she rejected him. But when he knocked on the door of room 252, and it opened, a stranger stood there before him. He'd glanced furtively past the man, into the room, demanding, "Where is she?"

"I think you've got the wrong room, pal," replied the annoyed stranger as he closed the door in Sil's face. He then raced downstairs, where the desk clerk informed him she'd checked out, and no, he didn't know where she'd gone. Sil ran down to the steamer pier, but he was too late---the ship had sailed. He caught sight of it pulling out of the harbor, cupped his hand across his forehead, and strained his eyes to catch a glimpse of her on the fantail, but to no avail. The *S.S. Catalina* was now too far out to distinguish individual faces. He stood there, on the end of the pier, until reality finally set in, and with it clarity.

"You really know how to hurt a guy," he said sadly. Then he walked along the waterfront, and the streets of Avalon, remembering the places they'd been and the things they'd done together. He felt very alone for the first time in many years. Nor had he felt this sense of loss before, except maybe when he was a child, and his dog had died. Now, out of the blue, he remembered that he was supposed to send J.T.'s belongings to him, and he felt guilty about not having done so. He had forgotten, and it seems he'd forgotten his friend as well. He wished J.T. were still around, so he'd have someone to confide in.

"I said rail it, Silenski!"

The Skipper's words suddenly brought Sil out of his head and into the moment, which was in the middle of the Saturday lunch rush.

"Oh, uh, aye, aye!" he replied distractedly.

Later on, when the rush had died down, and the Skipper ran out of beer and left the cooks' station, Sil had more space to think. He was alone now with Jimmy Fontana, who still wasn't speaking to him. It now occurred to Sil that he felt bad about that, as if maybe he'd been responsible for the rift between them.

Francie stepped up to the order window with a ticket in her hand. She held it up in front of Sil, as if it were something very important, before clipping it to the wheel.

"See that couple at the corner table?" she said. "This is their order. Make it special, they're honeymooners."

Sil looked over at the young couple, holding hands across the table and smiling sweetly as they talked.

"I'll do better than that," he said. "I'll pick up their bill. Tell them congratulations, and that the meal is on the house."

"Why, Sil," Francie said with a smile, "I never knew you were a romantic."

Sil glanced at Jimmy, who was cleaning the broiler with a wire brush. "Hey, Jimmy, did you hear that? Honeymooners!"

Jimmy ignored him, and went on brushing the broiler.

Sil tried again. "You want to go in on their meal with me? Give them a little wedding present from the Galley? C'mon, Jimmy, let's do it for love."

Now Jimmy looked up from his work and said coldly, "What the hell would you know about love?"

Sil was stung by the remark. He replied humbly, "You got me there, partner, maybe nothing at all. Up until now, I was never in love, only in heat. It was my motto, remember? But now I know that love is more than just a word. Maybe it's the most important thing in life. Maybe I'm just beginning to see that."

Sil placed an order in the window, and called Donna over the microphone. She picked the plate up wordlessly, avoiding eye contact with him. He watched as she walked away and delivered the food to a customer at the counter. Then he turned to Jimmy.

"Look, man," he began hesitantly, "I've been a chump and a louse. And I was wrong to come between you and Donna."

Jimmy looked up again, hurt reflected in his eyes now, rather than anger.

"Donna's a nice girl," he continued, "and she's unattached at the moment. You should go after her again. The way I see it, you still got a chance, and there's still some summer left. You deserve each other, and I hope you take my advice. I owe you an apology, Jimmy. You think we can ever be friends again?"

"No," said Jimmy, "we can't. But I accept your apology. I'm willing to bury the hatchet and chip in on the meal. For the honeymooners, though, not for you."

"Thanks." Sil replied. He'd wanted to add the word "guppy," but had restrained himself.

When the shift change came, Sil removed his apron, cook's coat and hat, and said to Jimmy, "Well, it's been nice knowing you, man."

"Huh?" said Jimmy.

"I'm clocking out for the last time. I'm splitting, leaving the island."

"How come?"

"There's someone I have to see again, on the mainland. I'm not sure I can find her, but I've got to try. Tell the Skipper to mail my check. And good luck with Donna. Don't let her get away again. Don't be a fool like me."

And then Bob Silenski was gone. He said goodbye to Shelly before he headed out the door and down the street. No one from the Skipper's Galley ever saw him again.

The Skipper flipped out, of course, when he heard Sil had deserted. His exact words remain unprintable, but they seemed to blister the very air around him. He retreated to his office, and slammed the door. A few drinks later he returned to the cooks' station, a little calmer, his face a little redder.

"Well, we'll just get along without that bum," he announced to those present.

"You're not going to put out the HELP WANTED sign?" asked Dan Burton.

"Nah. Labor Day's too close. We'll just have to make do. That means no more days off for the cooks. And I'll put Jimmy back on the day shift."

The Skipper's plan might have worked, if Phil had just kept his mouth shut. But he took the opportunity to give the Skipper his own notice.

"Maybe this isn't the time to bring it up, Skip, but this is going to be my last season. I'm going back to San Francisco after Labor Day."

The Skipper shot Phil such an angry look that his face contorted and went from red to purple, and his eyes looked as if they were about to pop out of their sockets. He began opening and closing his mouth like a fish out of water. Then he exploded.

"So you're going to abandon ship, too, eh Munday? Well, then go if you want to. Get out now, in fact. We don't need you. Clock out. I don't want to see your face around here anymore."

"What?" said Phil. "That's it? No gold watch? So much for doing the square scene. Adios, lame-o." He untied his apron, and marched off singing, "Free at last, free at last, oh my Lord I'm free at last," in a Negro affectation.

And so began what later came to be known as "The Mutiny." And now the event having been set in motion, it became an irresistible force, like a snowball rolling down a mountain.

As Phil Munday marched off, the Skipper turned to Dan Burton and said, "Okay, when the going gets tough, the tough get going."

"What's that mean?" asked Dan.

"It means it's up to you and me now. We're not quitters, are we?"

"No."

"Good. Then you'll just have to hitch up your pants and cover this shift by yourself. Okay?"

"Okay."

The kitchen was now under-staffed, but things could have still worked out. However, they did not.

Encouraged by her husband's outbursts and stormy moods, Sam O'Hara became increasingly caustic and abrasive in her dealings with the wait staff. A dark cloud of discontent descended over the Skipper's Galley, and morale plummeted. There was a song climbing the Top 40 charts on the three L.A. radio stations, which became the theme song for the coffee shop. It was "We've Got To Get Out Of This Place," by the Animals. One morning when it came on over the radio in the dishwasher's station, Luis turned up the volume and began singing along.

"We've got to get out of get out of this place, if it's the last thing we ever do...."

The Skipper, who was working by the broiler, picked up a wire whip used for scrambling eggs, and threw it at Luis. It sailed through the air and ricocheted off the dishwashing machine, just missing his head. Startled, he looked up to find the Skipper yelling at him.

"Shut that God damn noise off!"

Luis picked up the whip, tossed it in the trashcan, removed his apron and tossed it in the can as well, gave the Skipper the middle finger salute, and marched off. His parting words were, "Chingate, pendejo borracho!"

The Skipper pulled a bus boy off the floor and put him to work washing dishes, but it did not suit his temperament. He was gone the next day, and the Skipper's troubles were just beginning. Three-thirty rolled round, but the only cook left on the swing shift, Dan Burton, failed to show up. Unbeknownst to the Skipper, Dan had gone over to Phil's after work the night before and smoked some pot with him. Phil talked him into quitting his job, dropping out of school, and splitting up to Frisco with him. The Skipper asked Jimmy to stay on and pull a double shift in order to plug the hole. However, Jimmy only lasted the one more day as well. He walked out because of Donna.

Sam O'Hara had withheld money from Donna's tips on other occasions, accusing her of coming up short on her tickets, but on this day she withheld all her tips, which set Donna off.

"That can't be right," Donna complained. "I'm good with math, and know how to make change. I couldn't have been that much off."

"Not the way I figure it, DEAR," Sam said, caustically putting an emphasis on the work, "dear."

"This just isn't fair," Donna insisted. "I deserve those tips."

"I'll decide what you deserve, DEAR."

"Oh yeah? Well, you're not my mother, and you're not a good boss either. I'm sick of being taken advantage of by everyone, especially you. So you can keep my money, but you can shove this crummy job, Hatchet Face. I quit!"

When Donna walked off the floor, so did her new friend Shelly, as a matter of principal. Jimmy mistakenly heard that Donna had been fired, so he quit in protest.

The Skipper's ship was sinking fast, but he continued to plug leaks. The HELP WANTED sign went back in the window, but it was too late in the season to find anyone. The O'Haras closed down the third shift, and ran the other two shifts with skeleton crews for a while. The Skipper put the graveyard cook, Pete Martino, on the swing shift, for him to cover alone. Unfortunately, Pete was a Korean War veteran, quiet, and wound a little too tight. He did not handle stress well, which is why he worked the graveyard shift in the first place. But he gave his new shift an earnest try, and managed to get through it, barely. Then two more employees hit the bricks, and the Skipper and Sam became more crazed and short-tempered. The Skipper blew up at Manny over something insignificant, and Manny decided he'd rather spend what was left of the summer hanging out on the beach. He tossed his coat and hat on the floor as he walked out the door. Another leak to plug. The Skipper had no choice but to ask poor Pete to work a double shift. Early the next morning, Pete showed up, cinched his apron tight, and got to work cranking out orders. His eyes took on a faraway look after the first hour, and during the height of the lunch rush, he had a major meltdown. He bolted for the back door, and ran through the parking lot and up the street, babbling incoherently. Later, he had to be flown over town to the Veteran's Hospital for psychiatric observation.

By the end of the week, the Skipper's Galley had just enough of a staff left to run one shift. This lasted two days, with the Skipper and Lee, recently promoted from bus boy, handling the cooking. Jose doubled as bus boy and dishwasher, while Marilyn and Sam covered the floor. There was no longer a hostess. Jimmy Fontana walked through the parking lot one day, and caught sight of the Skipper, through the open doorway, scrubbing pots and pans in the big sink.

By the time Labor Day arrived, the Skipper's Galley ceased operations. The doors were locked, the lights turned out, and a CLOSED sign hung in the window. Someone spotted the Skipper at the bar of the Waikiki, drinking heavily. Rumor had it that Marilyn had left town, and Sam was sequestered in her house, curtains and blinds drawn. The ship had finally run aground, and other restaurants and coffee shops in Avalon received the windfall of extra business.

Up the street on Sumner, meanwhile, another drama was unfolding at the Travel On Inn. Waxie Shein finally broached the subject of college with Blackie.

"Why do you need to go off to college, son?" Blackie said, leaning back in his chair. "It makes no sense. I can teach you everything you need to know about the business."

"But they've got a lot of good classes at City College, pop, and the tuition is next to nothing. Anyway, what if I want to do something different with my life?"

"Something different?" said Blackie. "What could be more important than running the family business? This is tradition, son. Are you ashamed to be a Shein?"

"Of course not, pop. I'm not saying I want to do anything else, I'm just saying I want to keep an open mind about my future. After all, it's a big world."

"I've seen the world, son. Believe me when I say this, you're better off here in Avalon."

"But what if I get drafted? If I'm in school, I can get a 2-S student deferment."

"Who told you about that?" asked Blackie suspiciously.

"Lynn mentioned it to me."

"Lynn Robinson? The mainlander you've been seeing, the shiksa? She's putting fancy ideas in your head? Why can't you find yourself a nice Jewish girl?"

"That's not the point, pop. Maybe I just want to see what my options are."

"And to be a draft dodger, that's what you mean. This is an option? This is not my son talking. To serve your country, you should be proud. This is the best country in the world. Your grandparents came here from the old country. You know what they had there? Nothing. Repression, poverty, that's what they had. You should be proud to be an American."

"I am proud, pop. I know you were in the Navy in World War Two, but that was a different war. Vietnam is something else. I'd like to know what we're doing there, and until somebody explains that to me and convinces me we're defending our country, I'd rather not have to be drafted."

Blackie had no answer for Waxie's argument. He thought it over a few moments, then leaned forward in his chair and said thoughtfully, "Let's not discuss this anymore right now. I want to absorb what you've said, and I want you to think about things too. Consider staying here at home, where you belong, and helping your father run things. Maybe we can restore the Inn to its proper place in the world, to the prosperity it once enjoyed. In the meantime, I don't think you should see the shiksa anymore. She's a troublemaker, and she's an outsider."

"Okay, pop."

Waxie then approached his mom on the matter of college, but received a similar reaction.

"David," she said, "I want to speak to you on tradition and heritage. As you know, we are Jewish, which is a faith steeped in tradition. It is also your heritage. You're an Islander, which is also your heritage, because you are third generation. The Travel On Inn is not only your heritage, but also your legacy. You are a link in a long and strong chain. And as we know, a chain is only as strong as the weakest link. Accept your heritage, and who you are, and be proud. Should you choose another route, we will still love you and accept you. The bonds of family are strong. But if your choice is not right for you, we would be hurt. And should you choose to leave us, we will miss you, because we love you. Your life is your own, of course, but we hope you will stay her with your family, where you belong. I want you to promise you'll consider your future seriously before running off over town on a whim. Do you promise?"

"Okay, mom, I promise. Maybe you're right. Maybe it was just a crazy idea."

And so now, seemingly less confused about his future, Waxie took Lynn aside, after they had cruised to the top of the Chimes Tower Road on the Vespa, and were gazing down on the beautiful little town of Avalon, where he had grown up, and where he now wanted to stay forever.

"I talked to my folks about college," he began.

Lynn's eyes brightened. She looked hopeful. "Oh? What did they have to say?"

"They more or less said my place is at home."

"Oh, I see," she said, disappointedly. "And what did you decide?"

"Well, I tried to convince them it was a good thing, but, well, you know how it is."

"No, Dave, I don't know how it is. Why don't you tell me?"

"You know the old saying—blood is thicker than water."

"Is that what you want, to stay home and do what they tell you?"

"Look, Lynn, I don't know what you want from me. I'm trying to make you happy, and I'm trying to make them happy, and everyone wants something different from me," he complained.

"I asked what you wanted," she reiterated.

"And I told you, I don't know. Right now I just want to be with you, and to enjoy this night out, while it lasts."

"I'm sorry," said Lynn, "but I'm not enjoying it anymore. Please take me home."

"Why? What did I do wrong?"

"Nothing, Dave. It's just that I like you a lot, but I don't think things will work out between us. You don't know what you want in life, you don't assert yourself, and I guess you're just too young to be in a relationship. And I guess I'm too young as well. Also, I worry about you being drafted. If you were, and had to go to war, I just don't know what I'd do. I'm not very strong, I'd probably fall apart. Oh, Dave, we've had a wonderful summer together, but I don't think we have any future. I'd like to break it off now, before either of us gets more deeply involved."

They talked and argued for another half-hour, but in the end Waxie took her home. She kissed him passionately, and with tears in her eyes, said, "Goodbye, Dave. I'll always remember you and this Avalon summer."

After closing the door, Lynn watched out the window as he drove away. She shuffled into the kitchen, where Donna was sitting at the table, over a cup of tea.

"What's the matter?" asked Donna, concern in her voice. "You're crying. He didn't try anything, did he?"

"Oh, Donna," Lynn sobbed, "what's wrong with us? When I talked you into coming to Catalina so you could find romance, I didn't expect to find it as well, or that we'd both lose our hearts in the process."

"What happened, Lynn? Did he dump you?"

"No, he's too sweet to do something like that. I'm the one who broke it off. Now summer's almost over, and all we've got to show for it is two broken hearts. I'm so mixed up, I don't care if we stay or go."

"Hey, Lynn," said Donna, "ain't no big thang. I'll fix you some tea, and you'll feel better. Besides, there's plenty more fish in the sea. After all, this is the Island of Romance, remember?"

"No, it's not. They lied to us, Donna. Catalina is the Island of Heartbreak."

The dark cloud that had hovered over the Skipper's Galley now spread out over Avalon and settled over the house on Whitley Avenue, which hung precariously over a bluff. However, the new moon had passed, and now a full moon was on the way to signal not only the end of August, but also the arrival of a new season in the turning of the Earth.

CHAPTER 19

▼

FULL CIRCLE MOON

"Streets full of people all alone...."

Jimmy Fontana's portable radio, which was positioned next to his beach towel, was turned up just high enough for him to hear, without competing with other radios on the beach, because not all of them were tuned to KRLA, as his was. He looked about at the sunbathers and passers-by on Crescent, wondering if any of them felt as alone as he did.

"Everyone's gone to the moon."

"Jonathon King with 'Everyone's Gone To The Moon,' number twenty this week on the KRLA Top Forty survey. This is Casey with you for the next couple of hours, followed by Roger Christian at four. We hope you're enjoying this beautiful Saturday afternoon. This is the final weekend before the Labor Day weekend, so hang loose guys and gals, cause we've still got some summer left. And nothing goes better at the beach on a warm day than a cold Pepsi."

Casey Kasem launched into a Pepsi spot, while Jimmy got up off the beach towel, and headed for the cool, inviting water. He no longer had a job, and he still had over a month to kill before boot camp, so he was just lazing around, trying to enjoy the waning summer, but had no one to share it with.

His rent was paid up through Labor Day, but after that, he had no plans. It seemed he was just waiting for his life to enter a new phase.

Jimmy walked down to the water's edge and waded in. The water had a sensual quality that caused him to dive under and swim out a bit, to become immersed in its comfort. The water was so clear he could see the bottom, and little fish darting about. He surfaced and began dog-paddling, gazing all about, taking in the beauty that was Avalon, and had been his home for these many weeks. He viewed the *S.S. Catalina* tied up at its dock. He watched a Grumman Goose taxi out into open water and take off for the mainland. And then he gazed on the beachgoers, especially the young women. There was a volleyball game happening on a portion of the beach, and it caught his attention for a few moments. Then, sufficiently cooled down, and tired of dogpaddling, he swam back in and waded ashore, shaking water out of his ears and hair. He picked up the beach towel and dried off. Then after a long look around the beach, he picked up the radio and suntan lotion, put on his shirt and sunglasses, tossed the towel over his shoulder, and began walking toward the Hotel Glenmore.

Suddenly Jimmy spotted her in front of the drugstore on the corner, browsing through a rack of postcards. She stood in profile to him, and there was no mistaking her shape or the way her thick black hair fell around her face, framing it perfectly. She must have sensed his eyes on her, for Donna Forte turned her head, and in the instant of recognition, smiled openly. Jimmy returned her smile, and their hellos collided in mid-air.

"Looks like you've been getting some sun," she said.

"That I have," he said. "And it looks as if you've been shopping."

"Window shopping," she corrected. "I'm trying to find some postcards to send, and maybe some souvenirs for my mom and brother."

"I was sorry to hear about you losing your job," he said.

"I didn't lose it," Donna said proudly, "I quit. And I don't regret it one bit."

"Good for you," said Jimmy. "I quit that place too."

"So what will you do now?"

"Right now I'm just hanging out. My rent's paid up for the next week. Then maybe I'll move over to the Annex for a while. Blackie said I could stay there all of September if I want. I can trade rent for doing a few chores around the place or the Travel On Inn. Then it's anchors aweigh. What about you?"

"Well, Lynn still has her job, and our rent is paid through Labor Day. Then we'll go back home to San Diego and off to college. In the meantime, I'm just like you, hanging out."

Jimmy couldn't think of anything else to say, so he just stood there, feeling dumb, while Donna turned back to the postcard rack and began spinning it, looking for the right card. Then he recalled Sil's parting words, "Don't let her get away again." He realized if he were going to make a move, it was now or never.

"What are you doing tonight?" he asked.

She looked up from the rack.

"Lynn and I were thinking about going to the dance at El Encanto. Why?"

"Well, actually, I was thinking about going as well. Maybe we could meet up there."

"Sure, why not?" she said. "It might be fun to hang out together again."

"There's just one thing," said Jimmy.

"What's that?"

"Waxie was planning on coming along, but he and Lynn split up."

"That's okay," said Donna. "I won't tell. I don't know why they broke up in the first place, and I wish they would get back together and work things out."

"Then it's a date?"

"I'd like nothing more," she said They made some more small talk, and said their goodbyes. As Jimmy headed off to his room, he thought about Sil's parting words, and wondered if he and Donna could really have a second chance. He didn't know, but he was willing to find out. As far as he was concerned, the past was dead, and today was all that counted. He felt the loneliness of only a few minutes earlier leave him, and began whistling as he walked, the old bounce returning to his step.

That night, in the twilight glow when the sun had dipped behind Avalon's hills, but the night had not yet brought the darkness, a blue Vespa pulled up in front of El Encanto. It's two riders dismounted, and one of them kicked it up on its stand. Then the pair strode purposefully through the long entryway, and into the open-air plaza. They moved around the dancers, and found an area off to the side where they could easily scan the crowd. They soon spotted Donna and Lynn, who were standing over by the disc jockey, Donna making an apparent request. Jimmy nudged Waxie, and as the record began spinning, they worked their way across the plaza and asked the two girls to dance. Lynn declined, saying she wanted to "sit this one out," but Jimmy led Donna out into the middle of the dance area, and held her close as Barbara Lewis sang.

"Baby I'm yours, and I'll be yours until the stars fall from the sky...."

Donna rested her head on his chest, and Jimmy could smell the Wind Song perfume in her hair, and remembered the night they had first gone out together. His heart ached for her now. He felt the warmth of her hand in his, and the contact of his other hand in the small of her back. Her arm was around his shoulder. It felt so familiar and so right to Jimmy to be holding her again this way. All the time they'd been apart was now forgotten, like a dream upon awakening.

The song ended, but the couple stayed out on the dance floor for the next two, both fast numbers. It was only then that Donna asked to take a break and sit out the next one. They strolled off to the sidelines, where they had left Lynn and Waxie earlier, but didn't find them now, nor did they spot them dancing. Then Jimmy noticed his friend standing near the entrance, arms folded across his chest, staring down at the ground. Lynn appeared now, walking through the crowd and straight toward them.

"I'm leaving now," she said to Donna in an upset voice. "I'm going home. You can stay if you want to. It's okay with me."

"Would you like us to walk you home?" asked Donna.

"No, I don't want to spoil your fun. I'm fine."

"I can't desert you, Lynn. We came here together, and we'll leave the same way. Ain't no big thang, is it Jimmy?"

"No," Jimmy agreed. "Donna's right. We'll walk you home. I could use the exercise."

They walked together, but Lynn wouldn't say why she was upset, or what had transpired between her and Waxie. After the steep climb up the hill, Jimmy waited on the porch while the two girls went inside. After a few moments, Donna came to the door and said, "I'm sorry to keep you waiting. You're welcome to come in, if you like."

"I have a better idea," offered Jimmy. "Let's you and I go for a walk."

"Okay. I'll tell Lynn."

So they headed back down the hill, and Jimmy said, "How late can you stay out?"

"As long as I want to. I'm eighteen and un-employed. No more Skipper's Galley."

"Yeah, same here," laughed Jimmy.

"What did you have in mind?" asked Donna.

"I just want to spend some time with you," said Jimmy. "We haven't talked in quite a while. You want to go back to the dance, or just walk a while?"

"Walk," she said.

They stopped by the Casino and wandered around back, both recalling the Fourth of July, but not mentioning it. Next, they strolled over to Descanso Beach and the Hotel Saint Catherine. They entered the lobby, and Donna commented on the size of the hotel and its faded grandeur.

Once outside again, they headed to town, along the beach, and Jimmy said, "The moon is almost full again. I guess this will be the last full moon we'll see here on the island."

Then Donna said, "I'm sorry for everything, Jimmy."

"What do you mean?"

"For the way I treated you. For Sil, and all that."

"Forget it," said Jimmy. "That's all in the past."

"You were always so sweet, so nice to me," she said. "I don't know why, or why you're being nice to me now. I don't deserve it."

"I care about you, Donna, and I've missed you. It's nice just being here with you again."

"It's nice for me too. Thank you for being so forgiving."

"Would you like to get together tomorrow?" he asked.

"I'd like that," Donna replied, taking his hand.

"How about breakfast?" he suggested.

"Thank you, but no. I'm planning to go to mass in the morning. It's been a long time since I've been, and I really feel the need to re-connect with the church. Maybe we could have lunch together."

"Sure thing, lunch it is. What time?"

"Make it around noon," she said. "I'll be home by then." Then she added, "It'll be strange not to be working lunch rush on a Sunday."

"'Quoth the raven, nevermore,'" said Jimmy with a smile.

They kissed goodnight on Donna's porch, and she watched as he walked down the hill and out of sight. She lit a cigarette and thought about Chuck and Sil, comparing them to Jimmy, and decided that maybe football players were overrated.

When Jimmy showed up at noon the next day, Donna invited him inside the apartment.

"I made us some lunch," she said. "Since you're not working anymore, you should watch your money. I may not be a great cook, but I don't think I can mess up sandwiches and potato salad."

After lunch, they took a walk down to the beach, and Jimmy said, "Let's be tourists for a change. How about going on one of the tours?"

They bought tickets for the Glass Bottom Boat Cruise aboard the *Nautilus*, then took a walk down to Pebbly Beach and watched a Grumman Goose of Catalina Channel Airlines land and roll up the seaplane ramp. That night they went to the Casino Theater for a showing of *A Very Special Favor*, starring Rock Hudson and Leslie Caron. It was a romantic comedy, which put Donna in a happy and carefree mood. Afterward, they walked along the Via Casino, and had their pictures taken at a 25c photo booth in the Atwater Arcade.

"What should we do next?" asked Jimmy.

"Well, actually," said Donna, "before we do anything else, I need to find a ladies' room."

"There's one off the lobby of my hotel," said Jimmy. "It's just across the street."

They walked across Sumner, and Jimmy waited for her in the lobby. He didn't see the night clerk anywhere, so when Donna reappeared, he said, "Would you like to go up to my room for a minute? I'll be moving out of there soon. And anyway, there's a song I just learned I want to sing for you."

"I don't know," she said hesitantly, looking away.

"We won't stay," he said, moving toward the elevator. She didn't answer, but followed him mutely into the car, and when the doors closed, she suddenly felt claustrophobic. She panicked, and wanted to tell him she'd changed her mind, but before she could get the words out, they were at the fourth floor, and the doors opened. Jimmy led her by the hand to his room, not noticing her palms were sweating. He opened the door and switched on the light, and Donna had a sudden feeling of having been there before. It looked a lot like Sil's room, and arranged the same way: the same sink, bed, nightstand, table, chair, and the dresser with a mirror above it. Then she noticed the differences, the ones that were unique to Jimmy, like his record player on the dresser, and his guitar in the corner, and the window that looked out onto the street, rather than the alley. But above all, the room had Jimmy's presence, his vibrations, if you will. She walked over to the open window and peered out.

"Not much of a view, I'm afraid," he said, standing next to her. "But if you leave the window open, you can hear the music from across the street at the Bamboo Lounge. Speaking of music, I want you to hear this song I learned off one of Phil's Bob Dylan albums. Have a seat." He motioned her to the bed, while he took out his guitar, sat in the chair, and began strumming.

"Corrina, Corrina, where you been so long? I been a worrying' bout you baby, baby please come home...."

Donna listened to the song that seemed to be directed to her personally, and felt both embarrassed and enthralled. When Jimmy finished, she said, "Thank you. That was nice. I never told you before, but I think you have a beautiful voice."

Jimmy set the guitar aside, and sat next to Donna on the bed. He took her hand, and then kissed her.

"It feels so good to be with you again," he whispered.

He felt her stiffen, but she returned his kiss, and soon they were lying on the bed, in a passionate embrace. Jimmy could feel her tremble as she said, "Could you turn out the light, please?" While Jimmy was switching off the light, Donna removed her blouse and bra. When Jimmy lay beside her again, she helped him out of his shirt, placing his hand on her breast. They kissed and caressed, and then Jimmy began removing her bell-bottoms.

"Don't, please,' she suddenly sobbed.

"What's wrong?" asked Jimmy.

"Please stop," she repeated, "I can't go through with this."

"Are you okay?" Jimmy asked again, concern in his voice.

"No, I'm not," she said, sitting bolt upright and fastening her bra. "I'm all messed up."

"About what?"

"You, know, sex." She spit "sex" out as if the word was poison. "Don't worry," she added, "it's not your fault. It's my problem."

"Is there anything I can do to help you?" Jimmy said, taking her hand.

"No, nothing." There was a pause, as she looked away from him and out the window. "There's something you need to know about me, Jimmy. I'm not a virgin."

Jimmy had already figured that was the case, since she had been with Sil, so it was not a surprise to him. "That's alright, Donna. It doesn't matter to me."

"It matters to me," she said. "And there's something else I should tell you. I feel ashamed, but you may as well know. I haven't told this to anyone else, except my mom. But she didn't really believe me."

"Go on," encouraged Jimmy.

"It's about my evil stepfather, Carl. He used to do things to me when I was younger."

"I'm sorry," Jimmy said quietly.

"What have you got to be sorry about? It's not your fault or your problem. It's mine, for letting him touch me. He didn't rape me," she said. "It wasn't like he, you know, put it in me. But he used to fondle me. It happened when I was thirteen, and starting to develop. He'd sit me down on his lap, and run his hands over me, feeling me up. Ugh. I feel sick even talking about it. I can still feel his chin stubble and smell the beer on his breath. Just saying this makes me feel dirty." Then she put her hands to her face and sobbed.

"It's okay," said Jimmy. "He's not here now. You're safe with me."

Donna lowered her hands, stole a quick glance at Jimmy, and continued speaking. "Then a few months ago, I lost my virginity to my boyfriend, who dumped me immediately, like he was disgusted. And he's not the only guy I've slept with. So you can see why I'm messed up about sex. Not only do I not enjoy it, I'm afraid of getting pregnant." She paused, and then looked at Jimmy in a resigned way. "So now that you know all this, I wouldn't blame you if you never wanted to see me again."

"Are you nuts?" said Jimmy. "Of course I want to see you again, and to be with you. I think I love you, Donna, and nothing about your past can change that. All that matters is that we can be together. That stuff about your stepfather, well, that's not your fault. He took advantage of you when you were too young to do anything about it. He's a sick-o, that's all. But I would never do anything to hurt you."

"No, I don't believe you would," she said. "You're a good guy, and you've always treated me right. I don't deserve someone like you."

"Stop talking that way, Donna. You deserve happiness, and good things in life, and I wish I were the one who could give you that. But I'll be going off to boot camp soon, and I don't know if we'll ever see each other again after this summer. So all we've got is now, tonight. And tonight I'd rather be with you than anything else in the world."

"Do you mean that?"

"Of course I do."

"Thank you,' she said, managing a smile. "I feel so much better now, like a heavy weight is off me. Hold me, Jimmy, hold me close."

Jimmy took her in his arms and held her, her head resting on his shoulder. In the quiet of the moment, they began hearing the strains of a song drifting through the open window from the street below. The bartender at the Bamboo Lounge not only had a new song on the jukebox, but it had now replaced "Pearly Shells" as his favorite. Don Ho warbled the tune, which reached across Sumner Avenue to touch them personally.

"I'll remember you, long after this endless summer is gone...."

"And I'll remember you," Jimmy whispered in her ear.

"I'll remember you too, Jimmy. Forever, I hope."

They lay together a while longer, listening to each other's breathing and each other's heartbeats in the darkness of the room, and time passed as in a dream. Just before midnight, Jimmy walked Donna home, kissed her goodnight, and they promised to see each other the next day.

True to their words, they did see each other again, and in the ensuing days became inseparable, spending as much time together as they could. Each day they became closer, and more comfortable with each other, and more open. Donna found herself falling in love with Jimmy. They could be seen all around Avalon, laughing together, holding hands, kissing in public. One middle-aged tourist even mistook them for newlyweds. Time passed by in a blur, and paradoxically, seemed to stand still. For Jimmy and Donna, there was no past or future. There was only now, and Avalon, and each other.

On Friday afternoon, while Lynn was working at Molly's Gifts and Souvenirs, Donna invited Jimmy into the apartment on Whitley. She led him wordlessly into the bedroom, closed the door, and began undressing. Then she surrendered to his touch, his kisses, his soulful eyes, and they made love together. When Donna closed her eyes, it was not out of fear, but out of joy. She gave herself completely to him, feeling safe and loved in his arms. Afterward, as they lay close together, Jimmy confessed that he'd just lost his virginity. "You've corrupted me," he said, and they both laughed.

The full moon came and passed again, and time became a very special and precious thing to Jimmy Fontana and Donna Forte.

CHAPTER 20

▼

PEBBLY BEACH PARTY

Phil Munday, sitting on the small couch in his living room, glanced once again at his watch, and then felt irritated for having done so. Why the hell did he need to know the time? It wasn't as if he had a job to report to anymore. In fact, that was such a liberating thought that he removed the timepiece, walked across the room, and dropped it in his beat up old suitcase, which had sat in a corner for quite some time. Three years, in fact. Much longer than Phil had originally planned to spend in Avalon. The gig at the Skipper's Galley was to have been a temporary one. "Oh, well," thought Phil, "everything in life is temporary. I just got conned into the middle class security trip. Got trapped here, too comfortable. Forgot what it was like to live on the edge, where your senses are sharpened and your soul can breathe life into the art. Gotta hustle, man. Nobody gonna hand you nothin' in life, without there being strings attached." He took some solace, however, in the fact that the steady paycheck from the coffee shop had at least allowed him some creature comforts, while keeping him from the temptation of "selling out," of prostituting his art, painting landscapes and portraits and such. He knew he wasn't cut out to be a commercial artist. The very word to him was an oxymoron. Phil knew the purity of his muse was more important than any price tag he could put on it. He would rather scuffle, even if it meant selling pot on the side, than cheat his muse. He'd been at this game long enough to know that he'd never starve, and in time his art would find it's proper place, it's audience, it's niche.

Phil Munday looked forward to being back in Frisco, The City, and to living the life of a bohemian again. He thought about the crisp autumn of North Beach with its little cafes on steep cable car hills. In fact, it was the familiarity of the hills and ocean breeze that had always reminded him of North Beach, and had made life in Avalon an easy transition. But now it was time—no, past time, to move on.

Phil would have no need of a watch to know when to catch the boat out tomorrow. He would have all day to get around to that. He was about as packed as he was going to get for now. He took a long look around the old pad. It looked almost like the day he'd first moved in. It had been furnished by the landlord, so the furniture was still in place, and would stay that way. Phil's stereo was about to belong to the landlord as well, partly to cover the week's rent he owed on this Labor Day, but mostly because it was too cumbersome to take with him, as he'd be traveling light. He'd already sent along some paintings over town to be put on consignment in an art gallery. He'd given another painting to an Islander friend as a trade for the use of a golf cart tonight. His paints and brushes were securely packed in a sturdy case for tomorrow's crossing.

He'd donated his books to the Avalon Public Library, with the exception of a dog-eared copy of *On The Road*. His records, the jazz and Dylan albums, had been parceled out to Jimmy Fontana and Dan Burton (who had come to his senses and returned to Pierce College for the fall semester). Now, it seemed, there was nothing left for Phil to do but roll a joint for tonight's farewell party, and wait.

The party, an end of summer farewell to Avalon blowout, had been Jimmy's idea, and originally was to have been held here at the pad. But since Phil was uneasy about tipping off the landlord to his imminent departure, another place was needed. Waxie suggested Pebbly Beach, because of the privacy, and the waning of the moon. Somehow, a last quarter moon in the sky had lent the appropriate touch.

It was much later that Labor Day, as the sun was setting, that Phil made his way through Avalon's tourist-choked streets to pick up the borrowed golf cart. He then drove down to the liquor store on Sumner to buy a six-pack of beer. Now he swung by Shelly Green's place and collected her.

Soon the pair was cruising down pebbly Beach Road, a two-mile expanse of asphalt unbroken by stop signs. It was the closest thing Avalon had to a freeway, where Waxie Shein and members of the Islanders Motorcycle Club could roar along at speeds approaching 30mph. Phil and Shelly, however, slowly wound their way past the Cabrillo Mole, Abalone Point, and Lovers Cove to a small and rocky, pebble-strewn beach. Here was where the PG&E plant stood and the barges from the mainland tied up. Here also was the seaplane ramp for Catalina Channel Airlines, and Catalina Vegas Airlines. At night there were no planes, nor barge activity, and so it was rather peaceful. Usually the only sounds to be heard were waves washing up against the shore, and the cry of gulls. Now, however, another sound carried through the still air. It was the sound of a guitar being strummed and a rich baritone voice singing softly but clearly.

Shelly recognized the song as "There But For Fortune," a Joan Baez recording that had been getting a lot of airplay lately on KRLA. Both Shelly and Phil recognized the voice as belonging to Jimmy Fontana. In the dim moonlight, they could make out his form perched atop a picnic table in the middle of the beach. Nobody knew where the table had come from. One day this summer it had just appeared there, as if by magic. But it added the perfect touch to the party. Also sitting at or standing around the table were other partygoers: Donna Forte, Lynn Robinson, and Waxie Shein. Nearby, between the beach and the road, a sleek blue Vespa stood like a proud sentinel to the scene.

"Hi everybody," said a smiling Shelly Green as she alighted from the front seat of the golf cart that Phil had brought to a halt at the side of the road. He switched off the ignition, and swung his legs out onto the ground, then reached behind the seat and grabbed the bag containing the beer, and brought it over to the table. He set the bag down, pulled out a can of Coors, pulled the tab, and offered it to Jimmy.

"Thanks, man," said Jimmy, setting down the guitar and taking hold of the can. Phil repeated his motions, opening cans and passing them around until everyone had one.

"Is anyone else coming?" asked Donna.

"Just us hep cats and cool kitties," said Phil. "Everyone else done split the scene. And the Skipper regretfully declined our invitation, haw haw. And as for yours truly, I must hip you to the fact, no jive, that this is the first Labor Day since I came to The Rock, that I didn't have to make the scene at that greasy spoon known as the Skipper's Galley."

Jimmy said, "We ought to drink a toast to that place."

"Count me in," said Shelly.

"Groovy,' said Phil. "here's to that den of iniquity, that unholy alter of square-ness, that veritable slave ship of toil and trouble, the Skipper's Galley. May she rest in peace."

"Amen to that," said Donna.

Following Phil's lead, everyone lifted beer cans.

"I'd like to drink a toast to all our friends who couldn't be here tonight, especially Dan and J.T.," said Shelly. Everyone toasted again. "To the Island of Romance," said Donna. "And to the best summer I've ever had." Again, everyone hoisted beers and took a sip. Then Lynn offered a toast. "Let's drink to Crescent Beach, since that's where Dave and I met." Again, the ritual was performed. Then Shelly spoke again. "Speaking of beaches,' she said, "I can see why this is called Pebbly Beach. But I wonder why there's no sand, like at Crescent Beach."

"Because this is the leeward side of the island," explained Waxie. "There are only a couple small beaches on this side of the island that have any sand, and they're accessible only by boat, and aren't near Avalon."

"But what about all that beautiful sand along Crescent Beach?" asked Lynn.

"Because, my dear," said Waxie, "like every thing else on the island, it's imported from over town."

"You're kidding," she said.

"I'm not. It's all imported. Each winter, storms wash it away. And each spring, barges bring in fresh sand from Newport Beach, just in time for the tourist season."

"What happens in the fall?" asked Shelly.

"The tourists leave, and the town becomes ours again--small, quiet, and boring."

"It seems like summer just began," said Shelly. "Now it's already over. What's everyone got planned for the future?" She looked to Phil for an answer.

"Well, yours truly is splittin' this nowhere scene and going where the action is. Namely that Mecca of Hip-ness, that Casbah of Cool, that Bagdad by the Bay, the only city for me, San Fransisco. I'm gonna crash with an old Bohemian cat in the Haight for a while, and dig the scene. Then, who can say? But I'll be putting brush to canvas, that's for sure. But first, before this night gets one minute older, I'm gonna fire up this joint, and we're gonna get high."

He pulled the slender joint from his pocket, lit it, took a deep drag, and passed it to Jimmy. Then he said, "And you, daddy-o, you still got a date with Uncle Sam?"

Jimmy took a drag, coughed, and said, "Yeah, anchors aweigh. But not right away. I'll be here a few more days, helping out at the Travel On Inn. Then after a visit with my family, it's off to San Diego, where I'll stay with Donna's family before going on active duty."

He handed the joint to Donna, who took a hit, and said, "That's right. We have a guest room for Jimmy to stay in. I cleared it with my mom, and I could care less what my evil stepfather has to say about it. When Jimmy gets out of boot camp, I'll be waiting for him. And if he goes overseas, I'll still be waiting, because he's worth waiting for." She leaned over to give Jimmy a kiss.

"Yeah," said Jimmy, "I'm a lucky guy. And if I'm really lucky, I'll get a ship home-ported in San Diego, so I can see more of Donna."

The joint was next passed to Waxie, and after he had taken a hit on it he said, "As for me, in case you hadn't heard, I'm leaving The Rock. Yeah, it's true. But not forever, just to go to Long Beach City College. I went over town last week, took the entrance exam and enrolled for the fall semester. My Uncle Max and Aunt Rose agreed to put me up for a while. Then maybe I can get some grants and student loans and get my own place."

"You mean our own place, honey," said Lynn.

"But not right away," said Waxie. "The plan is for you to spend the first semester in San Diego, and then transfer."

"That won't be long to wait, only a few months. And anyway, San Diego isn't far. We can see each other on weekends," said Lynn.

"Not every weekend," said Waxie.

"That's right,' said Lynn, addressing the others. "Dave promised his family he'd come home one weekend a month, and then spend summers in Avalon helping out at home. That was the deal he made, and I'm so proud of him for standing up for himself and making up his own mind about what he wants to do with his life."

"I still haven't decided,' said Waxie. "I'm an undeclared major right now, but I've got plenty of time to figure it out."

Waxie now handed the joint to Shelly, passing up Lynn, who he knew would've declined. But Shelly also declined with a wave of her hand and shake of her head. The joint ended up in Phil's hand again. He took one last long drag, then pinched the glow out with his thumb and forefinger, and pocketed it. Then he addressed Shelly.

"So that just leaves you, Shel. What's going on in your world?"

"Oh, just going back home and back to Orange Coast College, then maybe transfer to a university. I'm thinking about changing my major to Nursing, though, so I can help the wounded boys coming back from Vietnam."

"How's your brother?" asked Donna.

"John's fine, thanks for asking. I just got a letter from him. He was in Saigon, and hadn't been assigned a unit yet. Maybe he won't see combat. Maybe he'll stay in Saigon where it's relatively safe."

"We all hope for the best," said Donna.

"Well, that's all the news I've got," said Shelly. "I'm flying back to the mainland in the morning." Then changing the subject, she said, "You know who I wish was here for the party? Bob Silenski."

Donna made an audible groan.

"No, really. Sil had his faults, but he was still a lot of fun."

"Guppy! Puma head! Flatus breath!" said Jimmy, doing a bad impression of Sil.

"I thought he was a cool cat," interjected Phil. "Wonder what he's up to?"

"Chasing women, no doubt," said Donna sarcastically.

"I think he's in love," said Jimmy. "Anyway, that's what he hinted at to me. I know it's kinda hard to believe, though."

"Fat chance," said Donna. Then, "I wonder what happened to the Skipper and Sam?"

"I saw the old pirate on the boat back from over town the other day," said Phil "He was holed up in the ship's bar, probably spending our paychecks. I waved to him, but he was too far gone to recognize me."

Jimmy, who had been quietly strumming his guitar, now set it down and peered off toward the road, squinting as if to make out something. Everyone's eyes began following his. Someone had just parked a bicycle by the side of the road, and was walking toward the group. In the dim moonlight, they could make out someone in the uniform of an L.A. County Sheriff's Deputy approaching. Phil called out, "Hey, Deputy Doug, is that you? Like, what's happenin' daddy-o?"

Doug Martin switched on his flashlight and quickly shined it on the group, and the empty beer cans, then switched it off and returned it to his utility belt.

"Phil," he nodded. "They put me on bike patrol tonight. What's going on here?"

"A farewell to The Rock party. How cool of you to make the scene. If I'd known you were coming, I'd have saved you a beer."

Doug ignored the remark and said, "Got any underage drinkers here?"

"No squares in this scene, daddy-o."

"Didn't think so. I hear you're leaving Avalon, Phil."

"That's right, dads. Tomorrow. When you splittin'?"

"Tomorrow as well. I'm in the home stretch of my last shift of the season. Then I get a few days vacation time before hitting the mean streets of L.A."

"You catching the afternoon boat?" asked Phil.

"That's a ten-four."

"Me too. Look for me in the ship's bar, and I'll buy you a beer."

"I'll take you up on it," said the deputy. Then he walked down to the water's edge, and stared up at the sky for a long time, while everyone watched, not saying anything. Then Doug Martin walked back to the picnic table and said to no one in particular, "Well, have yourselves a good time, and take your trash out when you leave." Just before reaching his bicycle again, he shouted out, "Take it easy. Maybe I'll see some of you again next summer." Then the deputy pedaled off down Pebbly Beach Road.

"I wonder if he will see any of us again," said Shelly. "I wonder if any of us will ever be here together again."

"Why shouldn't we?" asked Donna.

"Yeah, why don't we all meet up here again next year?" Lynn suggested.

"Well, for one thing," said Jimmy, "I can't guarantee where I'll be. Maybe Vietnam, or out on the high seas."

"How about five years from now?" said Waxie. "We could all get together here on Pebbly Beach on Labor Day, Nineteen-Seventy. Wouldn't that be cool?"

Everyone agreed to the idea, and promised to reunite in 1970.

"I think this calls for a song, Jimmy. Something appropriate," said Phil.

"Yes, sing something, honey," said Donna. "Something special."

"Something special, huh?" said Jimmy. "Okay, let me think for a minute."

He closed his eyes for a few moments, thinking, then opened them wide with a grin on his face. "Okay, I got it," he said, as he began strumming the guitar.

"*Twenty-six miles across the sea, Santa Catalina is waitin' for me. Santa Catalina, the island of romance,*" he sang, and soon everyone joined in, and the words floated through the night, echoing off the bluff across the road, and then out to sea, where they mixed with the sounds of wavelets lapping and gulls crying and boats creaking at anchor.

EPILOGUE

▼

The Hotel Saint Catherine was torn down that autumn, and Phil's painting was moved to the Casino's art gallery. When it sold the following spring, a check was sent to him in care of the Blue Unicorn, a coffee house and mail drop in the Haight-Ashbury section of San Francisco.

By the end of the decade, the steamer pier had also been torn down, and the *S.S. Catalina* began docking at the Cabrillo Mole. It was retired completely in 1975, and eventually ended up in Ensenada, Mexico, where it sat half-submerged for many years. Eventually it was cut up for scrap. When the steamship moved, so did the seaplanes, to a landing at Pebbly Beach. In 1979, they discontinued carrying passengers, and ten years later, ceased flying altogether.

Jimmy Fontana and Donna Forte visited Avalon again in the summer of 1966, while Jimmy was on two week's shore leave, before going on a Westpac cruise to Vietnam. They stayed at the Travel On Inn for a long weekend, and visited all the sights, including tours that they'd never been on before. They failed to show up for the intended reunion in 1970, but as it turned out, no one else did either, except for someone who hadn't even known about it. It was just by coincidence that in August of 1970, Robert Wayne Silenski, surf board shop owner and decorated Vietnam veteran (Bronze Star, Purple Heart), honeymooned in Avalon with his bride, Rhonda, a stunning redhead. As it turned out, he'd met her briefly once in 1965, on the *S.S. Catalina,* but only ran into her again by chance after his discharge from the Army. The Silenskis spent a weekend at the Hotel Glenmore. They stopped by the Skipper's Galley for lunch, but it had a new name and new owners. Next, they dropped by the Travel On Inn, but it was boarded up with a FOR SALE sign in front. Had he bothered to ask around, Sil would have discovered that David "Waxie" Shein still lived in Avalon. He and his wife Lynn were teachers at Avalon School.

Sil saw Candy Love only one more time in his life, on a drive-in movie screen, where *Catalina Caper* was showing. The movie had been a bomb, and after a brief run at the drive-ins, it disappeared without a trace. Decades later it showed up on "Mystery Science Theater 3000," a television show that lampooned some of the worst movies ever made.

Today Avalon has grown a little, and changed a little, but still retains its unique charm. A fleet of modern boats, aircraft, cruise ships, and helicopters bring about a million visitors a year to the little town. Glass bottom boats and submersible craft still cruise Lovers Cove, mariachi bands play in the square on Crescent Avenue, and sometimes couples still fall in love on the Island of Romance.

THE END